The Isabella Triangle

Janet Lord

AmErica House
Baltimore

First printing

ISBN: 1-58851-766-7
PUBLISHED BY AMERICA HOUSE BOOK PUBLISHERS
www.publishamerica.com
Baltimore

Printed in the United States of America

To my husband Erik, my uncle George, and my cousins Edward and Clement, whose brief lives brightened my world,

And

To my parents for their unflagging support.

Acknowledgements

I am deeply grateful to the following people and groups for their assistance in the research behind this book: Dr. Neil Hampson, Medical Director of the Hyperbaric Department, Virginia Mason Medical Center, Seattle; Colonel Ted Cieslak at the United States Army Medical Research Institute of Infectious Diseases, Fort Detrick, Maryland; Center for Disease Control, Atlanta; Professor Emeritus Milton Friedman of the Hoover Institute, Stanford University; Mr. Salvador Rodezno of the Embassy of Honduras, Washington, D.C.; Steve Winston and Dr. Bart Krawetz at Lockheed Martin and the INEL; Mike Fox at the Hanford Nuclear Facility; Bruce Banks and the Divers Institute of Technology, Seattle; Roger Brink of Equinox; and Gus Salvador, former director and operator of the dive chamber on Roatan, Honduras.

I am, also, grateful to Dr. Scott McLean, Dr. Dan Fairman, and Dr. Royal McClure for their internal medicine insight and to Dr. Keith Sivertson for his proofreading.

Much thanks to Rich Bray of Ex Libris, Sun Valley, Idaho for showing me the way into the writing world. Thank you to John Sack and Mary Claire Griffin for their advice after the book was accepted for publishing. Thank you to Lane Teachout for promotional photographs and to Mary Beth Cooper for computer assistance. Thank you to Byron Merritt for his writer's perspective about the book market and to Patritia O'Neill for her consumer insight into that market. Sincere thanks to AmErica House, Vice-President Aida Matic-Chaffee, and Senior Editor Christen Beckmann for taking a chance on a new writer.

Finally, to my family and all of my friends, who have offered moral support during this endeavor, a most heart-felt thank you.

1

Saturday

October 30, 1993

She could hear the crying and yelling in the background, as the emergency room physician at Mary Benson Medical Center related the details of the case to her by phone. By sheer coincidence, she had been in the department finishing another case when the hyperbaric charge nurse took the call, even though it was late in the evening. Dr. Carla Knight listened attentively to the ER physician, who urgently described a 19 year-old, unmarried, 34 week gestation pregnant, white female who, in a fit of despair, had tried to commit suicide in a car with its motor running, in a closed garage. The patient had severe carbon monoxide poisoning, suggested by her comatose state. It was believed that she had been in the car for several hours. Already, 100% oxygen by mask had been instituted, but it was felt that it was imperative to get her hyperbaric oxygen therapy. The Harborview Medic 1 physician had routed the patient to Mary Benson, as the hospital was the major hyperbaric treatment center for the city of Seattle.

She quickly surmised that the background sobbing was from distraught family members. It was funny how the sound of such voices still got to her after years of emergency room work. She ran her hand through her long black hair, nervously. Her defense had always been to maintain a calm demeanor, even in the worst of circumstances. However, this had been harder to do since her husband's death a few years ago, because she could relate more deeply to the grief others felt.

The emergency physician's voice distracted her from the lamentations and informed her that the patient had been stabilized, as much as possible, and that it was hoped that the patient could sent across the street to her, by ambulance, for hyperbaric oxygen therapy. She accepted the transfer and said she would meet the patient in the department. The patient's name was Tiffany Douglas. It was 11:40 p.m. After ending the phone conversation with the ER physician, she had the charge nurse notify the chamber operator, chamber specialist, inside attendant, and respiratory therapist on call that there would be another case.

Carla knew the fetus's prognosis was poor because it was more susceptible to carbon monoxide than the mother. The exposure caused more pronounced decrease in oxygen content of the blood in the fetus. It would also take the fetus longer to eliminate the toxic compound from its body. For that reason, Carla figured she would have to treat the mother and fetus longer with hyperbaric oxygen to dissociate the carbon monoxide from the hemoglobin. The emergency room physician had told her the patient's carboxyhemoglobin level (the amount of hemoglobin combined with carbon monoxide in the blood) was 55%. Usually symptoms, such as a headache, would occur at a level of 10%. However, carboxyhemoglobin levels did not bear a direct relationship with symptoms and, mainly, were used to establish the diagnosis. Carla would have to judge the patient's presenting symptoms, in order to determine the therapy needed.

Carla watched as a stretcher, carrying a frail form with a protuberant abdomen was wheeled into the main treatment room in the hyperbaric department by paramedics. The young woman was very pale and her long, dishwater blond hair hung limply from her head. She was not responsive to painful or verbal stimuli. The paramedics had intubated her in the field, as she had been barely breathing. They were bagging her, currently, through the endotracheal tube with 100% oxygen. Two IV lines dripped into her arms. There were multiple needle tracks on her arms, as well.

8

The inside attendant, who was a critical care nurse, started applying an external fetal heart rate monitor to the woman's abdomen. The respiratory therapist began adjusting the settings on the ventilator, in the multi place chamber, that would be attached to the patient's endotracheal tube, so they wouldn't have to continue bagging her manually. Carla proceeded to examine the patient. What bothered her, immediately, was that the young woman was showing a slight injury pattern on her heart monitor and her blood pressure was 80/50. The fetal heart rate was approaching 200 beats per minute. This woman was in real trouble. So was the fetus.

She had the critical care nurse, Cary Bishop, a generally upbeat person, start a dopamine drip for the patient's blood pressure. The pressure responded moderately to this measure. Her next task was to try to treat the patient's severe metabolic acidosis in her bloodstream. Lab results from the emergency room indicated that this condition was present. It occurred in carbon monoxide poisoning because there was poor tissue oxygenation and lactic acid was produced. Carla realized that the tube in her trachea had already improved the patient's ventilation and that would help, but the process that caused the poor tissue oxygenation needed to be corrected quickly. Therefore, they had to get the patient into the chamber in short order.

The hyperbaric charge nurse, Lisa Wickham, was on the computer terminal in the treatment area looking at the patient's past medical records while Carla was formulating the patient's treatment. She blurted out, suddenly, "Listen to this. In a note from the Obstetrical Clinic, it states that the patient is a heroin addict and has a drug dealer boyfriend, who got her pregnant. Here's the part that will get you, though. He got her pregnant on two previous occasions, and, following the birth of each infant, he sold the infant to make some big money fast. He kept our patient blitzed on heroin, so she wouldn't know what had happened until it was too late. Nice guy. Sounds like the woman had at least three reasons to do what she did. The funny part is, the note indicates

9

she came from a very upper class family." Lisa shook her blond head, in disbelief, as she made that last statement. The other members of the hyperbaric team that were in earshot shook their heads, too.

Carla responded, "No one said coming from money is a guarantee of a protected life. If anything, for a young person, it seems to be a license for rebellion." Carla proceeded to give the OK to the chamber operator and inside attendant to slide the patient's stretcher into the chamber.

As the operator, Chad Parker started to do this, a middle-aged, well-dressed Caucasian female burst into the room and delivered a barrage of questions to Carla. Her frosted blond hair was coifed perfectly, but her reddened eyes bespoke the anguish of her mental state. "Who are you?" she asked Carla. "Are you the doctor, or are you the intern? What are you going to do for my little girl? Why is it taking so long to get her the special oxygen in the dive chamber? Do you know who her father is? Ted, tell them." The woman was followed by a dignified-looking man, in his late fifties, who wore the saddest expression that Carla had seen in a long time. It was the look of someone that felt completely helpless in the current situation, and normally, was used to being in control of his business and life. "I'm sorry," the man replied. "My wife and I are very worried about my daughter's condition. My name is Ted Douglas." (Now, it was ringing a bell, thought Carla, the Douglas Aircraft CEO). "If there is a choice between my daughter's life and the baby's, we want my daughter spared," he went on, uncomfortably. "You see, the pregnancy was not desired by my daughter. It was forced on her."

Carla felt badly for these parents and their daughter, but she also felt badly for the baby, whose life was being disregarded. At this point, she introduced herself and her credentials. She noted that the patient's mother gave her a skeptical expression. "We will do everything that we can for your daughter, Mr. and Mrs.

Douglas. However, we must still consider the welfare of the fetus, as it, too, is a threatened life."

"I understand," Mr. Douglas answered, in a conciliatory manner, "but please expedite whatever you are going to do." It was obvious that he and his wife did not believe that the striking young woman, before them, with black hair and blue eyes, was a physician.

"Did the emergency room physician explain why we are pursuing this form of treatment for your daughter's toxic inhalation and the basic procedure involved?"

"Yes, he did," replied Mrs. Douglas, in an impatient tone, beating her husband to the answer.

"Good. I will ask one of you to sign a consent form explaining the procedure, briefly, and the risks and benefits for your daughter, and, then, I will have both of you wait in the entry area vestibule until we are done here. The entire treatment should take about two hours. We will admit her to the intensive care unit, afterward, to observe her mental status over the next 24 hours. Lisa will show you where you can sit down."

Mr. Douglas signed the consent and the charge nurse led him and his wife away, reluctantly.

Chad Parker commented, subsequently, "Those people are sure full of themselves."

"Yes, they are, but it sounds like they have had tremendous heartache over their daughter's past drug addiction and her current situation," Carla acknowledged.

"But how insulting to ask you if you are an intern," the respiratory therapist, Jackie, added.

"I actually took that as a compliment. It means I don't look that old, right?" They all smiled at that remark and kept working.

The nurse, Cary, climbed into the chamber on one side of the patient's stretcher, while the respiratory therapist, Jackie Drummond climbed in on the other side of the stretcher. A crash cart full of resuscitation drugs had been positioned in the chamber, earlier. Electrodes from the patient were connected by wires through the hull to the cardiac monitor, located outside of the chamber. Lisa and Carla would watch the monitor during the procedure. With an OK sign from Cary and Carla, the chamber specialist, Bernie Mellick, closed the outer air-lock door, and Cary closed the inner lock. The chamber had double-lock compartmentation. This allowed equipment or lab samples to be passed in either direction without interrupting the treatment. Chad began adjusting the valves on the chamber control panel. The chamber would be pressurized to 3.0 atmospheres absolute (equivalent to 66 feet underwater), where the patient would receive two 23-minute periods of 100% oxygen breathing. Chad would, then, decompress the chamber to 2.0 atmospheres absolute (approximately 33 feet underwater equivalence), where the patient would receive two 30 minute 100% oxygen periods. With some luck, Tiffany Douglas's mental status would improve following this treatment.

Carla could talk to Cary and Jackie through a wireless headset. Cary monitored the patient's vital sign every 5 minutes during the pressurization at 3.0 atmospheres. All went well enough, at the start of treatment that she and the respiratory therapist started talking about some movies that they had seen.

Carla, meanwhile, had called the second-year obstetrical resident on call to give them notice about the case. The patient had had very little prenatal care to date as evidenced in clinic records. The resident would have to work up the patient once she was admitted to the ICU to find out whether the pregnancy was at risk for any additional reasons other than the carbon monoxide. Dr. Jim Kinsey was not thrilled about the call. He had just lain down to sleep after several hours of delivering babies. His voice sounded groggy and devoid of emotion. Yes, he would see the patient later on the floor. End of conversation.

Carla was reminded of what it had been like being a resident. Most of the time, one was serious, tired, and focused on medical minutia. It was hard to show flickers of emotion after awhile. This trait was molded by a survival instinct to persevere through numerous long shifts of call and to outshine one's peers during daily jousts of rounds on the wards.

Her eyes returned to the instrument panels. The patient was still in a moderate tachycardia. A blood gas sample had just been sent out through the air lock after the first 23-minute period of therapy. A remote camera in the chamber showed calm administrations by the inner attendants. Her mind, therefore, returned to reminiscence evoked by the conversation with Dr. Kinsey.

She recalled an incident, as an intern, when she ran to help an elderly, emaciated, female cancer patient, who was found pulseless and without respiration's by the nursing staff. She was the first person to respond. The nurse's aide, who had discovered the patient's condition, asked her, frantically, to start CPR. Carla examined the patient and noticed that rigor mortis was already setting in. She was reluctant to start mouth-to-mouth respiration's, for that reason, but she was an intern and could not call off a code. She asked the nurse's aide if there was a "no code" order in the patient's chart, often prearranged by the patient or family in terminal illness. The aide didn't think so, but she told Carla to hurry and start mouth-to-mouth breathing, and then she bolted out of the room to find a nurse and have them call the patient's physician. There was no resuscitation equipment in the room except wall oxygen and a nasal cannula. The nurse did not come back with a code cart or a defibrillator. In fact, no one came back. Carla lifted the patient's chin, parting the clammy lips and pinched off the patient's nose, to deliver two quick breaths before starting chest compressions. The stench from the patient's mouth was one of a cold meat locker. There was crusted yellow particulate matter on the lips. Carla performed several cycles of breaths and compressions, and tried to cope with her revulsion. Yet, she simultaneously felt sorry that she was putting the woman through

13

this process, when the woman was already dead. A second-year resident showed up after several minutes and told Carla the code had been called off by the patient's attending physician. She went into a ward bathroom, shortly afterward, to wash her lips and rinse her mouth, and cried. Never again, did she show such emotion through the remainder of her residency training.

A second-year resident developed an unflappable personality, as a result of such circumstances, and was...

"The blood gas is back and doesn't look good," Lisa Wickham announced, suddenly, breaking into Carla's thoughts.

It was worse than the first sample taken in the emergency room! It didn't make sense. The patient was intubated and well-ventilated, reflected Carla, in amazement. She, suddenly, noticed a change in the cardiac monitor, as did Lisa. There was prominent ST elevation across several leads.

A voice erupted from headset and there was movement in the chamber on the TV monitor. "Hey, we've got problems!" stated Cary Bishop. The patient's radial pulse just dropped out. I think this woman is having some kind of heart event."

Carla answered Cary, "You're right, she is and she just went into v-fib. Do you have a carotid pulse?"

"No. I don't feel a femoral, either. I'm starting CPR."

Carla ordered over the headset, "Jackie, take the patient off the ventilator and bag her." Then, she turned to Lisa Wickham, "Call a code. Page Dr. Kinsey to come to the department STAT."

Bernie Mellick commanded to Chad, "Depressurize the chamber."

Chad quickly adjusted the controls. The chamber returned to surrounding room pressure in about two minutes. Meanwhile, the code team arrived.

The commotion brought the Douglases from the waiting area and they tried to get through the main treatment room door. Lisa stopped them. "I'm sorry, Mr. and Mrs. Douglas, but we can not have you in this room during a code. You will have to wait outside. We will keep you informed."

"No, you don't seem to understand something, young lady," said Mrs. Douglas, angrily. "This is our daughter, you are manipulating. We have a right to be here!"

A tall, male second-year resident from the code team intervened, "We have a job to do here and we have to do it well, so we must ask you to go wait in the outside area. Your cooperation is appreciated."

Mrs. Douglas seemed to accept more from a male than a female, and acquiesced, glancing at her husband and casting a woeful look at her daughter, who was now being wheeled out on the main treatment floor to be resuscitated. The Douglases retreated to the outer vestibule.

The code team took over. A nurse charged the paddles of the defibrillator to 200 joules at the resident's order. The patient was defibrillated. No change, still in v-fib. The defibrillator was charged to 300 joules and the patient was defibrillated. No change. Finally, the patient was defibrillated with 360 joules. She was observed on monitor to convert to a regular rhythm with somewhat widened complexes.

"Does she have a pulse?" yelled the second-year medicine resident to Cary.

"Barely," Cary replied, palpating the carotid artery.

"What about the fetal heart rate?"

"It's down to 70 beats per minute."

"We're going to have to maintain the mother's pulse. Give her an amp of epinephrine."

After a few seconds, "Given."

"Does she still have a pulse?"

"No, I've lost it."

"Does anyone feel a femoral pulse?"

Hands went for the groin areas. "No," was the answer in unison.

15

"OK. Resume chest compressions. Give another amp of epinephrine." A minute elapsed. "Any pulse?"

CPR was stopped. Hands again went to the groin and neck. "No," answered Cary soberly. "It looks like an idioventricular rhythm, now, with a rate less than 60. We've lost the normal fetal heart rate baseline variability, too."

"Then, the fetal central nervous system is not functioning," interjected Dr. Kinsey. "There is probably no benefit in performing a crash cesarean section. We would be delivering a brain-dead baby."

The second-year internal medicine resident nodded his head and continued, "Give 1 milligram of atropine IV and another amp of epinephrine."

Carla was having a hard time being quiet during these administrations, but she realized this was part of a resident's training experience. Finally, she suggested, "How about a fluid challenge?"

"Yeah. Let's give 200 cc normal saline as a fluid bolus." Another minute elapses. "Any pulse?"

Cary palpates. "No pulse. The rate picked up briefly on the monitor, but it is slowing again."

"Resume chest compressions. Give another 200cc fluid bolus and then give another amp of epinephrine," commanded the second-year resident, while a few other residents on the code team, stood by observing. Another couple of minutes. "Are we getting anywhere?"

"Now, we're in asystole!" replied one of the code team nurses watching the monitor, when CPR was halted, briefly. The flat line on the monitor was very evident.

"Any pulse?"

"No," answered several voices dismally.

"All right. Let's try the transcutaneous pacer."

Cary and one of the residents placed the two pacing electrodes on the patient. The device was activated at 80 beats per minute and

16

was turned to maximal output. A widened complex on the monitor indicated capture.

"We've got capture. Now, do we have a pulse?"

Everyone held their breath. Cary shook her head "no".

"I'm afraid we're pacing a dead heart. Resume chest compressions. How long have we been coding the patient?"

"Thirty-five minutes," announced the nurse, recording the code.

"OK. We'll try one more amp of epinephrine and one more milligram of atropine, and if we don't get a pulse, we'll call the code off. Does that sound reasonable to you, Dr. Knight?"

Carla was, technically, the attending physician for everyone operating in the treatment area, so she had final jurisdiction, regarding the code. She nodded approval to the second-year resident, reluctantly. No one liked calling off a code on a young person.

The final drugs were tried in succession to no avail. The code was ceased 45 minutes after it had been started. Tiffany Douglas had only made it through 15 minutes of her second oxygen breathing period at 3.0 atmospheres before she arrested. Her baby had ceased brain function and could not be rescued. The group in the room was very dejected.

"Thank you, everyone, for all your efforts," acknowledged Carla. We did the best that we could. I fear this young woman had pre-existing heart damage from her drug use, which was probably made worse by her carbon monoxide inhalation. I think we'd lost the battle, before we even started. There's a good chance she ruptured some heart muscle."

Several nodded in agreement. The group took some comfort from this explanation and started to disband. Lisa, Cary, and Jackie cleaned the immediate area about the patient's body of empty drug vials and syringes and detached the pacer and fetal heart rate monitor. The patient was left with the endotracheal tube in her mouth, as she would be a coroner's case, due to the

17

possibility of foul play in her initial circumstances. Her pale, lifeless frame was cold now and her lifeless abdomen seemed equally forlorn under the sheet.

Carla said to Lisa, aside, "I'll go talk to the Douglases. Let me know when you're ready to have them come in and see her." Lisa nodded. To Dr. Kinsey, Carla asked, "Would you mind coming with me while I talk to the Douglases, in case they have any questions about the fetus?"

"No, I would glad to help out."

They proceeded to the outer vestibule, bracing for the emotional onslaught. The Douglases were pacing when they arrived. A hospice counselor was with them. One look at Carla's crestfallen face drove Mrs. Douglas into exclamations.

"She's dead, isn't she?" Mr. Douglas clutched his wife's arm as she said this.

"Yes, Mrs. Douglas, she is. I'm sorry. We did everything we could. I'm afraid she suffered significant heart damage from the carbon monoxide inhalation and arrested."

Mrs. Douglas's face contorted and she blurted, "Don't make excuses! You killed my little girl! I knew you were incompetent from the moment I laid eyes on you! We'll get an autopsy and take you to court! You were so worried about the baby, you probably saved the baby in place of my little girl."

Carla's face had flushed and her heart was perceptibly racing. She saw the hospice worker's mouth drop open, in surprise, at the outburst.

Dr. Kinsey, also showing astonishment, intervened to break the tension, "The baby is dead, too, Mr. and Mrs. Douglas. It could not be saved. It had sustained too much damage."

Mrs. Douglas deflated with this last statement and let out a moan, and collapsed in her husband's arms in tears. Mr. Douglas looked at Carla and said, "Forgive my wife. We are both at the end of our rope over this. Let us know what we should do next."

18

Even though Carla was somewhat consoled by this apology, she felt the sting of the previous remarks. They went to her very soul. She tried to make a brave face and answered, "I'm sorry that your wife feels as she does. Once again, we did everything possible for your daughter. Mrs. Jacobs from Hospice," gesturing to the woman behind them, "will help you make any arrangements that you need. If you and your wife desire, you may go in and see your daughter in a few minutes."

"Thank you, Dr. Knight," responded Ted Douglas, his wife still sobbing on his arm.

"If you have any further questions, later, please feel free to have the staff find me." With that, she turned and walked quietly down the hallway to her office.

Dr. Kinsey followed. In her office, he said, "Wow that was intense. Are you OK?"

"Yeah, I'm OK. Unfortunately, it's one of the risks of our job."

"I think if someone said those things to me right now, I wouldn't be able to finish my residency, my confidence would be so shattered. You really hung in there."

"Thanks, Jim. Why don't you try to get some rest? I appreciate you coming down to help us."

"You won't have to work hard to convince me, on that front. Good night." He hurried out of the office.

Carla closed the door and walked over to her desk, and collapsed in her chair. She felt the tears coming. She leaned forward, on folded arms, on her desktop and cried softly for awhile. All the anguish came back. The years of relentless pimping on rounds. Always being doubted by her peers, as far as her dedication. Her husband's death four years ago. Philip had been her rock of Gibraltar. He had gotten her to ignore what other people thought of her. He was very much his own person and was not bothered by others' opinions.

She had been devastated that night she had received the ominous phone call from the police and learned that he had been shot and killed. Philip had been an attorney, and an angry client had stormed into his office and shot him, while he was working late on a brief. The client, a high-strung securities trader, had been found shot in the head, outside his office, in an apparent suicide, the murder weapon in his hand. The client had lied to Philip and it had come out during testimony in a trial. Philip lost the case, as a result, and the client had to pay huge monetary damages ordered by the judge. The client had blamed Philip for the outcome. Carla would never forget how upset her husband had been, when he learned that his client had lied to him. He had written a brilliant brief, and even the other side conceded that he would win the case. Then, the fatal testimony and all was lost. Her world had been turned upside down.

There was a gentle knock on the office door, suddenly. It opened and Lisa stuck her head inside, "Dr. Kinsey told me what that arrogant woman said to you. I'm really sorry. You didn't deserve that. Can I get anything for you?" She had noted Carla's reddened eyes.

"No, but thanks for your thoughtfulness, Lisa. You know Mrs. Douglas just doesn't know where to direct her anger at the moment, she is too grief-stricken. I've seen it before."

"Well, I don't care. It wasn't fair to you. Why don't you call it a night and go home?"

"Oh, I probably will soon. Thanks for your help tonight."

"Don't mention it. Hopefully, we will not see each other until Monday, and the chamber will stay quiet the rest of the weekend."

"I agree. Good night."

"Good night," and Lisa left, shutting the door.

Quiet, again. Rather than revisiting sad thoughts about Philip, she started thinking that she needed some time off. Her last vacation had been over a year ago. She had learned, the hard way, that one had to make the most of life and not waste it. A warm place near the water sounded good. She wondered what her good friend, Steve Terzien, was doing. He was a treasure salvager and she and Phil had met him on a dive trip to the Galapagos several years ago. They had stayed in touch ever since. Steve had been a good source of information about dive equipment for them. The last she remembered, he and a group of salvagers were headed to Honduras to look for treasure off the Bay Islands. Maybe she could offer to provide some medical coverage for them and get a vacation out of it. If only she could remember where she had put his contact number in Miami.

2

October 31, 1993

Several hours after Carla's ordeal in the hyperbaric department, an event was unfolding in a different world that involved her friend, Steve Terzien. It was sheer coincidence that she had been thinking of him, prior to the series of developments, which ensued. Steve was watching a side scan sonar, intensely, on the **Golddigger,** a 130 foot converted research vessel, for which he was chief salvage officer, as it plowed through the waters off Cabo Camaròn, approximately 51 nautical miles southeast of the Bay Islands of Honduras, in the Caribbean. There was no breeze and the sun beat down on the glassy water surface. This scene prevailed, despite the announcement by the National Hurricane Center on the console's marine radio that this was still hurricane season. Steve continued to look at the sonar for any unusual shape on the bottom that might be part of a shipwreck lying underwater.

They should be near the purported site of the **Isabella**, he thought. The name conjured up images of the Spanish galleon, which had carried one of the richest treasures from the New World in an attempted trip to Spain. Unfortunately, the ship had sunk during a storm. The exact location was unknown. However, it was known that she had sailed from Trujillo Bay in the mid-1500's, just 1 degree longitude west of the Goldigger's current heading, and was last seen by a group of Payan Indians on the eve of bad weather off Cabo Camaròn. Her cargo had consisted of Peruvian gold and silver that had been minted into coins. She also carried gemstones from the New World. Originally, her captain, Juan Alvarez, had planned that she would stop in Havana, en route to Spain, to pick up further supplies, but she never made it there.

Now, the Golddigger was looking for the galleon's underwater grave. But where?

A few more minutes elapsed and, suddenly, Terzien noted a large object on the sonar screen, that registered a depth of approximately 120 feet, resting on the top of a wall that dropped off to almost a thousand feet. He was a curly, fair-haired muscular man in his mid 30's, who was not subject to emotional outbursts, but on this occasion, he was. "Shit! There's something on the screen! Phil, get a GPS reading, quick. Tell Jack to cut the engine."

Phil McConkey, a crew member, who had been sunbathing, jumped to attention and scanned the GPS receiver for latitude and longitude. He, then, ran for an orange buoy on an anchor line and threw it into the water, while calling for Jack Frees, the skipper, to stop the vessel. They were approximately 12 miles offshore and the only landmark in sight, through the binoculars, was a heavily foliaged bluff to the north on the western horizon. Phil was short and wiry and had no trouble moving quickly. "Jesus, Steve! You scared the hell out of me," he exclaimed.

Steve started laughing. By this time, the remaining six crew members surfaced from various parts of the vessel and converged on the stern deck, from which Phil had thrown the buoy. The cook, Cindy Rogers, still had her apron on. Jim Dutke, chief engineer and first mate, crawled out of the engine room with grease on his face. Erik Slade and Bob Weber, both in their late twenties and chief divers on the vessel, in addition to Steve and Phil, ran back from a Zodiac raft, in which they were repairing a tear. Erik was an oceanography graduate of the University of Washington and Bob was a former police diver for the East Moriches, New York Police Department. Excitement showed on their faces. Skip Randall, the salvage equipment specialist and dive tender, and Dave Krueger, the underwater photographer on the trip, followed everyone, as they had been buried in the workshop on the boat, taking apart a portable pump.

By this time, Erik and Bob were already donning dive gear. The vessel's engine had been idled, and the anchor was released over a sandy area, away from the nearest reef wall. Steve gave a short briefing, "This could be it, guys, although I didn't expect us to find any intact structure after all these years. The two-sensor metal detector behind the boat does register a strongly positive reading. We haven't seen anything else, on sonar that would suggest a wreck after miles of cruising, out here. The sonar indicates we are in 110 to 150 feet of water over a ledge. The mass appears to be resting on this wall, which then drops off hundreds of feet."

Erik and Bob checked their dive computers as they had done a 60-foot dive earlier in the day and their tissue nitrogen pixules had all cleared except for a line of six or seven pixules. Both were using Edge dive computers with LCD matrices that displayed digital information about decompression status. This status referred to the amount of gas, in most cases nitrogen, which was dissolved in an air-breathing diver's bloodstream when they descended. The computer constantly reassessed it, permitting the diver to have longer dive times for a particular depth than the Navy Tables allowed. Black bars represented the amount of nitrogen absorbed, or pixules and their distance from a curved line called a Surface Nitrogen Limit line. A diver faced decompression diving if his tissue nitrogen pixules crossed the line, and he then would have to make a series of stops at different depth intervals, in an attempt to washout nitrogen bubbles, or face going to a decompression chamber. Erik and Bob's pixules were well above the nitrogen limit line.

Steve warned, "When you get down to the object, keep track of your depth as you may forget about it, if you're too busy scouting around." He had always been safety conscious, particularly, since a buddy of his had been severely "bent" as a consequence of a dive for black coral. The fellow was now wheel chair bound.

"We'll be careful," answered Erik with a big grin, and he and Bob jumped off the swim platform into the water.

Visibility was 80 to 100 feet much of the way down. A cluster of groupers hovered near the divers in their descent and became their constant dive companions. Colorful coral fans and sea sponges clung to a nearby ridge and disappeared at 65 feet. Bob saw the bottom at this juncture. In the grayness of the depths below, he could make out a long dark mass encrusted with coral and covered with silt sitting atop a rock ledge with a sandy surface. Not far from the mass was the edge of the wall and the dark expanse of a drop-off. The mass resembled a long cigar-shaped boat. My God, thought Bob, it's a submarine!

There was no apparent damage to the hull, but this was difficult to ascertain due to the heavy coral encrustation and silt. The sub was angled, on the uneven ledge, with the stern lying at a greater depth than the bow. The bridge of the vessel appeared intact. One closed hatch was visible forward of the bridge. It was heavily encrusted and appeared tightly closed. However, on the bridge, the hatch was open and the round hole yawned mysteriously.

Erik's computer now logged eight minutes bottom time at 110 feet; he was directly over the open hatch peering inside. He figured that he had another five to seven minutes if he stayed at that depth, otherwise a shorter period if he spent much time at the stern end which was deeper. Bob had already gone to the stern, however, and was noting a depth of 134 feet. He estimated the length of the vessel to be 300 feet. There was no major exterior damage suggesting a collision against a reef or blast from a depth charge, only cosmetic damage from the ravages of time, saltwater, and coral encrustation. The sub appeared to have been scuttled.

Bob turned to locate Erik and noticed the remainder of one scuba fin disappearing within the hatch on the bridge. He immediately swam back toward the hatch opening. He hoped Erik was watching his air consumption at this depth.

Within the sub's hull, Erik was exploring the remains of a control room that had been reduced to a jumble of corroded and encrusted equipment. His flashlight was out and in hand. A periscope was cemented in place on a raised platform by several coral polyps, none of which appeared healthy or living. A little labeling was still evident on the instrument and was not in English, but in German, Erik noted. Further scouting revealed several navigational instruments on one panel in the room. Another panel held a number of switches and buttons. Erik swam toward the aft end of the control room and spied a corroded metal box on the floor. He pried the lid off. It was empty, but big enough that it could have held a ship's log. He then noted the inscription on the inner side of the lid - "U-2359"! His mind was racing - German labels on the periscope, the inscription on the box. The answer seemed obvious. This sub had been a German U-boat, presumably during the Second World War!

Another look at the computer by Erik revealed the elapsed dive time to be 11 minutes. The pixules were nearing the no decompression limit line, but there was still a margin and he decided to take it. Making his way through an open bow passageway, he noted several skeletons of small dead fish lying on the floor. I wonder what killed them? thought Erik. He did observe that while he had been within the hull there had been no living fish in sight. Funny, most wrecks had fish swimming throughout them, he reflected. He came upon several small cylinders stacked within a large recess in the passageway. There was a skull and crossbones symbol on each cylinder. One was on its side on the floor of the passageway and appeared to have been damaged, as there was an irregular crack in its metal casing. Beyond, there was a ladder that advanced down half a deck and led to a tunnel entrance. The tunnel was closed, after a short distance, by a bulkhead door, which bore a yellow nuclear symbol, universally warning of radioactive material, and there were several German sentences with exclamation points beneath it. Normally, this would be where the torpedo room was located. Fear was starting to seize Erik. He was not aware of any nuclear submarines in World War II. As far as he knew, they were developed much later. Also, what about all the dead fish? He turned and retraced his path. The computer logged 13 minutes bottom time at a depth of 117 feet. His air was more than two-thirds depleted. He needed to ascend and make a safety stop so he would not risk getting bent, the divers' familiar term for decompression illness. He also needed to find Bob and alert him to this fact.

As he made his way into the control room, he noticed the beam of a flashlight illuminating the opening of a bulkhead door in the stern. He, suddenly, saw Bob's incredulous face behind a scuba mask in the beam of his own flashlight. Bob had made his own discoveries in the stern's stowage compartment. There, he had found three watertight locked chests, with the four-ring biologic hazard symbol emblazoned on their sides, lined up against the bulkhead. Erik pointed to his computer to indicate that they were approaching the limits of their bottom time and should ascend. Bob acknowledged, and turned and swam out of the hatch above them. Erik followed. They, then, made as controlled an ascent as possible to ten feet for a safety stop, while wrestling with a rapidly dwindling air supply, resulting from the depth of their dive and their eagerness to alert the crew of the **Golddigger** as to what they had found.

3

The swim platform of the vessel was the focus of activity as Erik and Bob surfaced. They were both out of air as they had used the last bit making safety stops for eight minutes and ten minutes, respectively. Gasping, they related their discoveries in bursts of short sentences. "You'll never believe it!" said Erik. "There's an old German U-boat resting on the bottom. It seems intact. It looks like there is some radioactive material on board, as there is a nuclear symbol over a gangway," he blurted. "Lots of dead fish, which is odd," he added.

Bob chimed in; "I didn't see any wreckage of a wooden ship. No **Isabella**, but the sub is amazing. It appears scuttled. There is biologic hazard material aboard, as well.

Steve Terzien frowned, "I hope you guys weren't exposed to anything serious. This is not your average salvage discovery."

Jack Frees, the skipper aboard the **Golddigger**, in his early 50's with peppered gray hair and a coarse beard, just shook his head in disbelief. He was a native of New England. Never, in his twenty-five years of skippering vessels, had he come across such a find.

"I need to get down there and take some photos, pronto," urged Dave Krueger.

"Not before we get some special equipment and suits from Miami," admonished Steve. "We don't know what Erik and Bob may have been exposed to in that sub and I don't want anyone to take any more chances. We'll radio Miami today and see if they can fly the necessary gear to the island of Guanaja." The island, that Steve mentioned, was one of five comprising the Bay Islands off the northern coast of Honduras in Central America, the remainder being Roatan, Utila, Barbareta, and Cayos Cochinos, which was actually a group of tiny islands. "What we need are dosimeters and special dry suits with attached dry hoods that can accommodate the Exo-26 full face mask. Also, in view of the potential for a radioactive or biologic contaminant, we need valveless suits. We can pick it all up at the Posada del Sol resort. Then, we'll motor back here ASAP and start working. Erik and Bob, you better shower off on the swim step." They nodded. "Phil will get some buckets of water for you to use."

Steve's reference to Miami alluded to the investment group, Beck International that had backed the treasure-hunting operation. The major partner and stockholder, Peter Beck, was a real estate mogul with a penchant for adventure. He had raced hydroplanes and cars, previously and, now, participated in mountain climbing expeditions and searches for lost ruins and treasures. Some said he had too much time on his hands and didn't know how to fill it. Others thought he was trying to make up for an unsatisfactory marriage by staying away from home as much as possible, since his wife's sole ambition was to be a religious devotee of the shops on Worth Avenue in Palm Beach and the lunch circuit. Nevertheless, he was extremely resourceful and was able to locate needed supplies and equipment readily, utilizing a number of salvage supply operators nationally and internationally. He had just visited the crew last week at the Posada del Sol resort and was anxious to go diving with them.

Dave Krueger asserted further; "I should be all right if I stay a distance from the wreck. I can shoot wide-angle with a powerful strobe and get most of the external detail."

"I know what you can do, but I've got to insist that we take the necessary precautions on this job," Steve responded.

Dave was not happy with this remark. He stuffed his hands in his pockets and looked off to the horizon trying to contain his impatience.

Cindy Rogers, the cook, nodded understandingly at him. She was a buxom, blonde-haired young woman in her late 20's, who was always in good spirits and very supportive of all the crew members. She had graduated from Oregon State

University with a degree in urban studies, but decided she would rather ply the waters of the Caribbean on dive boats or salvage boats, exploring new places and preparing meals for the fun-loving crews. "I'll get the equipment inventory," suggested Skip Randall, a balding man in his late 30's, who had run a small dive salvage business in San Diego, California. "Today is Sunday, so we won't be able to reach anyone at the Beck office until tomorrow."

"OK," said Steve. "Jim can radio Miami in the morning and we'll leave for Guanaja shortly thereafter."

Jim Dutke nodded agreement. Not only was he first mate, but also the communication specialist on board. His experience had come from a stint in the Navy. Miami was one hour ahead of Honduras, which was on Central Standard Time. They could radio at 0700, as it would be 0800 in Miami, and the Beck office would be open. Then they could be underway by 0730 for Guanaja. Little did anyone know, on the vessel, that this would be a mistake and cost them dearly.

***

The crew stayed busy all afternoon checking the operation of equipment and taking note of what they would need further in the way of supplies for work on the sub. That evening, Cindy made them a dinner of snapper, which Phil had caught earlier in the day. Talk at dinner was animated, as everyone was excited.

"What do you think is behind that sealed door?" asked Phil of Erik.

"You tell me, man. But whatever it is, it doesn't look friendly. I'm not sure that I can wait until we get our special suits, to find out, though."

Phil laughed. "Well, you'd better or you might end up as a glowing radioactive lamp for someone."

"Get out of here," Erik replied, as he playfully punched Phil. They had been friends for a long time, dating back to college years

31

at the University of Washington. Phil was slightly older than Erik was, and after graduating with an engineering degree, he had pursued salvage training at the Divers Institute of Technology in Seattle.

"I thought that you two guys were friends," kidded Cindy, watching the punching episode.

"Just getting back at Phil for making fun of me, because I'm eager to open that door." Everyone at the table chuckled.

Steve and Jack fell back into a discussion about approaches to the sub with various pieces of salvage equipment. "I'm less concerned about getting the right equipment for opening the door than about the length of time required for the operation at that depth," voiced Steve. "If we used a surface-supplied air system, the divers could stay down longer and they wouldn't need an on-site decompression chamber as long as they stayed above 130 feet. We may need to get the Navy involved in this venture, as we may be getting in over our heads, dealing with a potential nuclear entity." Steve had alot of experience salvage diving, particularly at depth. He, also, was an ex-Navy seal. His last major job assignment had been with an operation using a remote-operated vehicle on the Tortugas wreck. He had come a long way from growing up on a farm in Ohio.

"That's not a bad idea. I think that the nuclear concern is valid," agreed Jack, stroking his beard. "We've already got that surface capability on board. Beck wouldn't have to send us a portable chamber, but just to be safe, the Navy, here or home, should be notified.

"I'm sure the company wouldn't mind saving some expense and working with the Navy."

"You can count on that. The simpler and safer, the better, in my mind." Jack was anxious to get home to his wife and two college-age daughters for Christmas, and he was concerned that if the operation became too complicated, they would face delays and he would not return home in time. He had already been away a couple of months. Most of his earlier career as a merchant marine captain had been spent away from his family, too.

"Ah, you're getting short-timer's attitude, Jack." Steve grinned. He was happier with more complex operations, as he loved the new technology available.

"I'm afraid so, but it's because I miss Betty and the girls."

"I can understand that. I miss my girlfriend, but I can't conceive of going home until we unload the cargo from this sub."

"No wonder Beck hired you. You're as hungry for the excitement of discovery as he is."

Steve couldn't deny it.

"That sure was a great dinner, Cindy," praised Phil. Everyone else nodded their heads in agreement, mumbling various phrases of contentment.

"Thanks, guys. I can't let you all starve before you start working 24 hours a day."

"I don't think that's a problem on this boat. I've probably gained 10 pounds since I came on the trip. Understand, I'm not complaining," prodded Erik. Cindy pulled on his ear, playfully. He looked at her affectionately. It was obvious that there was more than crew comradery between them.

"Man, I'm going to hit the rack. I'm beat," yawned Phil.

Others nodded. The events of the day had exhausted everyone and they all turned in, that is, all except Dave, who had his own ideas. He had always been a rebel, even as a kid in Kansas City. His dad and he had never agreed on anything. When it came time to leave home, he was glad.

Dave waited until everyone was asleep and then crept out of his bunk. His watch said 11:30 p.m. . He knew that Jim would be on watch until Jack relieved him at 2:00 a.m., so he made his way silently through the salon and galley to the stern deck. There, the scuba tanks lined the gunwales, secured by bungee cords in their stands. All were filled with air, which was what Dave was counting on. He slipped quietly into his scuba gear with his

Nikonos camera in tow, making sure not to bang his tank on anything. After a check of his regulator and air pressure gauge, he eased himself off the swim platform into the inky black water with a tiny splash. Only upon his descent did he turn on his flashlight.

The sunken sub loomed eerily in the darkness, starting at approximately 90 feet. It did not look as menacing as Erik portrayed. Dave started taking pictures and traveled along the length of the sub. Steve always worried needlessly, Dave thought. He entered the open hatch and descended into the control room. He was so busy taking pictures that he did not notice that his dive computer had registered eight minutes at 140 feet before entering the sub. His path took him to the same tunnel with the nuclear symbol on the bulkhead door, that Erik had discovered. He made a point of taking a photo of this detail. Along the way, he had noted the cylinders marked with skull and crossbones symbols and the dead fish on the floor. Despite these warnings, he proceeded to stay in the tunnel and attempted to open the sealed bulkhead door by turning its wheel mechanism. It would not budge. He then pulled with his full weight on the wheel handle. No movement. Dave snapped a few more pictures of bulkhead detail and then he turned and made his way back to the control room, where he noticed the aft passageway in his flashlight beam. He remembered that Bob had mentioned about biologic hazard material in the stern. Just a few more pictures.

In the stern compartment, the metal chests were not stacked on top of one another, but were lined up side by side, obviously so they would not fall over. A couple had locks that were corroded. He pulled on one and it broke. More pictures. Then, he attempted to lift the lid. Since it was watertight, he had to wedge his dive knife under the lid to break the seal. If he had been out of the water, he would have been in a cold sweat. Instead, his heart was racing. Inside, were stacks of small, green metal boxes. All appeared to be sealed, as he couldn't open them. Maybe he'd just take one back to the boat. That would give them a head start analyzing some of the material from the sub. It could be sent back to Miami. He stuffed one inside his BC vest and glanced at his computer! It read 24 minutes at 130 feet and the pixules had intersected the surface limit line. He was now into a decompression dive and had to make decompression stops in order to reduce his risk of bends (the term used by divers for the musculoskeletal form of decompression illness - joint pain) after he surfaced. However, he only had 400 psi of air left and he had started with 3000! Oh, my God, he thought, I don't have enough air for adequate decompression stops. He turned immediately, went back through the passageway into the control room, and swam out through the open hatch.

Normally, his decompression stops would be at 10-foot intervals, but he did not have enough air for this precaution. Instead, his first stop was at a depth of 30 feet with roughly 200 psi left, as he had spent roughly half the amount of air that he left the sub with, on trying to ascend. His computer was advising not to go above a ceiling of 30 feet. He knew he must go to the surface and take the consequences because his air pressure gauge needle neared zero after a couple of minutes and his regulator had abruptly stopped supplying air. He dropped his weight belt and made a free ascent from 30 feet with no air. This increased the risk of contracting an arterial gas embolism, an entity caused by increased pressure in the lungs from overexpansion, as the surrounding pressure decreased on ascent. When the lung pressure suddenly relieved on surfacing, it allowed gas bubbles in ruptured pulmonary veins to enter the heart and subsequently the arteries. Varying effects could be caused by these bubbles depending upon where they lodged in the circulation, for example, in the brain, a stroke or loss of consciousness could result, or in the spinal cord, focal paralysis could occur in the extremities. On the surface, Dave gulped air.

As he pulled himself up on the platform, he noticed that his skin appeared mottled and while taking his tank off, he began to

35

cough. Shit, I hope that I haven't gotten bent. His question would be answered in the next several hours. He managed to get all his dive gear put away and he unscrewed his flashlight and replaced one of the batteries with the roll of film that he had just taken, and took it to his bunk. The box from the sub was in his hand. He planned to hide it somewhere until he could get a decent chance to talk to Steve. Just like Pandora, he was anxious to look inside, so he wedged his dive knife under the lid and was able to pry it open. Before he was able to appreciate the contents, he passed out and several sealed glass vials fell on the floor and cracked, rolling under his bunk. Dave was, unfortunately, in a bunkroom by himself, so no one discovered him immediately. The crew was still sleeping, except Jim, who was on watch and had not seen Dave enter or leave the water. The time was 12:51 a.m.

4

November 1, 1993

With first light at 5:30 a.m., Jack Frees noticed a large ship approaching them from a southwesterly direction on the horizon. He grabbed the binoculars in the wheelhouse and scanned the vessel, noting it was the gray color of a Naval Force vessel and was displaying the Honduran flag. It was gaining upon them at a fast speed and would overtake them in less than an hour. They must be patrolling the water for drug traffickers, Jack thought.

Meanwhile, in his bunk in the **Golddigger**, Dave Krueger had regained consciousness, but was faring poorly. He could not move his right arm and felt patchy areas of numbness in the extremity. His breathing had become increasingly difficult and his skin had become more mottled. The labored respirations had awakened some of the crew in bunks in the opposite cabin and they were now attending to him. "Hey, buddy, what's the matter?" asked Steve Terzien.

"You're going to be pissed. I went down and took photos. I stayed too long. I know it was stupid," he said, between gasps.

"Well, you undoubtedly have decompression sickness. We'll get some oxygen on you and get you to the recompression chamber on Roatan, fast."

"Appreciate it, Steve. I'm sorry."

"Forget it. We'll talk later." Steve was hoping that the uneasiness, he felt, was not showing on his face.

One hundred percent oxygen was placed on Dave's face by mask in order to relieve arterial oxygen deprivation and enhance the rate of bubble breakdown in the bloodstream. No one saw the broken vials on the floor. Dave was so ill that he forgot to mention anything about them or the green box, which was, now, empty and disregarded on the bunk. Unluckily, no biologic hazard symbol was on the small, individual boxes on the sub, only, on the large chests. The crew carried Dave up to the salon area and placed him on the sofa, lying on his back. The skipper was made aware of the situation.

At this juncture, Steve noticed a very large, gray, coast guard cutter-type vessel, with 76-mm cannons, closing on their port side. It was near enough that he could see several white-uniformed individuals on board, as well as a few tan-uniformed individuals who appeared to be officers. The name on the bow read **El Mundo**. It appeared to be a Honduran naval vessel. What luck! This ship could transport Dave to the island of Roatan, where the nearest chamber was located, as they probably had a medical officer on board. He ran out on deck to wait until the vessel came fully alongside. A dark-haired man with a mustache was visible on the bridge and he motioned to the crew to throw ropes to the **Golddigger** and secure the two vessels.

Jack Frees asked through a bullhorn, "Please state your identity and purpose." Then, he repeated the command in Spanish.

Surprisingly, the man on the bridge answered in English with a Hispanic accent. "This is the Honduran Naval Force. We would like to board your vessel and ask you a few questions, as we are doing brief routine inspections of all water craft in the vicinity."

Undoubtedly, looking for drugs, Jack thought. "Permission granted. We have a sick man aboard and we need your help. Prepare to make fast your ship."

Lines were thrown to the **Golddigger** and secured. It was at this point that a surprising turn of events occurred. Several of the white-uniformed crew members pulled out Heckler~Koch MP-5 9mm submachine guns and pointed them menacingly at the **Golddigger** crew. The apparent officer on the bridge yelled through a megaphone, "Captain, tell your crew to stand away from the lines while we board your vessel, or they will be shot. Also, have all your crew members report on deck."

Jack motioned to his crew to stand away and he asked Steve to get the remaining crew members on deck with the exception of Dave. " One of our crew members is very ill with decompression sickness and he is too weak to walk. He needs a recompression chamber."

The officer on the bridge, meanwhile, had descended to the main deck of the **El Mundo**, seemingly ignoring Jack's statement, and boarded the **Golddigger** with ten heavily armed men. He was a swarthy, hawk-nosed man of medium height and build. His gaze was piercing.

Jack said to him, "Surely, this is unnecessary just to ask us some questions." The **Golddigger** crew, minus Dave, and Cindy who was caring for him, had assembled on deck and were eyeing the boarding party uneasily.

"Not so, Captain, because, you see, we are not the Honduran Naval Force. My name is Hector Ramirez. You have found something we want and, unfortunately, we will not be able to let you go."

Steve gasped. Hector Ramirez was one of the chief lieutenants of the Cordillera Colombian drug cartel. He had taken over since the cartel's boss, Eduardo Rojas, had been arrested, extradited to the United States, and sent to the gas chamber over a year ago for the murders of several DEA agents. It had been his vow to get even with the United States.

"Ah, so you know who I am and are aware of my hatred for Americans," Ramirez said sardonically, gazing at the chief salvage officer.

Steve could only glare back. His mind was racing. What could he do that might create a distraction? He could think of nothing, as they were too outnumbered, both by people and arms.

It was, at this moment, that Cindy, who was caring for Dave in the salon and who was taking in the whole scene transpiring on the stern deck, decided to make a run for the radio in the wheelhouse. The route was through a corridor from the salon, toward the bow, and up a small flight of steps. Dave followed her glance and acknowledged her plan with a nod of his head. She made a dash down the hallway, but not unnoticed by one of Ramirez's men, who was near the stern entrance to the salon. His name was Alfonso Caldas and he was the most twisted member of the cartel. His face was dark, framed by thin greasy hair and a scraggly beard, and marred by a long scar on his right cheek. He had grown up during La Violencia, a civil war between the Liberals and Conservatives in Columbia, which lasted over a decade. His family had been murdered, brutally, by some of the Conservative Party members, because they sided with the Liberals, and it had been a woman in his village, who had tipped off the group that massacred them. He had been sent, by his mother, to a neighboring village to buy eggs from a farmer and, as a result, escaped death. Since then, his worst acts had been perpetrated toward women. He also took pleasure in killing people.

Cindy was almost to the wheelhouse by the time he charged into the salon. Dave, who was still under an oxygen mask, lying on the sofa, saw Cindy's attempt being threatened and he tried to yell a warning. However, it was muffled by his oxygen mask and stopped abruptly when Alfonso grabbed his chin in one hand and slit his throat with a knife in his other hand. Dave's eyes remained open as the life ebbed from his body and his limbs became cold. Luckily, Alfonso had not fired his gun in view of the oxygen tank present. The sudden silencing of Dave's warning made Cindy turn, but she kept running.

On deck, Steve and the others looked horrified and feared for the worst. He made a move to break through the ranks of Ramirez's men toward the salon, but was cut down by multiple submachine gun fire and collapsed into a bloody heap.

"The others of you should not be so stupid, or you will follow in his footsteps!" shouted Ramirez.

"You fucking bastards!" screamed Erik Slade, nearly hysterical, realizing that not only Steve but also Dave and Cindy were probably dead. He had not even been able to try to protect Cindy. Bob Weber restrained him for fear that he would be next. Erik broke into tears.

Meanwhile, Cindy had made it to the wheelhouse and had just picked up the handset on the radio and was about to dial frequency 2182, the international emergency channel, when Alfonso, who was not far behind her, fired a burst from his submachine gun, riddling her back with several bullets. Cindy fell to the deck with a brief gasp and was unresponsive. Bullets had severed her spinal cord and brainstem; she died quickly. Alfonso was not through, however. He rolled Cindy over and pulled out his switchblade knife to cut through her clothes. He, then, undid his own pants, straddled her, and drove his male part inside her. He liked them best like this - dead, empty stare, no screaming or resistance, yet still warm. He was surprised how fast he came.

Erik and Bob were beginning to lose hope for their crewmates and themselves. Ramirez had been smiling evilly through the previous submachine gunfire, and seemed unaffected by the reactions of the **Golddigger** crew. He had one of his men grab Jack Frees and force the captain to kneel in front of him. Jack's hands were tied behind him. Another man, designated by Ramirez, placed a gun barrel barely inside Jack's right ear, while keeping his finger on the trigger, and awaited further order from Ramirez.

"Leave him alone!" shouted Phil. "He's done nothing to you, assholes!" The words were barely out of his mouth before he was shot, subsequently falling against the stern bulkhead.

"Oh, my God," lamented Jack. He knew that he would never see Betty and his daughters again.

"Now, Captain, did you contact anyone by radio and notify them about the wreck and this location? Answer me quickly," Ramirez ordered, showing no emotion. "I will not tolerate any more impudence."

Silence. Jack feared that if he answered anything that he and the rest of the crew would be killed, anyway.

"Speak up!"

No answer. On a quick signal from Ramirez, the man holding the gun in Jack's ear fired it. Jack slumped forward unresponsive on the deck, blood pouring from his ear and the opposite side of his scalp.

This maddened the remainder of the crew and they tried to rush their captors, only to be mowed down by submachine gun fire, in the process. Not one of the crew was left standing, subsequently. Erik lay in a crimson circle of blood, moaning Cindy's name. Ramirez stood over him and pulled a gun from his pocket. He yanked Erik's head up by the scalp hair and held the gun to his forehead. "Did you radio anyone about this location?!"

"Fuck you." Erik then spit in his face. Ramirez let go of his hair, fired, and blew the top of Erik's head off. Any of the other crew, yet stirring, was shot in the head, also, by Ramirez's men.

"Now, we must make haste and finish our task," Ramirez said in Spanish to his men.

Alfonso appeared at the salon portal at this point, zipping up the fly on his pants. He appeared satisfied with himself. Ah, thought Ramirez, he has jumped another dead one. Alfonso had always been twisted. However, he was an effective hitman and soldier in the cartel's army and that was all that mattered, concluded Ramirez.

He and his men returned to the **El Mundo** and some set about donning special dive suits with dosimeters and protective seals against toxic materials. The plan was to complete their dive mission and pull up the **Golddigger's** anchor. They would, then, let the vessel drift in the current away from the site. Several divers descended on the wreck and entered the open hatch in the bridge. They all carried extra tanks of air for decompression stop purposes. Their course took them down the aft passageway from the control room to the tunnel on the lower deck. They faced the sealed bulkhead door with the radioactive material symbol on its surface. The divers had not expected the door to be sealed. They had been told that all doors had been opened when the sub was scuttled. There would be a delay in removing the material, within, because they needed further equipment. However, they removed all of the intact cylinders that they could find outside the bulkhead and the biologic agents in the stern.

Later, on the surface, they informed Ramirez of the unexpected complication. He was not happy, but was resigned to solving the problem. He gave instructions that any logbooks or written material with the wreck site coordinates, aboard the **Golddigger,** were to be found and confiscated, as well as any film within cameras or exposed film. Also, he gave orders that the GPS receiver was to be destroyed. This was all done with care not to leave fingerprints. They hauled in the **Golddigger's** anchor on its motor-driven windlass and watched her drift away to the southeast, carrying her massacred crew. Honduran Naval Force boats would be crawling all over this region, once they discovered the **Golddigger**, so Ramirez and his men would not be able to return for awhile, particularly in daylight. With this situation prevailing, the **El Mundo** made course for its safe haven to the south.

5

November 3, 1993

The crew of a Honduran fishing boat discovered the **Golddigger,** two days later. They noted that the salvage vessel appeared to be drifting aimlessly, without any signs of visible activity on board. As they pulled alongside and tied off on some cleats, Juan, one of the skipper's sons, pointed excitedly to some blood stains on the stern bulkhead. The stench of death was in the air. Quickly, another son, Felipe ran into the wheelhouse of their boat, on a nod from his father, and radioed the Naval Force, the American equivalent of the Coast Guard. Meanwhile, his father, Pablo, and his brother, Juan, climbed aboard the **Golddigger** and took in the carnage before them. Two days of sun exposure, out at sea, had left the bodies bloated and rapidly decomposing. Juan and his father had to see no more. They turned, rapidly, and went back to their boat to start the engine and idle it to hold their position, as it was too deep to anchor. There, they waited for the authorities. However, Felipe was curious and climbed aboard the stern of the **Golddigger,** despite his father's protestations. He was warned not to touch anything.

The aft companionway was open to the main cabin. Felipe, anxiously, skirted the dead bodies and made his way through this entrance. He immediately saw Dave Krueger's bloody body draped over a salon sofa. Sweat broke out on his forehead in the warm confinement of the cabin, smothered by the odor of congealed blood. He proceeded through the corridor to the crew quarters and bridge. Everything was in disarray. It was obvious that, whoever had boarded the boat, was looking for something. At Dave's cabin, he happened to look inside and noticed the vials on the floor near the bunks. Maybe there had been drugs on board, he thought, and someone had been looking for them and killed everybody. He bent down to pick up one of the vials. There was a wide crack in it and a brown substance in the bottom. He held the vial to his nose. He had smelled cocaine before. A friend of his had gotten some from some contacts in Nicaragua. Funny, this had no smell other than a suggestion of something old, like the skin on his grandmother's body. He quickly put the vial down.

Further, down the corridor, Felipe came to the bridge. An exposed, young woman's dead body confronted him on the floor near the instrument panel. He could tell that she had been pretty. Her eyes were open and had decomposed; leaving black orbs that accentuated the horror of the scene. Dried bloody handprints were evident on her body. Felipe was revolted and he felt something rise in his stomach. He ran, from the wheelhouse, out a starboard door and wretched violently over the gunwale into the sea. His father, seeing this, climbed back onto the **Golddigger** deck to come help him. He escorted his son to the fishing vessel with his arm around the boy's waist and his son's arm around his neck. Felipe would not talk, but only moan.

Juan met them. "Felipe, what did you see that made you so sick?"

Felipe looked at him with terror in his eyes; "A pretty young girl was dead in the wheelhouse. She had no eyes! It was horrible!"

"Papa, who do you think killed those people?" asked Juan, a sinewy teenager.

"I don't know, my son, but a guess would be drug dealers. They are renowned for execution-style killings. Whoever the murderers were probably had many guns. These people had no chance."

"It's so sad. The crew on this boat looks like they were diving, maybe for treasure. Do you think the murderers wanted what they were diving for, or are still in the area?" Juan fearfully scanned the horizon through the window of the wheelhouse after posing this question.

"So many questions, Juan. We will let the Naval Force answer them. Our job, for the moment, is to stay tied to this vessel and try to keep our position. If we see any suspicious activity, in the meantime, nearing our vicinity, we will abandon our post and make for home." Juan's father was an extremely patient man. He stroked his peppered black beard and waited.

The latter plan ended up unnecessary. It was necessary, though, to put the fishing vessel into gear several times to hold their position in the current. Felipe was silent through these proceedings. He was too stunned and scared by what he had seen. He, therefore, kept himself occupied with tasks aboard the boat. His father, occasionally, would pat him on the shoulder and tell him not to worry.

The true Honduran Naval Force arrived three hours later. They gave the fishermen some fuel for their trip home to Savannah Bight, on the island of Guanaja, because their boat had used up a considerable quantity trying to maintain the position. The skipper and his sons departed eagerly for their home north, not even giving a thought to setting more nets for the day. Felipe did not tell anyone about the vial.

The Naval Force loaded the **Golddigger**'s bodies in bags and stored them in the hold of their ship, taking precaution to wear gloves in the process. Nothing else was disturbed on the salvage vessel so that Honduran police could collect intact evidence. No motive was apparent. Captain Jose Martinez, captain of the naval vessel, decided that the **Golddigger** should be towed back to La Ceiba for further investigation. As a result, it took more than a day to put into port.

In La Ceiba, the police collected as much evidence as possible, but the motive remained unclear. One policeman discovered the vials that Felipe had found, and he also put one of them to his nose and smelled it. He submitted it for evidence, along with the other vials, in a plastic bag. Again, the green box with rubber seals was not given much attention because it had no labels. All these items were stored in a warehouse by three Naval Force sailors and were slowly processed by the local authorities. No equipment had been stolen, nor had any money in the personal possessions of the crew. However, the captain's logbook was missing and the GPS receiver was smashed. Cameras were found, but no exposed film was discovered in them or on board. Initially, the flashlight inside which Dave had placed his film cartridge had been collected for evidence, but not opened, so the film was not discovered. The only clear fingerprints they found were from bloody handprints on the breasts of the dead woman in the wheelhouse.

Eight days passed without any leads in the investigation by the Naval Force and the Honduran police. Naval vessels had searched the area, in which the **Golddigger** was found, to no avail. The police had not come up with any obvious motives for the crime. All that they did know, was that whoever had killed the crew, had not wanted the location of the **Golddigger** to be known. Meanwhile, the FBI had made inquiries about the deaths of the crew members, in view of their U.S. citizenship. The Honduran police decided to invite the FBI to participate in the investigation, locally. It was the FBI's idea to contact DEA operatives in the area, as they suspected drug activity, and drug cartel involvement in the crime.

The coroner assigned to the case by the Honduran police was Dr. Alberto Velasquez of La Ceiba. He had noted that some of the bodies displayed unusual skin lesions and markings, which he could not clearly identify. These did not appear to be associated with the causes of death which were fatal gunshot wounds to vital organs or structures, and in the case of one individual, death by bleeding from slashed arteries in the neck. He questioned whether the lesions were from some of the individuals having been exposed to a toxin or having decompression illness. This occurred to him as he was an avid diver and he had been recently to a meeting of the U.S. Undersea and Hyperbaric Society, of which he was a foreign member. There, he remembered hearing a lecture given by a young female physician on the physical symptoms of decompression illness. Her training had included a residency in internal medicine, as well as a fellowship in pulmonary and critical care medicine, and one in hyperbaric medicine. She was director of the hyperbaric chamber at Mary Benson Medical Center in Seattle. He remembered she was quite striking in appearance with black hair and blue eyes, and a slim, athletic yet feminine figure. She had been involved in a number of investigations of diving accidents and was considered an expert. Her name was Dr. Carla Knight. Since the investigation was already over a week old without leads, he decided to contact her. The police gave him their permission to do so.

6

November 12, 1993

Rain was coming down in a heavy curtain over Seattle and the sky was endlessly gray, the day that the coroner of La Ceiba called Carla. She was in the midst of treating a patient with a serious **Clostridial** skin infection with a chamber session. Hyperbaric oxygen was known to be an excellent deterrent to oxygen-avoiding bacteria and was achieving good results in Dr. Knight's patient. She had just returned from a meeting in Boston, where the skies had also been cloudy. It was about time for a vacation in the sun, she thought, as she watched cars splash through puddles on Seneca Street in front of the building. St. Lucia might be nice - beautiful island, Caribbean atmosphere, and a reasonable plane trip. The sharp ring of the nearby black touch-tone phone cut through her reflection.

The voice at the other end of the line, she answered, was heavily Hispanic, "Hello. May I speak to Dr. Knight?"

"Yes, this is Dr. Knight."

"Dr. Knight, my name is Dr. Alberto Velasquez. I am the medical examiner for the city of La Ceiba in Honduras. We have a rather unusual situation here, for which I believe we will need your expertise. Nine bodies were found either shot or slashed to death, three days ago, aboard an abandoned treasure-hunting boat called the **Golddigger**. They were all American citizens." Carla held her breath. "The motive is unknown at this time. However, three of the bodies have additional skin findings that do not appear associated with their cause of death. One of these same individuals has evidence of pulmonary edema, which leads me to think that the three corpses may have had varying degrees of decompression illness. There are some skin lesions that I can not identify, either.

51

Due to the homicidal nature of all nine deaths, an international investigation is inevitable, and it is important that the autopsies be as conclusive as possible. Is there any chance that you can come here next week to help us?"

Carla was alarmed by the call from Central America, "Why, uh - I'll see what I can do, but yes, I'd be glad to help you with your investigation. Can I ask, was one of the victims named Steve Terzien?"

The answer that she feared came. "Yes. Why do you ask?" Dr. Velasquez heard her gasp as he replied.

"He was a friend of mine." Carla was fighting the despair in her voice. "I was hoping to join him and his crew to do some scuba diving in Honduras."

"I'm sorry that you had to learn of his death in this manner. It sounds like your own life, by a quirk of fate, has been spared. I would understand if you did not want to participate in the investigation, in view of your friendship with Senor Terzien."

"No, on the contrary, I want to help find out who killed him. I'll have to see if I can get someone to cover for me while I'm gone. How long do you estimate that you may require my assistance?"

"Probably two to four weeks, as you will need to go to the island where the boat was last docked to inquire about the crew's circumstances and health prior to their departure, and then, out to the site where the boat was found. I understand that they had put in a couple of days at Posada del Sol, a resort on the island of Guanaja. Phone access has not been easy, so I have not had a chance to talk to anyone directly at the resort."

"I'm sure that I can get the coverage. I'll call my travel agent immediately and get back to you with my arrangements."

"Excellent! My telephone is 430229. We very much appreciate your assistance and I look forward to meeting you." This last statement Dr. Velasquez sincerely meant, as he wanted to meet the attractive brunette with blue eyes that he had seen at the conference. "I will await your phone call. Goodbye."

"Goodbye," responded Carla, with a mixture of sadness and excitement about the prospect of the task before her.

Thinking about Steve's horrible demise evoked more recollections of Philip. Her last memory of Philip, alive, was seeing him on the steps of his office building in his trench coat, with his dark hair blowing in the wind and his lively eyes scanning her face, after they had met for lunch at a downtown restaurant. It was later that night that he was shot and the ominous phone call came from the police.

Philip had only been 33 and she was 30 at the time of his death. They met while she was in residency training and had been married three and a half-brief, but good years. She had worked emergency rooms after her internal medicine residency and two fellowships because she did not have to take call on a beeper and could count on her time home. Children were not in the picture, as they had wanted to wait until she finished training and enjoy a few years of marriage, unencumbered. He had died before they were able to embark on this endeavor.

The first year after his death, she avoided dating and buried herself in work. She found that she could not handle the violent assault cases in the emergency room. They unnerved her and evoked bad memories of Philip's bullet wounds, which she saw when she had to identify him in the morgue. Therefore, she looked into pursuing a field of practice that was less unsettling and secured a fellowship in hyperbaric medicine at Duke University, after completing a fellowship in pulmonary/critical care medicine which was a prerequisite.

In hyperbaric medicine, diving accidents were not necessarily the predominant conditions encountered. Skin infections and poorly healing surgical wounds were more commonly dealt with. There were also certain toxic inhalations to treat, as in the sad case; Carla had just experienced the week before.

On the prompting of friends, she saw a few different men during her fellowship, none for more than three or four months at a time. Many had hang-ups about relationships, in general. Dating had been a disappointment.

She did realize something important after all her trials, though. Life was short and unpredictable. This was not a dress rehearsal. This was it! Therefore, she began to take advantage of more opportunities that came her way. She appreciated her friends and family more than ever. Her previous carefree nature had never fully returned, but was still there under a layer of reserve. Carla worked for two years in the hyperbaric medicine department of a hospital in Long Beach, California and then accepted the position in Seattle at Mary Benson Medical Center.

The consulting job in Honduras was just the sort of test Carla was willing to tackle. She wanted to find answers for her friend's death and she wanted to dive. Sure she would go.

Coverage was easier to get than she imagined. Four weeks loomed ahead of her without constraints. Her travel agent obtained all her plane and hotel reservations in short order. Dr. Velasquez had suggested that she stay at Posada del Sol on Guanaja for the length of the investigation, after a brief stay in La Ceiba to review the victims' autopsy findings. This was so she would have close access by dive boat to the area where the **Golddigger** was found and, hopefully, a better chance of securing answers to the mystery enveloping it's murdered victims.

7

November 14, 1993

While Carla prepared to leave for Honduras, further events were unfolding there. It had been almost 12 days since Felipe had sniffed the vial. He had started to feel badly on Day 11, since the exposure. Now, he had a raging fever and headache, and his eyes were sensitive to light. His parents were worried, but had no idea that his illness was related to his exposure to the vial. No one else in the family was ill. Felipe was so overcome with his symptoms that he was not able to get out of bed. His father decided he would wait one more day and then summon the doctor from Bonacca, further west on the island. Bonacca could only be reached by boat, as there were no roads from Savannah Bight and no phones. This definitely put Felipe at a disadvantage. His mother kept putting cool compresses to his head, hoping his fever would break. There was not much more that she could do other than give him fluids and food and hope that he would keep the ingested material down. However, it was soon obvious that not even this was possible, because he began vomiting.

Felipe and his family lived in a one-room hut on stilts, set back from the beach, with partitions made of sheets and blankets. Privacy was unheard of, not to mention the ability to isolate a sick individual. Everyone under this roof was, therefore, vulnerable.

Elsewhere, in Honduras, another individual was just beginning to develop some symptoms like Felipe's, within the same time frames from exposure. This was the policeman who had found the vial on the **Golddigger**, after the Naval Force docked the vessel in La Ceiba. He noted that he had diffuse muscle aches when he awoke in the morning and still felt tired. Odd, he thought, because he had no heavy physical exertion in the last few days. As was his usual routine, he went to work, kissing his wife and daughter good-bye on leaving the house. Eleven days had elapsed since his exposure.

At work, he sweated profusely all day, enough so that a co-worker asked if he was feeling ill. He answered to the contrary, but later that afternoon he developed a severe persistent headache. His superior told him to go home early, which he did.

The vials, now enclosed in a plastic bag, had been placed in an evidence room of a police warehouse that was heaped with articles from the **Golddigger,** and had been forgotten. Neither of the exposed individuals had made any connection between their symptoms and smelling the objects. This boded misfortune for the towns of La Ceiba and Savannah Bight.

8

November 14, 1993

Carla left late in the afternoon on Continental Airlines for Houston, where she stayed at an airport hotel, overnight. She flew to the capital of Honduras - Tegucigalpa, the following morning. The landing was memorable, as the large jet descended onto a downward sloping runway, with numerous adobe houses clustered about the ends of the runway. It seemed that the jet would hit one of these dwellings, but, miraculously, it didn't. The city lay nestled among a series of hills. In this respect, it reminded her of Quito, Ecuador, but there, the hills were actually large mountains that formed part of the Andes chain.

From her guidebook, she learned that Honduras was the second-largest country in Central America. It was predominantly mountainous, but had coastal lowlands with hot, humid weather. By contrast, the mountainous regions were cooler. Rainforests could be found in La Mosquitia to the northeast. Several Mayan ruins were located in the western section of the country. Christopher Columbus, who landed in Trujillo in 1502, had named the country. Tegucigalpa, or "Teguz" as it was familiarly called, was a city of roughly 800,000 people. It became the capital of Honduras in 1880. Originally, a silver mine, worked in the late 1500's, occupied the location. Tegucigalpa became a center of gold and silver mining, subsequently. The colonial influence had endured over the centuries on the architecture of the city. There were still many red-tiled roofs and several winding streets were cobblestone.

From Tegucigalpa, after a two-hour wait in the lone, terminal coffee shop, Carla flew Air Islena to La Ceiba, where the banana industry reigned strongly. Standard Fruit Company employed much of the town. The company was known to most Americans by its brand name, Dole, and owned a large percentage of the arable land in Honduras, along with the United Fruit Company, farther to the east. La Ceiba was a seaport from which bananas and pineapples were exported. It bordered the Caribbean, in which the Bay Islands were only a short distance away. Carla felt excited as she neared her ultimate destination.

Dr. Velasquez, who drove her to her hotel, met her. He was a dignified-appearing, Hispanic gentleman with a neatly trimmed, greying goatee and a portly profile. Since it was mid-afternoon, he told her that no work would be pursued until the following day. She, thus, had the remainder of the day to unpack, walk to the beach, and browse in the shops near the hotel. The air was humid, but there was a breeze blowing in from the sea. Carla did notice a medium-build, Hispanic man with long, limp black hair, who was standing in the plaza of shops and appeared to be watching her intently. He was wearing a tropical shirt and chinos, which was out of character with his otherwise unkempt appearance. His expression was notable for a pair of hard eyes and a lecherous grin, which wrinkled a thick scar on his right cheek, when she looked his way. Flirt, thought Carla, and she walked on.

Later, that evening, Velasquez took Carla to dinner at Ricardo's, a popular eatery on Avenida 14 de Julio at 10 Calle. They sat on a garden terrace and briefly discussed their careers and lives, and then launched into a discussion of the investigation at hand. Carla, at one point, glanced across the terrace and noticed that the same man, she had seen in the plaza, now was sitting at a distant corner table, scrutinizing them.

"Have you ever seen the man at the corner table before?" asked Carla of Velasquez. The doctor turned in his seat and looked behind him. The man at the table in question was, by this time, perusing his menu, with his head down. "Never. Why do you ask?"

"Well, he has been watching us and I saw him in the plaza today."

"I wouldn't worry. He's probably a local resident. He might even work for the Standard Fruit Company, here. Frankly, I can't blame him for watching you. You do tend to attract one's attention." At this, Carla blushed, uncomfortable with compliments. "I'm sorry. I did not mean to embarrass you," Dr. Velasquez responded. "If you would like, I can give the police his description and see if they can come up with any suspicious identities?"

"Well, it might not hurt since we are pursuing an apparent criminal investigation."

"Consider it done." However, Dr. Velasquez thought the concern unnecessary and he relegated the task to a low priority in his schedule for the next few days. Pretty women, he thought, when would they learn that a man's glance did not automatically imply a sinister action?

The rest of dinner was uneventful. However, Carla did notice, upon returning to her room, that her suitcase seemed to be in a slightly different location than where she left it originally, but nothing in it appeared to be missing. With that confirmed, she went to bed and slept fitfully after her long trip.

9

November 15, 1993

Later, the same evening, the fisherman, Pablo went to seek the help of the doctor in Bonacca for his son, who was still very ill. Felipe had not kept anything down and was severely dehydrated. He stared at the ceiling without expression. His mother was distraught.

"Felipe, please try to drink this soup," his mother, Meribel pleaded. "You need to keep your strength."

His eyes moved slowly to look at her. There were dark rings under them. Hoarsely, he answered, "I am sorry, Mother. I cannot." Even talking exhausted him.

Meribel turned away, frustrated. However, Felipe began dry heaving and she ran for a pan to hold under his chin. Where was Pablo? She prayed he would get back soon. With an arm around his back, she supported Felipe in a sitting position, while he vomited. Heat was radiating through his shirt.

Shortly, her prayer was answered by the arrival of Pablo with Doctor Torres of Bonacca. Dr. Torres was a very old gentleman with white hair and he took out a pair of spectacles, as he approached Felipe's mattress on the floor. "So Felipe, you have gotten yourself sick. We will have to make you better." His patient looked feebly at him, after this attempt to be lighthearted. Dr. Torres saw the degree of the boy's illness in his gaze and he was alarmed. Dengue fever could do this, but he hadn't seen it in the islands in years. Malaria was another less likely possibility. Turning to Meribel, he asked, "When did he get ill?"

"Three days ago."

"What was his first symptom?"

"The fever, then he began vomiting, yesterday."

"Did he have any cough or cold symptoms?"

"No."

"Any rashes?"

"No."

"Diarrhea?"

"No."

"Has anyone else been ill in the family?"

"No."

"Has Felipe traveled anywhere recently?"

"He went fishing with his father and brother last week." Meribel paled slightly, remembering the boat that they had found adrift. "They did come upon a drifting boat with several murdered Americans aboard."

"How were these people killed?"

Pablo interjected at this point, "They were shot or stabbed to death. Felipe did go on board and found one woman, who had obviously been violated and was shot."

Dr. Torres looked at Felipe. "Did you touch anything on the boat, Felipe?"

Felipe was mildly delirious and did not even hear the question, fully. He shook his head 'no.'

Dr. Torres was suspicious, but puzzled, as no one else was ill. "Meribel, does Felipe have any significant past medical problems?"

"No, Doctor, he has been healthy since birth."

"Is he on any medications?"

"No."

"He has no allergies to anything?"

"None."

"Has your family had any major medical problems?"

"Just diabetes in my grandmother."

"How about you, Pablo?"

"My father died of a heart attack."

"Very well. I will examine Felipe, now."

Dr. Torres took his time doing this because he was hoping to find some signs that would give him clues to the source of the boy's sickness. However, he only found evidence of severe dehydration. He decided to treat him symptomatically. "Meribel, I am going to give you a herbal preparation that will calm his stomach and will, hopefully, make him stop vomiting. Try to give him clear fluids during this time. I will come back and check him tomorrow. If he is still as sick, I will take him back to the infirmary in Bonacca and consider having him flown out to the hospital in La Ceiba."

Pablo and Meribel nodded gravely. On the mainland or in the United States, Felipe would have already received an intravenous line. They did not realize this, however. Nor, did Dr. Torres recommend an IV at this juncture, as he was used to treating illnesses with simple measures on the island.

Pablo, reluctantly, took him back to Bonacca by boat. Meribel, meanwhile, put cool compresses on Felipe's forehead. The humidity in the hut had caused multiple tendrils of her black hair to fall out of her bun, necessitating that she push them out of her face, while she swatted at flies. As the hours passed, Felipe's vomiting subsided with the herbal prep, but his fever raged on. He was quite delirious and would not take anything by mouth. Pablo returned home after a couple of hours, checked on Felipe's status, and then fell asleep in a corner, exhausted, his sweat-stained clothes clinging to his thin frame. Meribel continued to keep watch through the night.

***

In La Ceiba, that evening, the policeman was faring poorly, too. He had begun vomiting and had a high fever. His wife had taken him to the local hospital emergency room, where he had been given a couple liters of IV fluid and had been diagnosed with the flu. Strangely enough, the physician on duty had seen three Naval

Force sailors earlier in the day with similar symptoms. They had all received intravenous fluid. One had appeared severely dehydrated enough that he was admitted for continuous IVs. There appeared to be alot of flu going around, the doctor thought. He expected to see more cases because all of these patients had wives and children, not to mention friends. The patient sent to the floor had not been placed in strict isolation due to his apparently benign diagnosis. He was discharged late that evening, after receiving three liters of IV fluid. Had the emergency room physician been able to talk to Dr. Torres, on Guanaja, he might have considered, otherwise.

***

By the next morning, Felipe's fever had broken and he was not as delirious, but he was still very weak from lack of fluids. Several family friends had stopped by to pay their respects. His mother was encouraged except, for the fact, that she now noted that he had developed flat, red round lesions on his face. When she had him open his mouth, she noted that they were on the mucus membranes as well. He had had chickenpox as a child and this seemed similar, she thought. Maybe he was having another bout. She was relieved.

10

November 16, 1993

The day proved to be busy, and both disturbing and intriguing for Carla. Dr. Velasquez picked her up early in the morning and drove her to the La Ceiba's morgue. They had no idea what was evolving at the local hospital. On the way, she marveled at the majestic outline of Pico Bonito in the nearby Nombre de Dios mountain range. Its slopes were covered with lush green vegetation, as was much of the surrounding countryside. Farther along the Waterfront Boulevard, they crossed the central canal running through town, which was lined with Ceiba trees. In the distance, she could see a long solitary pier with a lighthouse gracing the end, projecting into the bay. The image was peaceful.

In sharp contrast, the morgue was sterile without any engaging scenery. It was housed in a plain, one-story stucco building. The interior was air-conditioned. One by one, Dr. Velasquez opened the chilly vault drawers containing the corpses of the **Golddigger** crew. When Carla saw the bloodstained body of Steve Terzien and his frozen stare, she gasped and tears welled up in her eyes. She had to take a moment to compose herself before she proceeded to the others.

"This is the gentleman who was your friend, yes?"

Carla nodded, gathering strength. "I was just startled by how brutally he was killed. It brought back some bad memories." In deference to Carla, Dr. Velasquez covered Steve's body with a sheet. She would say no more on the subject and approached the final drawer. The bodies of Erik Slade, Bob Weber, and Dave Krueger were most notable, as all of them had an unusual skin appearance, in addition to the liver mortis that the other corpses demonstrated. In Slade's and Weber's cases, both bodies revealed red scattered acne-like lesions. Dave Krueger's body revealed similar findings, but his body also displayed prominent blotchy purple markings.

"Dr. Velasquez, didn't you say that in the case of Dave Krueger, he was found to have a very red throat, fluid in his lungs suggestive of pulmonary edema, and subcutaneous gas in his neck tissue?"

"Yes, I did."

"Well, it would seem that he might have been in that state on the boat, as he was found wearing an oxygen mask and was near an oxygen tank. In addition, from the combination of his mottled purple rash, and lung and soft tissue finding, it would suggest that he had decompression illness, in particular the "chokes, from prolonged deep diving." With this last reference, Carla was alluding to the pulmonary form of decompression illness, which was a more serious entity, than the "bends", or musculoskeletal variety. "I am sure that you have already made that conclusion, as you are a diver and familiar with the risks."

"Yes, I did surmise that Senor Krueger had the full spectrum of decompression illness after noting, at autopsy, that the cardiac cavities were filled with air, air was in the splenetic vessels, and there was evidence of spotty hemorrhages within the spinal cord."

"However, the rash on the other two victims was not typical of that in decompression illness and would appear to be either from an infectious source or from contact with an irritant. The question is - what?"

"I totally agree, Dr. Knight."

"Please call me, Carla."

"As you wish, but you must call me, Alberto."

"OK." Suddenly, a thought dawned on Carla. She remembered some cases, a few years ago, in which a group of workers in a herbicide plant developed similar rashes. The skin ailment was later diagnosed as chloracne and thought to be secondary to exposure to dioxin in the herbicide. "Alberto, I think there is a possibility that we might have a situation of exposure to a chemical. Were there any herbicides or pesticides found aboard the Golddigger?"

"No."

"Well, I remember some cases of herbicide workers with a rosacea-like rash called chloracne from exposure to dioxin." By rosacea, Carla was referring to a rash comprised of small red bumps and pustules, which was also sometimes seen on alcoholics. "The exposure may have come from something that the **Golddigger** crew was working on underwater, as only three of the crewmembers display the rash, and they might have been the divers on the project," she added.

"Good point. However, unlikely, as they were found out to sea in water hundreds of feet deep and were a long distance from land."

"It was only a thought," sighed Carla. Any other unusual findings in the autopsies?"

"Two things. As you can see, the male decedent with a rash and the apparent decompression illness findings, had his throat slit and apparently died from this inflicted injury. Whoever killed him left their fingerprints on the oxygen mask when they held his head to cut his throat. The same person apparently raped the only female crewmember on the boat, and presumably killed her. Finding the same fingerprints on the woman's body, in her own blood, confirmed this. She had been partially disrobed and there was semen in her vaginal canal. Strangely, she was found lying on her back, spread-eagled, even though she was shot from behind. This would suggest that she was raped after she was shot. More than likely, she was already dead when she was violated, as one of the bullets severed her brainstem. We were able to make a positive ID on the prints with Interpol, and found that they belong to one Alfonso Caldas, a notorious member of the Cordillera drug cartel. He is known for being a cartel hitman and a vicious sociopath.

However, I did not bring you here to concentrate on these latter findings. They are criminal matters for the police."

"Why would the drug cartel be involved in this case?" Carla said, ignoring Dr. Velasquez's last comment.

"Nothing was found on the boat that might suggest the reason. The **Golddigger** might have surprised the cartel while they were conducting some clandestine smuggling operation. Perhaps, they were both looking for the same thing. The police are still wrestling with all the non-conclusive evidence. There are no leads, other than Caldas's fingerprints. No one saw the massacre on board the vessel, or what had overtaken it."

"What do you suggest that I do next, Alberto?"

"Go to the island of Guanaja, to the Posada del Sol resort, and see if you can learn anything about the health of the **Golddigger**'s crew while they were on the island to get provisions, and anything about their diving histories. I know the vessel often docked at the resort. Also, the resort's dive operation can take you out to where the **Golddigger** was found, and you can dive in the area and see if you can discover any new evidence. There is an underwater photographer on the dive operation staff, named Senor Rod Dalton, who can help you with underwater material you want documented. Rumor is that he used to do photographic surveillance during the Viet Nam War. I will have my assistant, Gonzalo, make your travel arrangements. When would you like to leave?"

"Would tomorrow be too soon?"

"No, by all means, we can arrange it."

"Good. I am anxious to begin work on the case." Carla was resolved to finding Steve's murderers.

"And we are most appreciative to have your expertise."

"I thank you for the opportunity to participate."

With that, Dr. Velasquez, summoned a taxi to take Carla back to her hotel. He indicated that the bodies of the **Golddigger** crewmembers would now be released to their families in the United States. She made some notes, meanwhile, about the post-mortem cases. The skin findings had her attention. What had happened to those people? Would they ever find out? Her curiosity about the resort, Posada del Sol, and the photographer, Rod Dalton, dismissed this thought. She was impatient for tomorrow to come. Others, unknown to her in Honduras, were uneasy for what tomorrow would bring.

11

November 17, 1993

Meribel was scared stiff. The rash on Felipe's body had become confluent and blood appeared to have collected beneath the vesicles on the skin surface. His general condition had taken a turn for the worse. He was now short of breath and coughing, occasionally hacking up blood-tinged sputum. His fever had also returned. He could barely speak. His mother was not convinced that this was chickenpox, any longer.

Pablo raced off, once again, to find Dr. Torres. His son, Juan, could only stand fidgeting at the door of the hut, unsure of what to do. He didn't feel so great, either. Meribel could not hold back the tears, even though she was trying to maintain a calm-appearing demeanor for her sons. She saw Felipe trying to get her attention.

"Is there something I can do for you, my son?"

"Mother, when Dr. Torres comes, tell him I smelled a glass tube on the boat we found two weeks ago. I think it made me sick."

Meribel looked puzzled. "What kind of tube was it?"

Before he could answer, Felipe broke into a paroxysm of coughing and became too short of breath to speak. Meribel decided to let him rest and asked no further questions. She wondered where he had found the object on the boat and if he still had it. What could it all mean? She was sorry that her family had ever found the boat.

Dr. Torres arrived with Pablo one hour later. Felipe was not alert and only moaned when questioned amid rapid, rasping breath sounds. Tears still streamed down Meribel's cheeks. Dr. Torres was greatly alarmed by what he saw. This was not chickenpox. The lesions he saw on Felipe's body were in the same stage of development, as opposed to chickenpox, in which the lesions were in all phases of development.   Also, there was a centrifugal distribution of the rash, which was unlike chickenpox. Maybe this was meningococcemia, taking into consideration the hemorrhagic nature of the vesicles. At least, there was treatment for this entity and prophylaxis for all contacts. But, what if this was smallpox?! The thought terrified him. He had only seen two cases in his medical career and these had been in some Indians on the Mosquito Coast in the 1950's. They had died, but the remainder of their village had been isolated from them and immunized. He knew that endemic smallpox had been proclaimed to have been wiped out globally by the World Health Organization in 1980, as a result of thorough past immunization programs. Smallpox had not been seen in Honduras in almost 40 years. However, here was a possible case and everyone in the room had been exposed. He shuddered, because there was no specific therapy for smallpox, other than supportive measures. Maybe others in Savannah Bight had been exposed.

As calmly as he could, he turned to Pablo and Meribel and said, "We need to get Felipe to the hospital in La Ceiba. I think he has a serious infection and he requires special medicine and treatment. I also think his illness might be highly contagious and we have all been exposed. Therefore, I have to place the rest of you in strict isolation with respiratory precautions. The best way to do this is to take you with Felipe to La Ceiba, where you can be observed. I will also have to be isolated, and thus, will send back other medical relief. We can't go by commercial airlines to La Ceiba because of the risk of spreading more disease. I will call the hospital in La Ceiba by radio and see if they can send a Naval Force helicopter to transport all of us."

Meribel and Pablo looked at each other, bewildered and scared. It was, then, that Meribel remembered to tell Dr, Torres about the glass object. "We will do what ever is necessary, Doctor. I must tell you about something that Felipe revealed to me this morning. He said that when he and his father and brother found the boat last week, he found a glass tube on board which he smelled. He thought it had made him sick."

"Did he bring it home with him?"

"He didn't say and became too ill to talk more."

"Pablo, did you see him carrying anything back onto your boat?"

"No. My son ran out onto the deck of the other boat and started vomiting. We had to help him get back on board. He had seen a horrible sight and it had made him ill. He was not carrying anything that we could see." Pablo wiped a rivulet of perspiration off his forehead, the sense of uneasiness building.

"It is important that we find that tube and the possible source of this infection. Look for it, before we leave for La Ceiba. I will go back to Bonacca and make arrangements for a helicopter. I will also get us some masks to wear. We must not breathe on any new unexposed contacts. Anyone else who visited Felipe, while he was ill, must do the same thing. Let them know this and advise them to stay near their homes. Pablo, I will have you take me back to Bonacca, now."

Pablo nodded. Meribel immediately busied herself, gathering items to pack for the family. There seemed to be so many questions that could not be answered at the moment.

Dr. Torres departed with Pablo and left the hut silent except for Felipe's labored breathing. His advice came, unfortunately, late for several in the village. Meribel, who put the husky boy to work packing, rescued Juan from his doldrums. She quickly ran down the main path through the village and knocked on the doors of the houses, where friends resided that had visited Felipe during his illness. This caused some hysteria as the nature of the illness was too unclear. Meribel encouraged them to stay near their houses and not to directly breathe on anyone should they fall ill, stipulating that this was at the request of Dr. Torres. She tried to reassure them that medical relief would be sent for any that became sick, saying this as she covered her own mouth and nose with a rag.

Not everyone would heed her advice and some quickly departed in boats to Bonacca in an attempt to get away from the village and its illness.

She watched people pushing and shoving each other out of the way to get into boats, and shook her head sadly. These were all individuals that she had grown up with and knew as gentle, respectful neighbors. The people, before her, now, were behaving like animals. No matter, she had Felipe to worry about, at the moment. Returning to the hut, she collected the remainder of items she needed to take with them to La Ceiba. Pablo returned, after an hour, and informed them that a Naval Force helicopter would be picking them up directly from Savannah Bight. Dr. Torres did not want Felipe transported anywhere, unnecessarily.

The helicopter arrived, a little over two hours later, and put down in a grassy clearing near the village. It had to be guarded at gunpoint, as several villagers tried to climb into the aircraft in an attempt to get away from the island. Naval crewmen carried a litter to Felipe's hut and he was transferred onto the stretcher. He and his family were, then, escorted back to the helicopter. There was no need for guns, at this point because the villagers kept a wide berth from the departing party. They did yell at them from a distance, though.

One swarthy man, Luis Guardado, a neighbor, shouted, "Who is going to take care of our families, if they get sick? Why does Pablo's family get special treatment? Several others in the crowd mumbled agreement with these questions.

Dr. Torres, who was now wearing a mask, stepped forward from the retinue surrounding Felipe and answered, "This Naval Force helicopter will return with other medical personnel from La Ceiba to monitor your health here in Savannah Bight and to assist anyone, who falls ill. They will also send similar personnel to Bonacca. I can not stay because I have been directly exposed to whatever Felipe has, without protection." Dr. Torres now wearing a surgical mask as were the other members of Felipe's family and the Naval Force crew attending them. "I would strongly recommend that anyone, who visited Felipe's house during his illness, wear a surgical mask when out in public and avoid close contact with others. When the other medical team arrives, they will quarantine any contacts for a couple of weeks to watch for symptoms. For now, I suggest that you return to your normal activities."

"How are we to return to our lives, when we don't know who will get sick and expose us next?", persisted Luis Guardado.

"We will, all, simply have to do the best that we can, reducing the risk of exposure to one another, exercising good hygiene, and having faith in God," offered Dr. Torres.

"That is little comfort. I think that you are flying away to leave us all here to die," replied the man.

"We are flying away to limit your contact to an obvious case of illness and to known direct contacts, and to get this boy needed treatment! Angrily, Dr. Torres turned away and followed the rest of the party into the helicopter.

The villagers continued to grumble and shake their fists, as the helicopter accelerated its rotors and lifted off the ground. Meribel looked down and could not believe she had lived with these people her whole life and had not seen this side of them before. Pablo stared out the window of the craft blankly, not able to fathom why this was happening to their family. On the stretcher, Felipe remained in a comatose state, his breathing shallow. Of all of them, Juan was in the best state of mind. He had never been off the island except on fishing excursions with his father and brother, and he had never been in an airplane, let alone a helicopter. This was becoming an adventure for him. He was sure his brother would recover.

12

The **Islena** flight from La Ceiba to Guanaja departed, mid-afternoon, the same day that Felipe was airlifted from the island. This left Carla time to walk the beach east of the town, listen to the tropical bird song, and make some purchases from the shops around the central Plaza. The day was sunny, the warmth in the air settling on her comfortably, despite the humidity, as there was a slight breeze from the sea. While at the beach, she sat and read a guidebook about the island of Guanaja.

Christopher Columbus had discovered the island in 1502. Prior to that time, Paya Indians, who were related to the Mayans, had inhabited it. The Spanish took several of the Payans as slaves. Those, that were not captured, either left the island or died of imported diseases. The Spanish, subsequently, used the Bay Islands as a provisioning stop on voyages carrying gold from Trujillo to Spain. For this reason, as well as the fact that ships could navigate the shallow waters and lie in wait for cargo-laden Spanish galleons, Dutch, French, and particularly, English pirates became interested in the islands. Carla could, now, understand why the **Golddigger** crew had been in the area around the Bay Islands, looking for treasure.

Her flight to Guanaja was not announced distinctly in the La Ceiba airport terminal. As a result, she ended up running to her plane when an agent gestured emphatically at her to go, and then, gestured at a small twin engine commuter plane, whose propellers were already turning. The plane was full of Honduran passengers and she took the last seat near a gray-haired, grandmotherly-appearing woman, holding a small dark-haired boy on her lap. It was obvious that the other passengers sensed that she was a visitor to the country, by the way that they looked at her. With her coloring, she could have passed for a local resident, but her sophisticated khaki clothing betrayed her, as did her notebook computer. Someone stuck a small piece of gum in her hair, while she napped briefly, deriding her foreign origin.

The flight only took twenty-five minutes. A lush green island, with a canal cutting through it , appeared out her window ahead of the plane. Carla noted that the main settlement on the island seemed to be built a distance out from the shore, on stilts, in the water. She could not imagine why this had been done. The beach did not appear marshy or flooded. However, the thick jungle vegetation did descend from the hilly terrain to meet the beach's sandy margin.

What an interesting place, thought Carla. It looked like a small version of Venice in the Caribbean. The town's name was Bonacca. She knew this from seeing a map of the island. It had narrow canals running in a grid pattern around stilted structures. Occasional palm trees poked their way out of the maze. There were no roads on Guanaja. Travel was by boat.

The plane touched down on a dirt runway spanning a grassy field, bordered on one side by the jungle and on the other side by the canal, which cut through the island. Several dark-haired children gathered around the plane after its engines quit. They helped to unload luggage from the plane and were seen to carry it away on large carts down to the water's edge, where there was a small dock and some motor launches.

Carla was, at first, alarmed, as she feared that she would never see her luggage again. However, a small boy with dark, close-cropped kinky hair walked up to her and tapped her on the arm. He could not be more than five or six years of age, thought Carla. The child indicated, in broken English, that his name was Pepe and he wanted to know where she was going and what pieces of luggage belonged to her. He said he would take her luggage to the boat bound for Posada del Sol, and that she should follow him. Suddenly, they were engulfed in a sea of children and luggage, but they eventually made it to one of the boats with her belongings.

The Honduran driver spoke English with a British accent. This, Carla learned when she asked the driver, was the case with many Bay Islanders, who were the descendants of Carib slaves and English pirates. The Black slaves came from elsewhere in the Caribbean, when they rebelled against the British government. They subsequently settled in the islands. Pepe was the descendent of a Carib slave and a mainland Honduran, and thus, he spoke Spanish.

The driver was named, Manuel, and explained that they would have to stop in Bonacca for fuel. Pepe, meanwhile, was beaming, because Carla had given him a healthy tip in American dollars. He preferred dollars to Honduran lempira, as the exchange rate was better. He promised to be her luggage bearer when she departed.

The boat churned through the water, sapphire-colored in the late daylight, toward Bonacca. There was a slight, cool breeze and, after the sticky-feeling air in the terminal and aboard the plane, it was a welcome change. Questioning Manuel, Carla learned that Bonacca was built on stilts to avoid the sand flies on shore. It actually rested on what was called Hog Cay and Sheen Cay, in addition to some landfill, which supported the stilted structures. This was not the case with Savannah Bight and Mangrove Bight, the only other two villages on the island.

Pepe and a few of the other children had hitched a ride in the boat to the town. They jumped out hastily when the boat docked at the gasoline pier, chattering happily. Manuel apologized for the stop, but soon returned with the fuel for the motor, and they were off again across the bay, heading southeast. No one seemed aware of the recent events that transpired at Savannah Bight.

Carla began to wonder when they were going to arrive at the resort, after they passed a few miles of thick, jungle beach. Suddenly, out of the dense growth, the resort appeared. It looked like something out of the old television series, "Fantasy Island." She expected to see Ricardo Montalban and his assistant Tattoo. The architecture was Spanish colonial with stucco walls and a tile roof. The balconies were hung with colorful bougainvillea. There was a neat gravel path to the main entrance from the dock through well-tended gardens. The resort manager, Bryan Reynolds, and the front desk personnel met Carla at the dock. Her luggage was hustled up to her room, which bordered the pool deck. From there, down stone steps leading into terraced gardens with a stream, sprawled the remainder of the resort which consisted of secluded stucco bungalows. All around could be heard sounds of the jungle, contributing to the exotic air of the resort. She fell in love with the place immediately.

There was an hour, or so, to unpack luggage before dinner, and she took advantage of the time. It finally struck her how tired she was, and she lay down for a short nap and didn't awake until she heard knocking at her door. It was Bryan Reynolds asking her if she was going to come to dinner, as they had saved a place for her. His demeanor seemed friendly and outgoing, almost fatherly. She was startled by the sudden interruption of her sleep, but acknowledged the invitation to come to dinner, eagerly.

The dining room was full that evening. It was wood-paneled and had the air of a captain's room on an old schooner. She spotted Mr. Reynolds holding a chair out for her at his table and noticed a particularly handsome, yet rugged-looking man, sitting next to her place. He had dark brown hair with brown eyes and a tall, muscular frame. He was smiling widely, as she approached the table.

"Dr. Knight, let me introduce you to the group that helps run this resort. This is Rod Dalton, on your right, who is our underwater photography pro. He does some very fine work here and, also, has done a lot worldwide."

As her eyes locked with his, she felt a very perceptible rise in her pulse. She knew that there was immediate mutual attraction. He grinned and shook her hand firmly, saying, "Nice to meet you. I understand that you are an avid diver."

"Yes, diving is, definitely, a passion of mine."

"Good. We'll, undoubtedly, get a chance to do alot of diving together, while working on the **Golddigger** mystery. Bryan has given me leave from my normal duties to help you in whatever capacity you may need." He had been taking in her presence while talking to her and was struck by her fit, yet graceful figure and her luminous blue eyes. It had been a long time since he had felt such attraction for someone.

Carla, likewise had been captivated by her new acquaintance. His face was so interesting - gently lined with tanned, chiseled features and lively brown eyes, and a small, central starburst scar on his chin. He appeared to be in his late 40's as suggested by his lined face, but his body was that of a younger man. It was hard for her to avert her eyes and receive her next introduction.

Other people at the table included the front desk manager, Rachel Vega, a very pleasant young Honduran woman, and the resort manager's wife, Noreen Reynolds, a middle-aged, sandy-haired woman , who seemed to mother everyone.

Conversation, at dinner, focused predominantly on the fate of the **Golddigger.** The crew had just been visiting the resort, several weeks before their murder. Some of the resort guests had even gone aboard the vessel for a tour. They had enjoyed the affable crew, who seemed enthusiastic about their work. It was everyone's conclusion that they had been murdered for treasure that they had found. Carla was skeptical. Rod did not miss this in her demeanor.

"Dr. Knight, you seem to disagree with the theory about the crew's deaths?"

"Please, call me Carla. Yes, I'm not convinced that the deaths were necessarily tied to the discovery of a treasure. From what I've heard, there's nothing on the vessel to suggest that they found anything. Also, the location, where the **Golddigger** was found, was in water that was too deep for conventional diving operations and would have required remote vehicles."

"Valid points, but the vessel may have been set adrift, and the location, where it was found, may not be where it was overtaken," Rod responded.

"You may be correct."

"Piracy wouldn't seem to be the motive as their personal possessions weren't stolen and the vessel wasn't taken. It makes me wonder if they found something that they weren't supposed to, or that was desired by others. That, "something", must have been fairly significant, as it cost them their lives."

At this point, Bryan Reynolds followed Rod by asking, "Did you know, Carla, that they were looking for the wreck of the **Isabella** ?"

"No. What was she carrying?"

"She was a Spanish galleon that set sail from Trujillo Bay in the late 1500's, laden with a heavy cargo of gold, coins and gems from the New World. She is believed to have been sunk in a storm somewhere off the southeast coast of Honduras. Her treasure was deemed to be one of the richest in the Western Hemisphere. The **Golddigger** crew had been looking for her for three years."

"Were there any rivals looking for the same treasure?"

"Yes, in the beginning, three years ago when an old map surfaced in Trujillo." However, the others eventually lost interest or ran out of money. The **Golddigger** crew was fortunate to have Peter Beck of Beck International backing their operation. His funds are limitless. His wealth comes from holdings in oil, computer technology, and telecommunications."

"I would assume that he has been informed of the tragedy?," interjected Carla.

"He was notified as soon as the vessel was boarded by the Honduran Naval Force, as he is its legal owner. Also, I might add that he is the owner of this resort. He has been here in the last week to gather facts about the murders, so he could try to answer questions for the victims' families. A few of them have been down to claim remains of their loved ones, but the government has, unfortunately, prohibited the reclamation because the post-mortem investigations are still being concluded."

"You might be relieved to know that the coroner of La Ceiba told me that the bodies would be released to families, today," interjected Carla.

At this point, the conversation was interrupted by the approach of a middle-aged, redheaded gentlemen with a wide smile and inquisitive eyes. He was accompanied by a woman, who appeared in her late 30's, with strawberry-blonde hair and an overly friendly manner. Bryan Reynolds introduced them. "These people are Bud and Gloria Campbell. They practically meet everyone who comes to the resort, as they stay down here every winter for three or four months, at a time. Unofficially, they are part of our welcoming committee."

"Nice to make your acquaintance." Carla shook hands with both of them. She felt the deep penetrating gaze of Bud Campbell's eyes try to make a quick assessment of her. It was obvious that he was trying to figure out if she was visiting the resort by herself.

"Are you traveling alone, Dr. Knight?"

"Yes, I am."

"Dr. Knight is here to investigate the deaths of the **Golddigger** crew," added Bryan Reynolds.

"Well, I certainly hope that you get some time to enjoy this lovely resort."

"I'm sure that I will, Mr. Campbell." She didn't care to be on a first name basis with him because her initial impression was that she didn't like him. She was sorry that Bryan had divulged the purpose of her visit.

"If you have any questions about things to do, please feel free to ask us. We are in Bungalow 28," Gloria Campbell volunteered.

"I appreciate your hospitality."

Rod Dalton gave Bud and Gloria Campbell a thin smile at this remark, and remarked, "Bud and Gloria are hospitable to everyone, Carla. Changing the subject, might I steal you away to go over the dive equipment that you brought, before it gets any later? We have an early morning departure and I'd like to get it stored in the scuba shop."

"Why, of course. I also brought some underwater cameras for evidence documentation that I'd like to show you."

"Great. Let's go." With that, they said their 'good nights' to the dinner group and walked out into the heavily scented tropical night air. Bud Campbell watched them leave and thought, lucky guy - for now.

13

The walk to the scuba shop was over a stone path, bordering a tranquil cove that was wreathed by lazily, a curved palm tree. Carla and Rod had picked up her equipment from her room and were now toting it, between them, in a large duffel bag over the path. Only an occasional croaking toad or calling bird, and the quiet lapping of water on the beach broke the silence.

Conversation centered on where they each were from and where they had gone to school. It moved around to discussion about their respective personal lives. Carla divulged that she was widowed, when Rod asked if she was married. He wondered how her husband had died and she answered him, by giving a brief account of Phillip's untimely death. Rod was struck he was by her confidence and optimism about life, despite her past tragedy. Joanne, his ex-wife, had been fun loving, but couldn't handle any adversity. In fact, when he was listed as missing in action for over a year, she was so uncertain of his return from Viet Nam, that she started living with his best friend from high school. She began divorce proceedings shortly after his escape from prison camp and, subsequently, married his friend. The sequence of events was so painful to him that he had held women in low regard, since, and had simply used them for his pleasure over the years.

He did not relate all of these intricate details to Carla, other than to tell her about his wife leaving him before he came back from Viet Nam and marrying his best friend. She could see the remote look of sadness in his face when he related this, and felt badly that someone had rejected a man, who had fought through such a difficult war and managed to survive. She had been devastated to lose Philip, but was glad that they had loved one another to the end. Her description of her marriage proved to Rod that some people were devoted to their relationships.

Despite her physical attractiveness, Rod found himself not regarding her in the usual manner that he did most pretty women. She was different. She had depth and was interesting, and appeared to be a caring person. However he was distrustful of this apparent sincerity as he had no past experience with it.

He launched into a discussion about her underwater photography equipment. "I see that you brought a Nikonos camera with a 35mm lens. We'll need some still shots. Did you bring other lenses with you?'

"Yes, I brought a wide angle lens, too."

"I have some other lenses for varying range, if you need them. Have you ever used an underwater video camera?"

"Yup. I rented one on a scuba vacation a while ago, but, now, I own one."

"Good, because I think it's a better way to document the area that we'll be investigating. However, we'll still need the Nikonos for detail."

Carla noted his sudden business-like manner and wondered what had caused the change in his demeanor.

"Do you need to borrow any equipment other than a tank and weight belt?"

"No, I brought everything else with me, including my own regulator." The regulator was a diver's most important piece of equipment, as it was the mouthpiece and connecting hoses to the tank through which the person breathed. Carla brought hers on her travels, like most divers did, to insure familiarity with use.

"OK. We'll store your gear here, near the boat, so you can find it easily in the morning," offered Rod. He hung her wetsuit and buoyancy vest on a peg on the wall of the boathouse, and put her gear bag beneath them. "Let's go into the photo shop and I'll show you some of the equipment that I have."

They proceeded into a white-walled, neat appearing room, which was brightly, lighted. Every serious piece of underwater photography equipment, which Carla had ever seen in a scuba magazine or camera magazine, appeared to be in the shop, along with a variety of computer hardware and video dubbing equipment. Her eyes rested on a picture, hanging on one wall, of a grinning, sandy-haired male toddler. "Who's that?"

"That's my son, Robbie, when he was a little boy. I haven't seen him, except for pictures, in eighteen years. He's now 20."

"Why such a long time?"

"When I got home from Viet Nam, he was two years old. He'd been born while I was away on duty and I had only seen him through pictures, until my return home. I'd been in a Viet Cong prison camp for the last 14 months of my tour in Viet Nam, and my wife had, by that time, been living with my best friend from high school for a little more than a year. As far as my son was concerned, he was his father. The combination of the shock over my wife's infidelity and the lack of recognition by my son pushed me over the edge. I left town and spent several months on the road, doing odd jobs here and there. The divorce became final and I, eventually, lost touch with all of them. After a couple of years, I started making child support payments, but when I tried to visit my son, he didn't want to see me. This has been the case on a number of subsequent attempts to visit, so I stopped trying. I do have pictures of him when he was older, but I prefer to remember him as I last saw him, in person."

Carla didn't know what to say, initially. His story struck her deeply, because she knew what it was like to grieve over losing someone close to you, and subsequently, to detach yourself from the emotion of it, stuffing the feeling out of the range of everyday life, knowing it was hovering there on the periphery. "I am sorry to hear that you haven't been able to watch your son grow up."

"Don't be." Rod did not even give her a chance to reply further, but continued, "I've been buried in work since, and have been too busy for other people in my life. Two adults in a secure home setting have raised my son, and I couldn't ask for anything more than that. Now, is 7 a.m. too early to meet on the dock to leave for the **Golddigger**'s last known location?"

"No, that's fine," replied Carla, thankful that the tension had relieved, but stung by his abruptness.

"Great, then I'll meet you at 6:45 a.m. here, first, to get your weight belt and equipment together. Do you drink cola, lemon-lime, or orange pop?" Those are the choices with lunches."

"Cola."

"I'll bring a few cans for you on the boat. Get some sleep tonight. We'll have a long day tomorrow. By the way, bring your toothbrush because we'll be staying out overnight on the boat due to the distance that needs to be traveled and the time spent diving. Night."

"Good night."

They parted and walked to their separate lodgings. Carla felt as though she had put her foot in her mouth, while talking to him. Rod felt her sympathy for him, but was reluctant to respond to it. Morning would come soon enough, and they could both start a new day working together.

14

November 18, 1993

It had been 16 days since Felipe had sniffed the vial. In that time, four other individuals remote from Savannah Bight had become ill with similar symptoms. They had exposed a number of individuals, either at work or in their respective homes, to their illness. No one had taken any infectious precautions. The policeman had actually returned to work because, like Felipe, he felt briefly better when his fever defervesced after several days of vomiting. However, he noticed that he had developed some odd lesions in his mouth, which he could not explain, and showed them to his wife. She was struck by their similarity to chickenpox. The memory was fresh in her mind, as she had two young children, who had experienced the viral syndrome a few years ago. Her recollection was that she had been told that they would not get it again. The funny thing was that her husband had had chickenpox as a child. So had she, for that matter.

On this particular day, following Felipe's air evacuation, one of the Naval Force sailors returned to the emergency room in La Ceiba with a rash and worsening fever. The emergency room physician, Dr. Jorge Lopez, was convinced that the patient had symptoms similar to Felipe's, as he had seen the boy the night before. He, thus, thought it prudent to put the sailor in isolation. Large doses of IV antibiotics were ordered for the patient to cover him for meningitis, after Dr. Lopez attempted a spinal tap for fluid to culture. He had done the same thing for Felipe. The only thing that bothered him was that the patient and Felipe did not have stiff necks.

On reviewing the patient's old records, he realized that he was one of the three sailors who presented the week before with flu symptoms. That meant that there were two other individuals that probably had this man's symptoms, now, and very well might be exposing other people to meningitis, or worse, smallpox. He would have the authorities go look for them.

Felipe was in isolation, also, but in the intensive care unit. He had arrived the evening, before, comatose and in severe respiratory distress. His chest x-ray had showed an extensive bilateral pneumonia. Due to his deteriorating respiratory condition, it had become necessary to intubate him. He had not spoken to his mother since his conversation about the glass vial. Meribel was losing hope seeing her young son, unresponsive, with a tube sticking out of his mouth to help him breathe. She had been the only family member allowed to room in with him, in isolation, and she continued to wear her surgical mask. Pablo and Juan were isolated in a separate room on the medical ward and Dr. Torres was in, yet, another room. All were under strict respiratory precautions and skin precautions.

Blood, sputum, skin lesion, and urine cultures had been taken on everyone. Meningitis prophylaxis was given to Felipe's family and Dr. Torres. This consisted of taking Rifampin tablets daily for four days. Smallpox was not strongly suspected, as it had not been seen in decades. However, Dr. Lopez did order smallpox vaccine from the health department in Tegucigalpa, as this was the only repository for the vaccine in the country since routine vaccination had ceased over 10 years ago. He wanted to be prepared. The vaccine would take a day to be delivered by plane to La Ceiba. The only problem was that, if this was truly smallpox, the people that had been exposed to these cases should also receive immune globulin along with the vaccine, within the first week post-exposure. The nearest supply of this was in the United States, held by the U.S. Army. There was, otherwise, no specific chemical or anti-viral treatment for smallpox. It was unlikely they would need any of this because the illness, probably, was not smallpox. He dismissed it from his mind, for the moment.

He did not have to wait long for his next case to present. His wife brought the policeman into the emergency room, late that afternoon, severely ill with a persistent cough and diffuse, hemorrhagic-appearing lesions over his body. His chest x-ray showed a diffuse bilateral infiltrate suggesting pneumonia. The physician gave him large doses of antibiotics, like the others. He placed the policeman in a room near Felipe and the sailor's. The man's wife was able to stay with him, but only by honoring strict respiratory and skin precautions. She was under observation, as well. Dr. Lopez was very worried that there might be a widespread epidemic in progress, because Felipe was from the island of Guanaja, off the coast, and these other patients were from the mainland. He was going to have to question the patients or their families, extensively, to see if there had been any common pathogen exposure amongst them. It was, also, obvious that he would need outside help to deal with the problem. Upon questioning the policeman, sailor, and Felipe's family, he learned that the three patients had all, either, been on the **Golddigger** after it was found, or had been exposed to objects that had been on the **Golddigger.** More importantly, it was divulged that all three individuals had sniffed, or simply opened, a glass vial that had been discovered on the vessel and that had been submitted for evidence. The physician realized that they had to find this vial to identify what may have made these people ill.

When he dispatched some Naval Force personnel to find the object in the evidence room, neither it, nor its companion vials, could be found anywhere. This was because Ramirez had ordered two of his men to break into the warehouse and retrieve all of the vials, the night before. Erroneously, the physician thought that the police must have misplaced them during their investigation. They would have to continue looking for the objects, realized Dr. Lopez. Meanwhile, he would talk to the coroner of La Ceiba about the bodies that were found aboard the **Golddigger**. This individual might provide some answers.

His train of thought about solving the current medical dilemma was interrupted by a nurse, who frantically reported that his young patient, Felipe, was dropping his blood pressure and had developed a worse sounding chest. It was, now, early evening and too late to call the coroner, anyway. The doctor ran down the hallway with the nurse to the intensive care room. Felipe's face appeared dusky, despite the fact that he was on mechanical ventilation, and his eyes revealed subconjunctival hemorrhages. There was blood issuing from his nose. On listening to his chest, the young Honduran physician was struck by the minimal excursion of air heard and the extensiveness of the wet sounds in his lungs. The patient's blood pressure was 70/50. Meribel stood by, tears streaming down her face, her hand clapped anxiously over her mouth.

Dr. Lopez was responsible for the intensive care unit because no other physicians were in the hospital, that evening. He started giving rapid orders to the nurse, who had alerted him. "Juanita, start a dopamine drip on this patient STAT. Also, make certain that the patient is on 100% oxygen and have the respiratory therapist draw blood for an arterial blood gas analysis."

The result was returned, shortly, still showing a moderately low oxygen level. Dr. Lopez instructed the respiratory therapist, "Please, place 5 centimeters of positive end-expiratory pressure on the endotracheal tube. I want to try to prevent further collapse of the lungs from fluid build-up." It was becoming apparent that the pulmonary capillaries had been injured by Felipe's infection and were allowing the lungs to flood with fluid from the circulation. Felipe had what was called "shock lung." His kidneys had shut down and he had not produced urine in the last hour. Dr. Lopez decided to try some diuretics, judiciously, to try to drive fluid out of the lungs and increase the urinary flow. "Juanita, give the patient 40mg of furosemide IV. Have lab come and draw a white blood cell count, hemoglobin and hematocrit, platelet count, prothrombin time, blood type, fibrinogen level, electrolytes, and a BUN and creatinine." He was worried that the patient was also developing a condition called DIC, disseminated intravascular coagulation. Felipe's infection probably was releasing tissue factors that were triggering his body's coagulation system to operate overtime. This would cause small fibrin clots to form in many of his small blood vessels, thus producing extensive vascular or tissue injury, or in some cases, extensive bleeding from depletion of clotting factors. The biggest risk was that Felipe's heart would fail, as a result of the combination of septic shock, flooding of his lungs, and the latter condition. There were limits as to what the La Ceiba hospital could do. Felipe needed a more technologically advanced intensive care unit with access to critical care specialists. The lab at the hospital had to send many of its non-routine tests out of the area for processing and there was an excessive delay in receiving results. He might even need to be airlifted to the United States, where there was more advanced infectious disease expertise.

That was a luxury he would not experience, however. Despite multiple doses of diuretic medicine, large volumes of normal saline IV fluid, and the continual adjustment of his dopamine drip, he could not produce any urine per his foley catheter and his blood pressure could not be maintained any higher than 80/65. His lab work showed a markedly elevated white blood cell count, elevated kidney function tests suggesting his kidneys were failing, and a low platelet count. They were losing ground. Dr. Lopez decided to try a norepinephrine drip along with the dopamine drip to hold the pressure and buy some time. Additionally, he directed, "Juanita, after you start that norepinephrine drip, tell the lab to send up 2 bags of fresh frozen plasma and 10 packs of platelets. I don't like the extent of the hemorrhagic pustules on his body nor the evidence of submucosal hemorrhage in his mouth." Juanita, a diminutive dark-haired woman, nodded. He stepped, aside, to talk to Meribel. "Felipe's prognosis is grave. He has an extensive infection that we haven't identified yet, he is in shock and has fluid in his lungs, and his kidneys have stopped working. We are doing the best that we can, but it may not be enough."

"What are you saying, Doctor? That he might not live?"

"Yes, Meribel. I will have one of the nurses go get Pablo for you. You should be together through this." Meribel's face whitened behind the surgical mask. A sob broke from her lips and she crumpled into a chair.

A few minutes, later, Juanita replied, "I have the drip started and I have called the lab, Doctor. His pressure is still dropping."

"Turn up the drip by 2 micrograms per kilogram per minute."

"Done." The nurse felt Felipe's pulse, at his wrist, after the drip had been increased for one minute. She looked up at Dr. Lopez, alarmed. "I can barely feel his pulse."

Dr. Lopez looked at the monitor. He saw some sign of regular electrical activity with wide complexes. Then, he reached to palpate the patient's neck and check the pulse in the carotid artery. There was none. He shook his head. "Call a code, Juanita." He had the respiratory therapist take Felipe off the ventilator and bag him. He, himself, started chest compressions. While doing so, he said to Meribel, "Your son's heart has stopped. I am going to have you wait in the next room with Pablo, while we try to start it pumping again." He said this as calmly as he could.

Meribel left, in defeat. She could barely meet Pablo's dumbfounded gaze. They were escorted to an adjacent room, where they sat, wearing surgical masks and holding hands, anxiously. She tried to explain Felipe's circumstances, but he would not believe what he heard.

The code continued in the next room. Several nurses clustered around Dr. Lopez and the patient. They, all, wore protective masks, gowns, and gloves. One administered drugs through the IV and another recorded what was given. Felipe regained a pulse, briefly, after one dose of epinephrine, but then it disappeared. The monitor finally showed no further regular electrical activity and only a flat-line rhythm. They had tried a number of resuscitation drugs over a period of forty-six minutes and even tried shocking Felipe three times to no avail. His rhythm remained flat-line and he had no pulse or spontaneous respirations. The code was terminated after 47 minutes.

Dr. Lopez, reluctantly, left the room to talk to Felipe's parents. He ran his hand wearily through his thick, black, wiry hair. One look at his face told them everything. Pablo was the one to sob, this time, crying, "my son, my son," over and over again. Meribel looked stonily off, in the distance, her emotions drained. She realized that they would have to tell Juan about Felipe's fate, soon, because he would be worried why his father had been summoned away.

Dr. Lopez offered, "Pablo and Meribel, you can go see Felipe for a few minutes, but after that time, we will have to put his body in a protective covering and transfer it to a safe place in the hospital, where it will not expose others."

"You are talking about my son!" said Pablo, indignantly.

Meribel grabbed his arm, gently, and said, "You must go tell Juan what has happened. He will be frightened."

Pablo nodded sadly. He turned, and left the room without another word.

Meribel would go see her son for the last time. "Thank you, Dr. Lopez. I know you tried to save Felipe."

"You are kind. I am sorry, but I must return to the emergency room. The nurse informs me that I have many patients waiting. We must still keep you in isolation. It's more important than ever. I am sorry."

With that he rushed off to the ER, leaving the poor woman with her grief. He was not uncaring, only apprehensive that there was a serious epidemic facing them. Additional assistance was needed. Felipe's body would have to be cremated. He would call the local internist, Dr. Hurtado, to come in and assume care of the other surviving patients on the floor. This was the first documented death and there might be others they didn't know about. They had to find the source of the illness. He had to talk to Dr. Velasquez, the coroner, tonight. It was 10:30 p.m. He would call him at home.

15

November 18, 1993

The sun had barely crept above the horizon, when Carla left her room, that same day that Felipe died. There was already a soft breeze in the palms. Hummingbirds were busying themselves about the feeders hung throughout the resort, as Carla walked to the dining room for breakfast. Despite the early hour, the Campbells were seated and eating their meal. No one else was in the dining room.

"Good morning, Dr. Knight," remarked Bud. You must be getting an early start on your investigation. Are you and Rod going out to the site where the **Golddigger** was found?"

"Yes, very shortly."

"Well, I certainly hope you find some clues as to who killed those poor people," chimed in Gloria Campbell. "By the way, did you hear that a strange disease has appeared on the island in Savannah Bight?"

"No."

Well, it apparently surfaced in a teen-aged boy and he had to be flown out to La Ceiba with his family. Everyone in Savannah Bight is in a fright. It seems no one has a clue why he got ill," replied Gloria coyly. She appeared to know more than she divulged and seemed to be probing for more information.

"I have heard nothing about the situation. I, certainly, hope that the disease does not spread over the island and that they find the source." Carla grew uneasy at the line of questioning.

"I hope so, too," patronized Bud. "I, also, hope you find answers to the **Golddigger** murders. Good luck to you. We'll see you at dinner."

Carla did not finish her breakfast, but instead, wrapped the remaining toast in a napkin and hurried off to the dive shop, as she had looked at her watch and realized it was 6:47 a.m. The Campbell's watched her departure with interest. Rod was filling tanks with air when she arrived. He smiled widely, upon seeing her.

"Your BC is still hanging in the gear room, with your bag beneath it. You can fit the BC on one of the filled tanks on the boat, and put your gear bag in the V-berth, forward," instructed Rod. The term, "BC", he used, referred to the buoyancy compensator vest divers used to descend by releasing air stored in its bladders through an exhaust valve, or ascend by driving air in from a hose on the regulator which was attached to the tank. A diver's tank was attached to the BC like a backpack.

Carla found her BC in the humid gear room. Upon reaching for the nylon web handle by which it hung, a thin green snake stuck its head out of the BC and darted down the front of the vest, falling to the floor. It slithered out of sight. Not before Carla let out a small scream, however.

Rod dashed around the corner and laughed when he saw the tail of the snake disappearing into a crack in the wall. "Looks like you had a green boa in your BC. They're harmless. Frequently, they show up in the equipment in here, looking for a nice dark place to rest out of the sun."

"Great. I'm deathly afraid of snakes."

"Well, you've come to the wrong place. Honduras has several varieties of snakes - boa, coral, bushmaster, fer de lance, worm, and rattlesnakes, just to name a few. However, the Bay Islands only have boas and vine snakes and they are harmless."

"I don't plan to do a lot of jungle walking."

"If you do, just wear boots," smirked Rod and he returned to his preparations.

With the gear finally loaded, they headed out to sea on a 37-foot twin diesel dive boat. A crew of two Honduran divemasters accompanied them. One drove the boat, while the other tended to the equipment. The captain was named Luis and his crewmate was named Rico. Both spoke good English with a slight British accent. Rod later explained that this was because several Honduran Bay Islanders were of mixed African and English ancestry due to the cohabitance of slaves and pirates, which Carla had previously read about.

During this discussion, Carla stood on the flying bridge, drinking in the glittering sun on the water and the salt air. The marine radio crackled with an American voice from the National Hurricane Center in Miami, announcing a building tropical depression in the southeastern Caribbean. She noted some tiny, low islands off the main island, a few of which appeared inhabited. The largest Cay had a spacious, clapboard house on stilts at one end. She asked Rod who owned the house.

"That's Bird Cay, and the house and island belong to Kurt von Kreitler. It is rumored that he came here after World War II. Many Germans came to Central and South America at that time. Little is known about his past. He is pleasant enough, however, and he is in his mid-70's. He has a small landing strip on his island and keeps a Piper Cherokee, there, that he uses to get to the mainland. One curious thing that the locals have noted, though, is occasionally, late at night, a bonfire will be lit on the island and a plane will land and take off again, after a short interval. Other than that, Kurt's life draws no attention from anyone, as he tends to keep to himself."

What Rod was not telling her was that the Cay had actually been under surveillance for some time by the DEA, because it was suspected there was some drug activity there. He had originally been sent by the DEA to the resort to work undercover as a professional dive photographer, but in actuality, he was there to do a photoreconnaissance of the Cay. He had worked for the DEA since he had returned from Viet Nam. In Nam, he had been part of covert CIA operations, again doing photo reconnaissance, but he quickly became disenchanted with the organization's tactics in the war, when he was caught along with some South Vietnamese who were trying to infiltrate several Viet Cong installations. The U.S. government and CIA subsequently forgot him and the Vietnamese commandos. A lucky break occurred after 14 months of incarceration, however, when the camp, in which he was imprisoned, was damaged from an airstrike by U.S. forces and he managed to escape with a few others. During the commotion, he managed to slip from a work field into a nearby river. For nearly 12 miles, he stayed submerged using bamboo shoots as snorkels and crawled or floated over muck and dead animal carcasses and refuse, and occasionally, a dead human corpse. By the time he surfaced, it was night, and he heard American voices among the reeds on the riverbank, and realized that he had come upon a U.S. patrol. He later learned that he had reached South Vietnamese territory, again. The patrol retrieved him from the river and flew him out by helicopter, due to the fact that he had developed a severe case of dysentery during his ordeal and was dehydrated. His field training in the CIA had helped him to survive.

Back in Saigon, surprised CIA operatives told him that the war was near an end and his tour of duty was done in Viet Nam. He, subsequently, flew home and discovered the fate of his marriage. A year was spent in depression and drunken stupor until one of his friends from the CIA, who had resigned and joined the DEA, found him passed out in a seedy bar and managed to get him into an alcohol treatment facility. After maintaining sobriety for an extended period, he joined the DEA as a field operative photography specialist. He spent several years documenting the activities of Hector Ramirez and Eduardo Rojas, and became familiar with their particular brand of treachery.

"Wasn't Von Kreitler a U-boat commander during World War II?" queried Carla, noticing Rod was deep in reflection about something.

Rod looked at her surprised and answered, "Why yes, he was. How did you know that?"

"I was something of a history buff in high school. I remember reading that Von Kreitler and his U-boat disappeared at the end of the war. Do the authorities know that he is here?"

"Oh, probably, but he appears to lead a clean life and wasn't accused of any heinous war crimes, so no one is after him."

Carla mulled over this last bit of information with interest. Rod seemed to be holding back some information. He was a complex man - so outwardly charming, yet reserved in other regards. She was convinced that his past was convoluted and harbored many skeletons. His company was reassuring, though, and she enjoyed standing next to him on the flying bridge during the remainder of the trip to the site where the **Golddigger** was found.

Anchoring was impossible because the water was too deep, so the boat's engine was kept running to maintain its position in the current. Equipment boxes were opened. Much to the dismay of Carla and Rod, they found that the lenses on both of their cameras had been smashed. Even more suspicious, the cameras had been in different boxes, and yet were both damaged similarly.

"It looks like someone is trying to hamper our investigation," Rod said, frowning. "Which also means that we are being watched."

Carla was alarmed. All of a sudden, this was not a nice vacation in the sun. "We needed those cameras for documentation of any findings. What will we do now?"

"I have some additional photo equipment in the shop, but it means returning to the resort and losing a day. What if we push on and dive here, collect what we can, and return to Posada del Sol?" encouraged Rod.

"Very well. I can collect some water samples. We will not learn much, anyway, as the depth gauge reads 234 fathoms, or 1404 feet, and the bottom is far out of reach. The vessel must have been boarded in a shallower location because one of the **Golddigger** crew showed signs of decompression illness, and was obviously diving not long before his death."

"That does appear to have been the situation. Taking into account the finding of the smashed GPS receiver aboard the vessel, someone, obviously, did not want the **Golddigger's** original location known. One strategy we might pursue, after diving here, is to go in a direction directly opposite to the course of the current two weeks ago, and see what bottom contours we traverse. We have tidal current charts for the region with us. They can help us determine the direction and speed of the current for the rough time we estimate that the **Golddigger** may have been set adrift. Did Dr. Velasquez tell you how many days had elapsed since the deaths of the crew members?"

"Yes. He estimated two days."

"OK. That puts the day that the vessel was probably boarded on November 1st because it was discovered by the fishermen on the 3rd. Knowing the current direction and speed for that particular day and allowing offset for wind and windage of the vessel, and the roughly 48 hour period of elapsed drifting time, we should be able to come up with an approximate location, where the vessel might have been overtaken. Who knows? We might even find the underwater wreck that the **Golddigger** crew was looking for."

Carla and Rod set about donning their dive gear, which took some time to put on due to the multiple protective seals that had to be checked. Dr. Velasquez had arranged for hazardous materials protective suits exposure to be sent by Beck International to La Ceiba, in view of concern over the appearance of some of the **Golddigger** corpses. The suits had seals at neck, glove, and boot junctures. Full-face masks with a hood that sealed at the neck of the suits had also been supplied. They had their own one-way exhaust systems. At one point, Carla caught Rod eyeing her physique, appreciatively, as she pulled on her suit. She blushed and continued what she was doing, trying to act oblivious. Rod smiled and finished gearing up.

The two divers were in the water within twenty minutes. There was not much to see except big blue expanses of water, as bottom was out of scuba range and there was no shallow reef wall. Carla took a water sample, anyway. The only animal life in the area were some seagulls above the water and fish, called yellowtails, grazing the surface for food. Rod signaled to end their dive after about 15 minutes. The boat motored to pick them up because they had drifted off a distance in the current.

On the swim platform, the crew as a precaution against clinging toxic residue hosed them off completely with fresh water. They removed their equipment and conversed, agreeing that clues about the demise of the **Golddigger** crew must lie elsewhere. After a word with the captain of the **Yolanda**, the boat was headed northwest, 180 degrees opposite the set of the current on November 1st with a slight offset for wind. This was estimated from the weather report, for the same date, which was obtained from the Honduran Naval Force on the marine radio. Rod frequently would glance at the sonar unit to see what bottom contours they were motoring over. The instrument was good to a depth of 2500 feet. It was almost noon, so Rico distributed their sandwiches and soft drinks. They ate while motoring.

Carla was into a discussion of how she had gotten into diving, and Rod was listening intently. She related that her mother had been a marine biologist and had interested her, early in life, in the sea. There had been walks along beaches, searching tide pools and collecting specimens. Finally, in high school, she had taken a PADI dive course, and a whole new world had opened up before her.

Rod was curious how she trained for a hyperbaric medicine career. She explained that she had taken a heavy physics curriculum in college and then, after medical school, an internal medicine residency, followed by a fellowship in pulmonary and critical care medicine, and, finally, a hyperbaric medicine fellowship. Following three years of emergency medicine practice in Seattle, she had ended up running the hyperbaric chamber at Mary Benson Medical Center.

Rod was impressed by the path she had taken to her ultimate career. She, however, was not his concept of a physician, that being of a fatherly appearing, middle-aged male with a stethoscope around his neck and a supercilious manner. Her interests were varied. She liked to ski and scuba dive, play golf, and travel. She certainly seemed to grasp life with gusto, he thought.

His interest in her conversation was interrupted, abruptly, by the sudden appearance of shallower contours on the sonar screen. The deepest depth was 200 feet. There seemed to be a long ridge-like reef beneath them. They had traveled approximately five nautical miles from their first dive site. Rod's sudden riveting gaze on the screen caught Carla's attention.

"What do you see?"

"Some sort of reef wall which appears shallow enough to dive on. Luis, stop here."

"OK, Senor Rod."

Once again, Carla and Rod put on their protective suits and strode off the swim platform to begin their descent. The wall was roughly 65 feet below them. Visibility was to about 100 feet. An inquisitive grouper met them at about 40 feet and followed them down. They could discern color on the wall consisting of purple tube sponges and lettuce coral. Deepwater lace coral also punctuated this garden. There was a profusion of triggerfish, parrotfish, and butterflyfish swimming just above the wall edge. No wreck was in sight. Initially, they swam against the current, along the wall at a depth of 60 feet, for approximately 15 minutes and, then, they descended to the mouth of a cave, interrupting the wall's coral-encrusted exterior. The cave's depth was approximately 70 feet. A crevice in the cave entrance revealed the protruding antennae of a spiny lobster. The crustacean's beady eyes locked onto their movement. A cloud of silversides, small glass-like fish, parted as they passed further into the cave. Suddenly, a large shape could be seen in the beam of Rod's flashlight charging toward them. Its dorsal fin and thick fusiform body was unmistakable. It was a bull shark and it was followed immediately by two others. All three sharks rammed into Rod and Carla, knocking them aside and cutting their vulcanized rubber suits in the process. Subsequently, the sharks darted out of the cave, leaving Carla and Rod to fumble for their full face masks with regulators that had been pulled off their faces. The shock of the charge left them both winded. They had come upon a bull shark den and had cut off the sharks' exit. The fish had become alarmed and charged. They were lucky that they had not been hurt worse. They would have to exercise caution leaving the cave and ascending to the boat, as bull sharks were known to attack humans.

Rod motioned to Carla to turn and depart the cave. Carla still looked terrified and Rod had to grab her arm to get her attention. They carefully swam out of the entrance and ascended to the top of the wall. There, they let the current carry them for ten minutes, at a depth of 60 feet. The bottom time on their computers read 35 minutes. They would have to ascend toward the surface in the next five to ten minutes, but right now, they were scanning the surface of the wall for clues. None were apparent. Carla collected a water sample. A lone bull shark appeared from the blue depths beyond the wall and swam by them into the current, eyeing them suspiciously. Carla's pulse rate started to rise. It did not approach further and swam off into the blue. She breathed a sigh of relief into her regulator. Since nothing had been found and their air was running out, they decided to ascend to the boat which had been following their bubbles in the current.

Late afternoon sun bathed the swim step. Rod exclaimed to Carla, after he removed his mask and made certain that they, both, were safely out of the water, "Boy that was a close call."

"You can say that again," Carla agreed.

"I didn't consider the possibility of running into sharks in that cave nor the ramifications of blocking off their exit from the cave. That was not an attack, but a charge to leave, as a result of fear. Even so, we were lucky to escape injury."

Carla nodded. "Especially, when you consider their size. One looked to be almost seven feet in length and was chunky."

"You're right. Those bull sharks can actually grow up to eleven feet in length."

Carla shuddered and then shook her head in amazement. They proceeded to relate the details of the shark encounter to Luis and Rico. Their suits would have to be patched once the protective garments had been decontaminated and dried, before they dove in them again. This would be done much like a bike inner tube was repaired. Rod had a brief discussion with Luis about the weather and it was decided, since the weather was forecast to be calm for a couple of days that they would anchor there overnight. Approximately 200 feet of anchor line and chain was released to set the anchor, due to the current. With the boat secured, they put out a few fishing lines to try to catch dinner. They were rewarded shortly with two strikes by blackfin tuna, which they were able to land successfully on deck.

Rico had brought a hibachi and he began making preparations to grill their catch. The sun approached the western horizon, signaling it was cocktail hour. Rod passed out beers to everyone. There was barely a ripple on the water, except for that made by the current.

Ah, this is the life, thought Carla. She eyed the wasabi that Rico planned to serve with the tuna, hungrily.

Rod caught her glance and smiled. "Hungry?"

"Starving."

"We can have some chips and salsa while we're waiting for the main course. Dinner shouldn't be too long. Rico is a quick cook."

Rico, who was a shy fellow with widely spaced teeth, looked up and grinned at this compliment. Carla then asked him where he was from, since she had marveled at what perfect English both he and Luis spoke. "Savannah Bight," he answered. "Luis is from Roatan. Most of us in the islands are not from the mainland. Our families settled here long ago. Where are you from?"

"Seattle, Washington."

"Is that in the U.S.A.?"

"Yes, in the far northwestern corner of the U.S.A."

"You have come from far away."

"Yes, I have." Rico's comment about Savannah Bight reminded her of the conversation that she had had with the Campbell's that morning. Turning to Rod, she related, "Rico just helped me remember something that the Campbell's said to me at breakfast. Gloria asked me if I had heard anything about a strange disease appearing in Savannah Bight this week. Of course, I hadn't, but she still kept trying to ply me for information. She already seemed to know a moderate bit about the circumstances. Have you heard anything?"

"As a matter of fact, I had, from Bryan Reynolds this morning. The island is on an alert for further cases. The local authorities were going to try to do this, quietly, so as not to cause panic, but several Savannah Bight residents showed up by boat in Bonacca, and told locals that there was a plague spreading over the island. There has only been one case of illness, involving a boy, and he was flown to La Ceiba for medical attention. Bryan said, by the way people were arriving in Bonacca, you'd think there were dozens of cases."

"Did Bryan happen to mention what the boy's symptoms were?"

"All he said was that the residents from Savannah Bight kept talking about this ugly rash on his face and body, that looked like the 'childhood pox.' I'm assuming they were referring to chickenpox."

"You're probably right. People can get quite ill having chickenpox later in life, either as a teenager or as an adult. It

107

sounds like they're overreacting to the problem. They could have managed the situation with good hygiene and limiting close contact with infected cases, by anyone who has not had chickenpox, previously, or anyone who is pregnant."

"That sounds like it would have been the more reasonable approach to the problem."

"Well, I hope the boy survives the illness and there are no further cases in the town, for everybody's sake. On a different subject, you told me, previously, that you grew up in Minneapolis, Minnesota. What suburb did you live in?"

"Are you familiar with Edina?"

"Yes, I am, because I worked one summer during college for Donaldson's department store, downtown Minneapolis, while staying with a sorority sister out around Lake Minnetonka. I remember that it appeared to be an upper middle class community."

Your recollection is correct. My dad was an attorney for a firm in Minneapolis. He was always disappointed that I didn't follow in his footsteps. My mom was the consummate housewife and entertainer. She was the perfect mate for my father because she kept his life running smoothly in Edina. My choice of careers didn't bother her, because she just wanted me to enjoy my life."

"Are your parents still alive?"

"My mother is and she still lives in Edina."

"Do you have any sisters or brothers?"

"One sister, Jen, short for Jennifer, who's an investment banker in New York. How about you?
Brothers? Sisters?"

"I have two brothers, one older than I am, who is a dentist, and one younger, who works for a computer company. My father is an engineer for Boeing and is due to retire soon. Everyone still lives in Seattle."

"It sounds as though your family has varied backgrounds."

"Yes, it makes for interesting dinner table discussion when we all get together."

"Oh, Rico is giving me the high sign. It looks like it's time for dinner."

They all sat on the aft deck in director's chairs and ate their meal. Carla learned from ensuing conversation that neither Luis nor Rico had ever left the islands. Their vision of the outside world consisted only of what others had related to them. She marveled at this seclusion, and in some ways, envied it. Dinner concluded with an assortment of local fruit, consisting of bananas, pineapple, and papayas.

Rod and Carla then climbed out onto the bow, and sat, watching the light drain from the sky. They discussed a rough game plan for the next day and, also, what Carla should do with the water samples that she had collected. Rod indicated that she would probably have to go to Tegucigalpa to find a lab, which could process the samples. That would mean an overnight trip because she would have to hand carry the material. He was concerned about her safety, making such a trip, in light of the discovery of their vandalized cameras. He, therefore, decided to give her contacts in Teguz should she have any problems. Carla appreciated the caution.

Rod abruptly asked her, "You haven't remarried since your husband's death. I'm surprised because I imagine that you would have had lots of offers. No Mr. Right?"

Carla became slightly detached, answering, looking off in the distance. It was obvious that the question bothered her. "I don't know. I've been buried in my work for a long time, and haven't had a lot of opportunity to meet many people, but more so, I haven't found anyone who was as good a friend."

" I can appreciate that. My ex-wife and I were close friends through high school and through our early marriage. However, my problem was that after I went to Nam, all of that changed for good." What he intended to say, further, was that he had never wanted to get close to someone again, but, suddenly, he could not say this to her.

Carla nodded and Rod grew silent. She tried to give some words of encouragement, "It's a risk to trust another human being, but it's also wonderful to find someone, in whom you can have complete confidence. They do exist." She smiled, no longer detached, looking straight at him.

He returned her smile with his own, warmly. He looked down at his watch. "Gosh, it's almost 10 o'clock. We've been talking for hours. I think that we better catch some shut-eye. Why don't you take the V-berth and the rest of us will sleep in the stern? You've probably found the head earlier in the day, but it's aft of the V-berth and I left some towels there. Breakfast will be at 6:30 a.m."

"OK. Sounds good to me. See you in the morning. Good night."

"Good night, Carla." He watched her thoughtfully, as she made her way from the bow, along the foredeck, to the stern and into the cabin, then, he found Luis, who was smoking with Rico, on the flying bridge, and they briefly conferred about departure times the next day. Both Luis and Rico planned to take different shifts of watch throughout the night, because the boat was in an unprotected anchorage. After the **Golddigger** mishap, no one wanted any further unfortunate incidents.

16

November 19, 1993

Carla awoke to a pronounced rocking of the boat and the sound of its inboard engine starting. She stuck her head out of the salon doorway and saw Rod standing on the stern, watching Luis reposition the boat. He noticed her look of concern, and informed her, "The anchor came loose and the boat moved in the current, a short distance. Also, some wind developed and that contributed to the movement. No need for alarm. Luis has it under control."

Carla nodded acknowledgement and ducked back into the cabin to run a comb through her hair and brush her teeth. She heard the anchor being hauled in and knew that they would be departing soon. By the time she stepped back out of the cabin, Rico was lighting a small propane stove on top of a cooler on the stern deck. He was planning to heat some water for instant coffee. Rod was no where in sight. She found him up on the flying bridge with Luis, looking at the sonar screen. They greeted her as she climbed off the top step of the ladder.

"Good morning. Did you sleep well?" inquired Rod.

"Like a baby in a cradle."

"I'm glad to hear it. Some people don't tolerate being on a boat, especially in deep water, in swells. Feel like some coffee?"

"I'd love some."

"Rico." Rod leaned over the flying bridge rail. "Could you hand up some cups of coffee?"

"Sure."

"Do you take anything in your coffee?" Rod looked back at Carla.

"Black will be fine."

"OK. Rico, give us two black coffees and a white for Luis."

"Roger." The steaming cups were handed up the ladder one by one.

"Thanks, Rico," Carla and Rod uttered in unison. Rico smiled.

"We'll motor further into the current, heading northwest, while we eat breakfast. That way, we'll gain some time," Rod explained. Carla nodded.

Bread and preserves were passed up the ladder, as well as fruit and more coffee, while they motored. Rod kept his gaze on the Twinscope scanning sonar. The marine radio crackled with the following announcement: "This is The Tropical Weather Outlook from the National Weather Service, Miami Florida, at 0930 Eastern Daylight Time, Friday, November 19, 1993. The National Hurricane Center is issuing advisories on Tropical Storm Vicki, recently upgraded from Tropical Depression 16, located about 150 miles southeast of the Virgin Islands. Storm warnings are in effect for Antigua, Guadelupe, Dominica, and Martinique ..." The rest was referral to public advisories on various radio headers. It did not even get Rod's attention. It was too far away.

An hour passed, and half of another. They were in shallower water, again. Rod estimated that they had traveled 18 nautical miles. The GPS read latitude 16 degrees 1 minute North and longitude 85 degrees 1 minute West. Land was barely visible on the western horizon.

Rod suddenly exclaimed, "There's an odd-shaped object! Luis, slow the engine and put us in neutral. Look's like a cigar-shaped structure at about 100 to 140 feet. Could be the hull of a boat, but it's so long and thin. Let's anchor here. Carla and I'll go down for a look. How many miles are we from where the **Golddigger** was found, Luis?"

"Almost 18 nautical miles."

With that said, Carla and Rod began donning their dive gear for yet another attempt to obtain answers to the mystery before them. They descended and could see the hazy, dark outline of the wreck below, because the visibility was to 100 feet. It appeared to be a long hull, which was fully covered by a fine layer of silt-like sand. This covering was disturbed in a few places by what seemed to be some recent physical activity. Also, there appeared to be a conning tower located just forward of the middle of the hull. A hatch cover was visible on its bridge and was in the open position. Rod quickly came to the realization that he was looking at the wreck of a sub! He nudged Carla, who was next to him, and penciled out on his dive slate the word, "SUB". Carla's eyes widened in her mask in acknowledgement.

The two made their descent eagerly toward the structure, but watched their dive computers the entire time. Rod pulled a flashlight from his BC pocket and entered the same hatch that Erik Slade and Bob Weber had entered, only 12 days before. Carla was close behind. Darkness engulfed them except for the arc made by the flashlight. Rod glanced at his dive computer and noted that they were at 112 feet and they had eight minutes of bottom time left. He recognized that they must be on a German U-boat by the German inscription on several instruments in the control room and the barely visible call numbers on the conning tower. He also noted that the sub had a "schnorkel", which was abreast of the conning tower, and was an innovation during World War II to allow operation of diesel engines, while submerged, for longer cruising range. Yes, this definitely was a U-boat, he thought.

Carla, meanwhile, was making her way through the aft passageway with the use of her own flashlight. What alarmed her were all the dead fish of various ages that lined the corridor. Rod turned to follow her and noted that she had already pulled a bottle out to collect a water sample. Before he had turned, however, he found a sealed green metal box on the floor of the control room, which he picked up and stuffed into his BC pocket. It had fallen out of the opened chest, when Ramirez's crew was taking the chest to the surface. As a result, it was not encrusted like everything else on the sub.

After the above exploration, they didn't have much time left before exceeding their no-decompression limits, only three or four minutes. He signaled her that they needed to ascend, and just at that moment, Carla saw the yellow nuclear symbol that Erik Slade had seen, over a bulkhead door closing off an apparent tunnel half a deck below her. There was German inscription beneath the symbol. She waved emphatically to Rod. He swam down and took a good look at it, as well. He knew how to read German from his work with the CIA, and was able to read, 'Die Gefahr!'(Danger!) - 'Das Material Radioaktin!' (Radioactive Material!). The tunnel was closed by a tightly sealed door, which Rod tried to open by turning the wheel on the door, but it would not budge. Undoubtedly, encrustation had sealed it. Carla noted a small steel cylinder, approximately 30 inches long and 8 inches in diameter, in a recess near the door, also, overlooked by Ramirez's crew. It was badly encrusted and had a skull and crossbones on it. Another similarly encrusted cylinder lay behind it and was cracked. Several dead fish lay nearby. Carla grabbed the intact one and towed it behind her.

At this point, Rod gestured at Carla and then at his computer, indicating that they need to make all haste for the surface. Therefore, they made their way back to the open hatch over the control room and swam out. They had little air left, so their ascent was faster than that advised on the computer display. A safety stop at ten feet was barely accomplished due to the dwindling air, but they did manage three minutes at that depth before surfacing. Divers routinely performed safety stops to reduce the risk of decompression sickness, by allowing reduction of the bubble content in their blood, when they remained at 10 to 20 feet for three to five minutes.

It was a relief to see their boat, and also to see that it had not been overtaken by another vessel. The horizon was clear and calm.

They quickly removed their gear after they were hosed off well, and stowed all of it in safety containers that had been brought along on the boat. Rod signaled to Luis to head for home. The **Yolanda** turned and headed northeast toward Guanaja.

Rod pulled Carla aside on the deck and said to her, with some concern, "There's something strange about this wreck. The structure is completely intact. It doesn't appear to have run aground. I keep thinking about von Kreitler and the fact that he was a U-boat captain, and today we find the wreck of a German U-boat, as well as a strange cargo aboard. It makes me uneasy that the **Golddigger** was found south of this location. The fate of the crew might be related to this wreck. They might have discovered something that someone didn't want them to find. Especially, since the sub appears to be carrying weapons of mass destruction."

Carla paled slightly at this realization. "You mean that nuclear symbol over the bulkhead door." Rod nodded his head. "The cylinder might tell us something. Look at the skull and crossbones symbol on it." Rod took the cylinder from Carla and turned it over to read the symbol. "It's curious that there were so many dead fish near it, however, the other cylinder was cracked and had obviously spilled its contents."

"Yes, we might find it contains some chemical weapon," Rod answered, ominously. "Luis, what reef areas are we near?"

"We are near the edge of the Serranilla Bank and Cabo Cameroon. It is rumored that the galleon, **Isabella**, sunk somewhere here in the 1500's."

"I forgot that, Luis. Interesting thought, and another possible reason that the **Golddigger**, was in these waters."

The vessel motored approximately another four hours until it reached the resort's cove. During this time, they studied the cylinder, further, making certain to wear protective gloves. There was some faint German inscription on one side opposite the skull and crossbones symbol. Part of a word, 'Das Gift' was legible. Rod interpreted this as 'poison'.

"Curious that a German U-boat might be carrying cylinders of a potential toxin. It's not as though they could use the material underwater. Obviously, they were transporting the cylinders somewhere. Stranger still, why was radioactive material aboard. No atomic bomb had been completed successfully by Germany during World War II," Rod mused. To his knowledge, no nuclear technology had been developed for submarine propulsion at that time, either. He, suddenly, remembered the green metal box in his BC pocket. "Look what I also found in the sub," pulling the box out and handing it to her.

"The box is clean. There is no encrustation," Carla marveled. "I can't seem to open it. It appears sealed."

"Here, let me try to open it." Rod reached for the box, taking a dive knife out of his gear bag.

"No, wait. In view of everything we found on the sub, let's exercise some caution. I know you'll think that this might be overkill, but I think that we'd better get back into our protective suits and masks, before we open this box."

"You really think that's necessary?"

"Yes, I do." Carla's demeanor was so serious that he decided not to argue and started pulling the gear out of the locker.

It took them five minutes to suit up. He wedged the blade of the knife under the lid and pried. There was a dull pop, and the lid opened revealing a rubber O-ring seal. Inside, were two neatly arranged rows of vials. Their tops were sealed in the manner that Carla had seen biologic materials contained, before. She saw Rod take one of the vials and look at its contents in the light. There appeared to be a small quantity of undefinable, brown material in the bottom. Her medical instinct made her warn, suddenly, "Don't even think of opening that vial. If your hunch is correct about weapons, there might be a biologic agent in that tube. That green box you found was too clean to have been on the sub that long, unprotected. It must have been contained in something else and was dropped out of that container, recently. Which also fits with the fact that the **Golddigger** was in these waters, not long ago."

"You're right." Rod placed the vial gently back into the box and closed the lid. They proceeded to remove their gear, again, and wash it off.

Carla, meanwhile, was puzzling over the findings of the **Golddigger** crew's autopsies and what relation might be drawn between them and the toxin in the cylinder and material in the vials. She was trying to remember what might cause a rosacea-like rash similar to that on the faces, neck, and hands of three of the crewmembers. Suddenly, a thought occurred to her. What about Agent Orange? It was known to cause an acneiform rash in humans and subsequent other ill effects. She remembered reading articles on the defoliant, which contained the toxic compound 2,3,7,8 tetrachlorodibenzo-p-dioxin, and which had been sprayed over central and southern Viet Nam between 1962 and 1970. Not only American soldiers, but also numerous Vietnamese had been exposed. Studies of those exposed had shown them to have a number of similar findings - cancer, ischemic heart disease, and chloracne - to name a few. Chloracne consisted of an eruption of acne-like lesions, plus pustules and cysts on face, neck, chest, back, and extremities in those exposed. Carla was excited. This could be the answer, but how did the Germans have an agent in 1945 that only had surfaced in the 1960's. Perhaps, it was not the exact same agent, but a similar compound, she speculated. Her face lit up as she told Rod what she suspected. He was impressed by her deduction.

"You know we must get this information and material to Tegucigalpa, as soon as possible, and contact U.S. authorities, particularly the FBI," Rod emphasized.

"I can go, because I need to update Dr. Velasquez in La Ceiba, en route, and I need to find a decent lab to run these water samples."

"OK. I'll stay at the resort and keep watch for any unusual activity."

It was at this juncture, as the crew was tying the boat to the dock, and they were finishing washing salt water off their equipment, that Bud Campbell strolled up to them. "How did it go today? Any luck finding more answers?"

Rod answered him, impatiently, "We may have found some leads, but we have more work ahead."

"Well, I'm delighted that you have made some progress. What have you learned?"

"We're not at liberty to say, Bud. This is a criminal investigation."

"Oh, I understand. I just get excited, because it's like watching a mystery on television." With that, he sauntered away.

"Tourists," muttered Rod, in disdain, after Bud was out of earshot. Carla, nodded with a grin. They collected their equipment and the evidence from aboard the sub, and made their way to the photo lab to find something, within which, to transport the cylinder, green box, and water samples to Tegucigalpa. The resort dinner gong sounded in the distance, signaling the end to a day full of unsettling discoveries.

17

November 19, 1993

Dr. Lopez had called, the morning of the 18th, after conferring with Dr. Velasquez, to the Pan American Health Organization for assistance dealing with the epidemic. They had, in turn, called the Center for Disease Control, in Atlanta, to invite the institute's participation in the task and they had referred the specialists, consulted, to Dr. Lopez, who was able to give great detail about the course of illness, but little information about the cultures done on the affected patients. This was because the cultures had not grown out any significant bacteria. In fact, the spinal fluid showed a viral profile and sputum specimens were sterile. There was great concern that a poxvirus was involved, but which type was a mystery. The CDC had dispatched a team that afternoon, flying via Miami to Honduras. The team arrived by noon, the following day, but not before the policeman succumbed to the same complications that Felipe had experienced. His body was cremated, as well. Now, there were two deaths within a week of onset of the illness, in each individual. This made the CDC team apprehensive, because if the entity was smallpox that was causing the disease, then it was producing the worst form of the affliction - the hemorrhagic variety. They had brought much of the existing civilian store of smallpox vaccine with them, in the event that mass immunization of the region may be needed. However, it was felt that vaccination of all known contacts was probably sufficient to break the chain of transmission, once smallpox was proven. Besides, the supply that they had available to them in the United States was small compared to the numbers of people that they, potentially, would have to immunize. There had not been much vaccine manufactured since the United States stopped routinely vaccinating military

119

troops in the 1980's.

Vaccinia-immune globulin(VIG), also, had been sent with the team, to treat close, household contacts. There was no guarantee that this latter treatment would successfully limit the number of secondary cases or decrease the severity of symptoms in contacts, which contracted the illness, because there was no definitive treatment for smallpox. Everyone simply hoped that the illness was not from the dreaded virus and would be found to be the result of some other healable entity. In 1752, smallpox infected over 30% of the population of Boston, Massachusetts and had killed one third of that same number of people. It produced 1700 cases on the island of Java in Indonesia in 1969, despite 95% of the population being previously immunized. The virus was capable of great infectivity, as well as high morbidity and mortality. What was more unnerving, was the ability of the variola virus, which caused smallpox, to persist for years in the right mediums and conditions.

The CDC's first job in La Ceiba was to come up with a firm diagnosis, as the hospital lab staff had not found anything definitive under a light microscope or by conventional culture methods, except that the pathogen appeared to be a virus, since bacterial assays were negative. They had some lab supplies with them, but most of the advanced tests would have to be done back at the CDC. The team had packed a few light microscopes to look at skin vesicle scrapings for smallpox virus particles, called Guarnieri bodies. While they were performing these tests, some of the members of the team proceeded to treat close, household contacts with VIG and vaccine, so as not to waste time in the event that these contacts had been exposed to smallpox.

Dr. Paul Jonas, one of the CDC physicians and, actually, the head of the mission to Honduras, was examining Meribel that afternoon, because she had developed flu-like symptoms. He bent his balding, middle-aged head, draped with a surgical mask, over her chest and listened with his stethoscope. The lungs were still clear. Being the detail-oriented individual that he was, he asked her several pointed questions, through an interpreter. "Meribel, when did your son, Felipe, become ill?"

"About a week and a half after he had been on the boat."

"What boat?"

"The boat where all the Americans were killed."

Dr. Lopez, who was also in the room, interjected, "She's talking about the **Golddigger**."

Dr. Jonas nodded. He and Dr. Lopez had discussed the boat's incident, earlier. Dr. Lopez had told him about Felipe finding the vial aboard and sniffing it. He, also, related that the sick policeman and sailors had done the same thing. Dr. Jonas turned back to Meribel, "How many days after Felipe became ill, did he develop sores in his mouth?"

"Three days or so."

"And you became ill today?"

"Yes, doctor."

"What were your son's first symptoms?"

"He had a headache and fever."

"How do you feel, right now?"

"I feel achy all over and tired, and I feel like I am hot."

"Have you been near anyone with similar symptoms?"

"No. Only my son."

"You haven't been traveling recently?"

"No, except to come to La Ceiba with Felipe, when he was very ill." A tear streamed down her cheek with this last remark.

Dr. Jonas decided that he had questioned the poor woman enough, for the moment. He left her to the care of a nurse, and walked out of the room with Dr. Lopez. He was very worried. Pulling Dr. Lopez aside, he said quietly, "If this is smallpox, which I think it is, the second generation cases are showing a shorter incubation period. That is not a good sign. It means that the virus is mutating into a more rapidly multiplying organism and can reach a massive viremia in the bloodstream, faster. Thus, the patient develops symptoms more quickly. We had better immunize all contacts and not wait." Dr. Lopez nodded, gravely.

At that juncture, another member of the CDC team, Dr. Bruce Tapper, walked up and interrupted them. He had just come from a makeshift, isolation lab in the basement of the hospital, near the morgue, where everyone wore biohazard suits with self-contained oxygen units. "Paul, we just identified Guarnieri bodies in all of the vesicular scrapings we took from the teen-age boy and the adult male, post-mortem. It looks like we're on the right track. We're waiting for culture confirmation from lesion scabs that we have sent to the CDC. The bad news is that it does appear to be the hemorrhagic variety. The white blood cell counts in both patients were elevated 30-40%, instead of decreased, with several precursor forms, suggesting stimulation of the bone marrow. Also, their platelet counts were markedly decreased, unlike other types of smallpox and there was bleeding within the skin layers, underlying the vesicles."

"No wonder those patients died so quickly. Get Colonel Neal Standish on the phone at U.S. AMRIID and ask him if the Army will release their supply of VIG to us ASAP, as we will need more than what we brought with us. I doubt that the military in Honduras keeps adequate stores." Dr. Jonas looked at Dr. Lopez for an answer, and Dr. Lopez shook his head. "Bruce, tell Dr. Standish, too, that we would appreciate whatever help he can spare down here."

"Will do."

Turning back to Lopez, Jonas said, "I'm going to need some of your staff to accompany the CDC team into the various neighborhoods of La Ceiba and the outlying villages to look for symptomatic individuals. It would help to have your military assist us in this effort. Will that be possible?"

"Yes, it is not a problem. I can have everyone you need by tomorrow, in the morning. I will make the necessary phone calls, now."

"Good. Oh, and one more thing. We need to institute a tight quarantine on the area. No one leaves or comes into La Ceiba for, at least, the next three weeks, until we are sure all contacts don't manifest symptoms and any sick individuals have their scabbed lesions separate, completely. As long as anyone has scabs, they are infectious. It will be necessary to post police and military at all points of entry and exit from La Ceiba, including the airport and harbor, to make certain that the quarantine is honored. Marshall law will have to be established."

Dr. Lopez nodded soberly. He thought of his elderly father, whom he had planned to visit in Teguz next week. That excursion would have to be postponed.

"By the way, Dr. Lopez, I want you to know that you and your staff have done a excellent job, handling the cases that have presented so far, with the limited resources that you have had at your disposal." Jonas respected the young physician's courage and stamina dealing with the epidemic. He knew that he hadn't slept in a couple of days.

Dr. Lopez beamed at this complement from the CDC physician. He was tired and he ached in every muscle, but the remark buoyed him. He agreed to meet Dr. Jonas, in an hour, to discuss a further plan of action, after he secured the assistance of Honduran army and Naval Force. Then, he would try to get some sleep. It was, now, 7:14 p.m.

Upon returning to the two-room emergency department, he discovered that another of the previously ill Naval Force sailors was there with his family. The man was covered with pustules and had a fever. His face was most affected. He did not seem as ill as Felipe and the policeman had been. Dr. Lopez had the patient sent immediately to the isolation ward, along with his family, to be seen by the CDC team. He, like others in the hospital, now wore a protective mask and goggles, all the time, as well as a gown, gloves, and shoe covers, which were disposed of in biohazard containers, after each patient encounter. These containers were, then, incinerated. Strict hand hygiene was enforced. It was the best they could do, under the circumstances.

Dr. Lopez returned to his task of making phone calls. He received a pledge of support from both the country's army and navy, and the La Ceiba police. They agreed to send representatives for a briefing by the CDC team, late that evening, at the hospital. He related this to Dr. Jonas at their subsequent meeting. Jonas reminded him that the same military forces would have to help set up a quarantine on the island of Guanaja, tomorrow, as well. He managed to stay awake through the final briefing with the military and police. Dr. Velasquez and the FBI were there, as well. They had been aware of the illness affecting the town and were curious about its possible association with the **Golddigger**. The proposed plan involved showing civilians World Health Organization, smallpox photo cards, in order to identify cases as soon as possible. Also, public markets in the surrounding area would be surveyed for cases and teams would survey all villages. With this strategy discussed, the meeting was adjourned and the groups dispersed to make their arrangements for early morning implementation. Finally, Dr. Lopez was able to get some sleep, even if it wasn't fitful.

18

November 20, 1993

Carla set off on the first Air Islena flight, the next morning, to La Ceiba, just missing the quarantine imposed two hours later. Rod took her to the airstrip and waited with her in the bus stop-like shelter until her plane arrived, as he wanted to make sure that she departed safely. His concern was growing that something big was going down, and whatever that something was, boded ill consequences for many. He was not sure what part Kurt von Kreitler might play in the scenario, but he was convinced that he was a player, especially after seeing the sub.

Carla had Dr. Velasquez contacted by the resort, before she left Guanaja, and learned of the quarantine in La Ceiba, as a result. This complicated matters because she was hoping to stop in La Ceiba to talk at length with Dr. Velasquez. He did manage to convey to her, through the resort radio, that there was an apparent smallpox epidemic in La Ceiba and that the boy transferred from Guanaja had died from the same illness. He emphasized that the boy and the other affected individuals, thus far, had all been exposed to the same items on the **Golddigger**. This comment struck her like an ice pick, making her suck in her breath. The green box that Rod had picked up in the sub! The glass vials, inside, probably did contain a biohazardous material, as she had thought. Dr. Velasquez got her attention, further, by telling her that the Honduran police had been looking for the items in the evidence warehouse, that the patients had contacted, but they had disappeared. She responded, telling him, only, that she had to get something to him at the La Ceiba airport that would help with this investigation. It was urgent. She didn't want to reveal, over the radio, that they had found a sub or what they had found in it. Dr.

Velasquez agreed to meet her at the airport, even if he had to get military and CDC approval to do so.

The next problem was how to transfer the cylinder and vials, so that they would not be confiscated by airport security checks. Carla decided to put the cylinder in her suitcase, along with some scuba equipment, so it would not attract undo attention. She felt that it would be fairly safe, because they were in a prop plane, not traveling at great altitude. The vials and water samples would be carried in her hand luggage to avoid breakage. Luckily, she would not be going through customs on this trip because she was not leaving the country. There, also, would be no security check at the airstrip on Guanaja. She would have to pass off the glass vials in La Ceiba, though, or run the chance of them falling into the wrong hands. Her suitcase would be checked through to Tegucigalpa.

Dr. Velasquez managed to meet her at the gate at the La Ceiba airport, by bringing Dr. Paul Jonas with him, in person, for clearance. He had explained to Dr. Jonas why Dr. Knight was in Honduras and that she might have found some answer to the origin of the epidemic. It was not necessary for him to say more. Jonas arranged to come to the airport that morning, and he brought clearance papers for Carla to return to Guanaja, after completing her trip to Tegucigalpa. The only stipulation for this clearance was that Dr. Knight be vaccinated for smallpox at the airport, before she went on to Teguz. She would not learn of this condition until meeting Dr. Jonas at the airport.

The plane landed, uneventfully, and taxied to a stop in front of the one story terminal in La Ceiba. Carla could see Dr. Velasquez waving from a window. That was reassuring. She disembarked from the plane onto the tarmac, outside. The humidity hit her like a wall. She clutched the Cordoba nylon shoulder bag, containing the box with vials, against her as she made her way into the building. She did not have to walk far, before Dr. Velasquez intercepted her and escorted her to an anteroom off the concourse.

Dr. Jonas was already there and extended a hand in greeting. "Very nice to make your acquaintance, Dr. Knight. I'm Dr. Paul Jonas, head of the CDC's team, here, in Honduras."

"Oh, I'm so glad you have come here to meet me," shaking Jonas's hand. "I have something for you to analyze that we found on a wrecked, German U-boat, underwater. It was found a few miles away from where the **Golddigger** was discovered adrift in a current. Rod Dalton and I believe that the **Goldigger** crew came upon this wreck, too, and were murdered for the knowledge, they had, of the cargo that was carried aboard it."

Velasquez could barely contain himself. "Carla, you won't believe a development in the case, that just occurred, yesterday morning." She looked intrigued. "It supports your hypothesis. Honduran police and FBI officials from the United States discovered a roll of film in a flashlight that had been aboard the Golddigger, after a more thorough search of the evidence room. Upon processing the film, they learned that the crew had found the underwater wreck of a submarine that appeared to contain hazardous materials."

Carla's eyes widened. "You mean hazardous materials, as evidenced by radioactive and poison symbols on objects?", hopeful that there would be a connection.

"Precisely." Carla's pulse quickened and her face lit up with the revelation. Dr. Velasquez continued, "There were also biohazard symbols on some things, which is what interests Dr. Jonas."

"Like what kinds of things?"

"Well, on a few large, metal chests for example."

"Alberto," Carla clutched his arm, "someone else besides the **Golddigger** crew, Rod, and myself have been on that wreck, recently. I know, because we found no such chests aboard when we explored it, only this small, green metal box, containing glass vials, on the deck of the control room," pulling the metal box, wrapped with duct tape, out of her bag and handing it to Dr. Jonas.

"Someone must have retrieved them since the murders and before we got there."

"That possibility causes me a great deal of concern," Dr. Jonas emphasized, taking the box, gingerly, from Carla after donning some rubber gloves. "What's in this box?"

"We only opened the box once, while wearing protective suits, but what we saw was a couple of rows of glass vials that were sealed with metal screw caps. In each vial, was some brown material at the base."

"If my guess is correct, these are old scabs of smallpox lesions, mixed with some enviroculture cell media. Smallpox is particularly hardy, like anthrax, and can last several years under the right conditions. However, we must get this box back into a cool environment for transfer to the laboratory." He picked up a Styrofoam ice chest with dry ice and placed the box inside. From another case, he took a sheath of papers. "Before I leave you, I'm going to give you these clearance papers to get back to Guanaja, Dr. Knight. But, in return for them, I am asking that you get a smallpox vaccination, now."

"I understand and agree."

Dr. Jonas opened the Styrofoam cooler, once more, to take a syringe with a bifurcated needle from it. He gave Carla the immunization in her shoulder.

"Thank you, Dr. Jonas, for all your efforts to assure my safe passage back to Guanaja."

"You're welcome. If I hadn't made the effort, there was no way you would have gotten back through the quarantine established there, this morning."

"Oh, I was not aware that one had been established. Thanks so much." Carla was relieved that she would be seeing Rod, again, soon. "I hope that what we've found will answer some questions about the epidemic."

"I'm sure that it will. Be careful traveling to Tegucigalpa. Also, make certain when you return to Guanaja that you wear a

128

protective surgical mask if you are near any identifiable sick individuals with any suspicious rashes or symptoms." Carla nodded. "I will talk to you later, Alberto."

"Very well. Goodbye, Paul."

An armed, airport guard was summoned and escorted Dr. Jonas from the room and out of the airport for security reasons. They did not know whom the transfer of this material might anger and the potential knowledge gained from it. Someone might be lying in wait to inflict more harm. All precautions were necessary.

Carla talked briefly with Dr. Velasquez before she had to catch her connecting flight. She told him about the cylinder that they had found and her Agent Orange hypothesis. She emphasized that it was urgent that she gets the cylinder and water samples analyzed to see if they held answers about what had affected three of the **Golddigger** crew.

Dr. Velasquez agreed, and gave her the name of a reputable lab in Tegucigalpa, where she could get the material processed, but also informed her about some of the blood tests that had been returned on the **Golddigger** victims. "Your Agent Orange hypothesis would appear to be correct. Three of the crewmembers - Dave Krueger, Bob Weber, and Erik Slade - showed varying levels of a compound identified as TCDD - 2,3,7,8 tetrachlorodibenzo-p-dioxin, a toxic contaminant of many herbicides, otherwise known as Agent Orange during the war in Vietnam."

"Wow. Alberto, this clinches it. We're on the right track. The **Golddigger** crew discovered something that others didn't want them to - something that had potential for harm to many people and they were murdered for it. Alberto, get Rod on the radio. He has the coordinates for the sub's location. The Naval Force and FBI need to get out there as soon as possible. I'm going to run and catch my connection to Tegucigalpa," Carla said looking at her watch. Thank you for the update and all of the arrangements that you made for me. I will stay in touch." And with that, she exited the room and ran across the concourse. Dr. Velasquez could only hope that no bad fate would befall her.

19

By the time Carla's plane arrived, it was dark in the city. She secured a taxi, quickly, and had her luggage loaded in the rear seat with her. The cylinder was in a metal camera equipment suitcase with a tight seal. Carla had placed scuba gear around the object to cause less suspicion. The water samples remained in a plastic pelican box in her shoulder bag. Her taxi driver eyed her suspiciously when she wanted to keep the suitcase with her rather than having it put in the trunk. This whole sequence was not lost on the driver of a grey sedan, parked across the street the loading zone, where the taxi was located. He had dark hair and wore sunglasses, but the car's tinted windows obscured his facial features. The grey sedan pulled out, a couple of cars behind them, in traffic, as the taxi left the curb. Carla did not notice this. Neither, did the driver.

She gave the driver the address of the lab, which she hoped might be open late running analyses. She did not want to delay getting the material to a safe place, by searching for a hotel, first. The driver seemed a little uncertain about the address that she gave in broken Spanish, but he managed to leave her on the opposite side of the right street, a short distance from the building. As the taxi pulled away, she picked up the metal suitcase and her shoulder bag. The grey sedan was not far behind her, and as soon as Carla stepped into the street to cross over to the lab building, the car accelerated directly toward her. She looked up, in surprise, on hearing the approaching sound, the headlights blinding her, and realized her life was about to end if she didn't make a leap in some direction out of the car path. Carla threw the suitcase and shoulder bag off in front of her after making a running dive, landing on the cobblestones, prone, as the car squealed by her. It did not stop, because several cars were approaching from the same direction, and it swerved around a corner, out of sight.

A couple of cars stopped upon seeing a woman lying in the road. A portly gentleman with a kind face got out of one of the cars and inquired if she was "OK" and if she needed help. Carla, by this time, was getting to her feet and acknowledged that she was fine. He helped her pick up her strewn possessions. The metal suitcase was intact, but it sounded as though one of the water sample bottles had fallen out of its plastic container and had broken within the shoulder bag. What she didn't know was if one of the two bottles from her first two dives had broken, or the bottle from the dive on the wreck. Luckily, when she opened the bag, it was the former. She thanked the considerate gentleman for his assistance. He waited until she reached her destination across the street. Shaken, Carla made her way to the front of a brick building, where she could make out the word "Laboratorio" on the sign over the doorway. She did notice a few windows displayed light suggesting that someone might be working late. Her knock on the door was urgent. Soft footsteps were heard, finally, on the other side of the door, and it was opened by a neat-appearing Hispanic woman in her 30's, who was wearing a white lab coat.

"Can I help you?" queried the woman in Spanish, while scrutinizing the metal suitcase held by Carla's right hand.

"Mi nombre es Dr. Carla Knight. Por favor, I need you to analyze these materials para una investigacion de policias," replied Carla in broken Spanish.

The woman smiled and said, "I speak English, so you need not struggle with your Spanish. I appreciate your efforts, however."

Carla was greatly relieved and she launched into her story about the **Golddigger** investigation. The woman had heard about the incident and let her in the door upon learning of her close call in the street. The lab building appeared moderately old in architecture with a dated, diamond-patterned linoleum floor, but everything was spotlessly clean. Carla followed the woman to a large room in the rear of the building, which had several counters with flasks on stands and Bunsen burners in operation. There were also some newer computerized machines evident for chemical analyses. The quiet of the lab seemed soothing to Carla and safe.

At this point, she opened the metal suitcase and shoulder bag, while explaining to the woman, "We found these materials at a wreck site off the Bay Islands. We are afraid that the cylinder holds a toxic substance, as might the water samples, so you will want to take precautions. Also, one of the water sample bottles has broken during my fall in the street. It was one, however, not retrieved at the wreck site. There is additional potential for biohazardous agent contamination of the wreck's water sample, as we found evidence aboard of storage of such agents. We believe it may be smallpox."

"Thank you for letting me know. The lab has an enclosed protective hood, within which I can open the cylinder and sample it. By the way, I should introduce myself. My name is Maria Hernandez."

"It is nice to meet you and good of you to help me. Do you have a phone that I can use to call the United States?"

"Why, yes. You simply dial the international AT&T operator, and they will put the call through for you. We are lucky to have a phone here, because we do mining analyses for many companies outside Honduras."

Carla was thankful that Rod had given her a phone number to call in Washington, D.C. for a friend, Brad Jacobs, in the DEA. Rod had said that Jacobs would get her in touch with any agencies that she needed to reach in D.C. She was thinking along the lines of the FBI, CIA, and possibly the National Security Council. He, also, told her that Brad could get them any equipment that they needed. A recording answered, initially, because it was after business hours in the United States, but it instructed the caller to hold on the line for emergency pages. Agent Jacobs answered shortly, thereafter.

"Hello, my name is Dr. Carla Knight. Rod Dalton, here in Honduras, gave me your number to call in reference to developments in the **Golddigger** crew murders."

"You've got my attention," acknowledged Jacobs.

"Is this line secure?" asked Carla, nervously.

"Quite, on my end. I can't speak for your end."

"You must forgive me, but I'm anxious because I was just followed from the airport in Tegucigalpa and nearly run over by a car that the person, tailing me, was driving. I fear that they wanted what I was bringing to this lab, or wanted to make sure that I didn't get it to this lab."

"Did you contact the local police?"

"Not yet."

"Well, you might want to hold off notifying them. I will contact the FBI about the matter, and alert our local field personnel, so you can get some protection while you are in Tegucigalpa. Fill me in on the developments."

"We discovered a wreck of an old German U-boat some distance north of where the **Golddigger** was found. Within that vessel, we found cylinders, which appeared to hold a toxic material. Also, we noticed a nuclear symbol over a bulkhead door, which we could not open. In addition there were biohazardous agents aboard which may have led to a current smallpox epidemic in La Ceiba. I brought a water sample from within the sub to be analyzed by this lab for toxic substances, and also, one of the cylinders for the same purpose. I suspect that some of the physical findings on the bodies of the **Golddigger** crew may be the result of a toxic exposure, and we have evidence that the crew was at this site. What is not totally clear is who killed the crewmembers, but we do have one lead on some fingerprints on a couple of the bodies. According to the coroner of La Ceiba, they belong to one of the Cordillera drug cartel, which is why Rod thought the DEA should be involved in the investigation. What is so perplexing is why a drug cartel should be trying to salvage weapons of mass destruction from a German U-boat wreck? We need to get back to the site as soon as possible, and try to get beyond the sealed bulkhead door. We will need some extra equipment for that purpose, and, for that reason, we need to enlist your help." Carla had talked so fast, relating all of this that she was out of breath.

"Whoa," commanded Jacobs. "Your leads are substantial, but you don't know who you are dealing with. A heavily armed adversary at the site could easily overwhelm you and Rod, so I suggest that you let the FBI intervene and conduct the remainder of the investigation. Where are you basing your operation at the moment?"

"We are staying at the Posada del Sol resort on the island of Guanaja. The dive boat, that we have been using, is docked there."

"Very well. I will have the FBI get some heavy salvage equipment and some field agents there in the next couple of days. Tell Rod that I will come down, as well, on this one. It reminds me of when he and I tried to find large arms shipment in a sunken Viet Cong barge in the Mekong River. We ended up in a real hornet's nest."

Carla interjected, at that point, "Agent Jacobs, I plan to go back to Guanaja on the first flight tomorrow morning."

"Please call me, Brad. That won't be a problem. I will get one of the DEA's field agents to you this evening. Where are you staying?"

"I haven't gotten any lodging, as yet. I came straight from the airport to the lab. Just a minute." Carla held the phone away and called to Maria, "Can you suggest some place that I might stay in Tegucigalpa this evening?"

"Try the Hotel Honduras Maya. It is very nice," she replied, while donning a protective apron and gloves, before transporting the cylinder and water bottles to the hood.

Carla leaned back toward the phone, "Brad, tell your personnel that they'll find me at the Hotel Honduras Maya, within the next two hours."

"Good enough. By the way, the agent who meets you will use the greeting, 'Hi, fellow diver, so you will know it's him. Do not repeat this aloud, now. Call a taxi and go directly to the hotel. I will contact the appropriate authorities for the help we will need. I'll, also, send two field agents to the lab, tonight, to protect the lab technician while she runs her analyses. What's her name?"

"Maria Hernandez."

"Give me the name and address of the lab."

"Laboratorio del Honduras Central, 22 Avenida Paz Baraona."

"Let Ms. Hernandez know that I'll have two men there within the hour. She should only answer the door, if they answer the question, 'How was the weather today?' with the reply, 'Snowing lightly'."

"I understand," affirmed Carla.

"Well, good luck, and I'll see you in a couple of days on Guanaja. Say 'hi' to Rod for me."

"I will. Thank you for your help. Goodbye." With that, Carla hung up the phone and walked over to Maria Hernandez, who was about to use the sealed hood. Two long, rubber gloves protruded into the hood and their linings were open to the lab, but sealed off from the interior of the hood, as they were affixed to the hood's wall. Maria slipped her hands into them from outside, after she had enclosed the cylinder and water bottles in the airtight area under the hood, by closing a side door with a rubber seal and hydraulic lock. The cylinder cap proved too encrusted to remove, but she took a sample from each water bottle with a pipette and put the liquid into glass test tubes and sealed the openings. They were then placed in a small receptacle, like a bank teller box, in the hood floor and a door, opening with a lever, slid over the receptacle. A fine mist of water was ejected over the material, and then the side door opened outside the hood and Maria collected the tubes wearing a pair of latex gloves. She took the tubes to a centrifuge.

"I will get someone to open the cylinder tomorrow, with special equipment. The results of the samples should be available in the next few days," offered Maria.

"I very much appreciate your efforts. Could you please contact a Rod Dalton, or myself, at Posada del Sol on Guanaja, when you have the results? You may have to have someone contact us by radio. I'm not sure that they have a phone at the resort."

"Of course, it is no trouble."

Carla then proceeded to inform Maria of Jacob's plan to protect the lab technician, while the tests were being run. Maria was grateful for this arrangement and helped Carla call a taxi. She also made certain that Carla got into the taxi safely when it arrived. It, then, whisked her off into the dark, cool night on winding cobblestone streets. She decided, en route to the hotel, that she would stop at the local police station to report the night's events, as she felt it was important that some law-enforcing body try to locate the car that almost hit her and its driver.

Maria Hernandez, meanwhile, returned to her work area. She collected the water sample tubes from the centrifuge and took aliquots from each and placed them in the analyzer. The remaining contents were kept in their tubes and placed in a large glass container. She labeled the container, "Golddigger tests," and put it in a steel safe with a combination lock in the rear of the lab. She did not realize how smart she was to do this.

20

Carla arrived at the Palacio del Distrito Central, a few blocks away, without incident. The building was well lit up at one end and parked police cars were visible on the adjacent street. Inside, activity was at a minimum due to the late hour, but there was a slightly overweight, Honduran, middle-aged male wearing a police uniform at the front desk.

"Por favor, senor. I tiene necesidad de su asistencia (I have need of your assistance)."

The officer could tell by her pronunciation that she was foreign, but he asked, "Hacen usted quiere informar algo?(Do you want to report something?)"

"I esta triste (I am sorry). I do not understand. Mi espanol es minimo (My Spanish is minimal)," answered Carla.

"Simplemente un minuto (just a minute)," and the officer went into a back office to find someone who spoke English. He returned with a solemn-appearing, uniformed man who regarded her curiously. She suddenly realized that she was still scuffed and abraded from her fall on the street, and her clothes were streaked with dirt.

"May I help you, senorita? My name is Captain Ortiz."

"Yes, Captain. My name is Dr. Carla Knight. I am here in Honduras working on the **Golddigger** murders' investigation at the request of the coroner of La Ceiba. Tonight, I flew into Tegucigalpa from La Ceiba to have some tests run on some evidence that we collected and I was nearly run down on the street by a car that had been following my taxi."

"How do you know the car was following you?"

"I am convinced that it was by the fact that it was lingering behind my stopped taxi, and then accelerated toward me when I stepped into the street."

"Did you see the driver?"

"No, it was too dark."

" Could you tell what kind of car it was?"

"It appeared to be a compact grey sedan with a black hardtop. I could not make out the license plate except for the number eight on the plate."

"About what time did this happen?"

"Approximately 10 p.m."

"Did anyone witness the incident?"

"Yes, a gentleman got out of his car to help me off the street and said his name was Victor Lomez."

"Where did this happen?"

"On the Avenida Baroana in front of the Laboratorio del Honduras Central."

"Why were you at that location?"

"To find out about processing some water samples at the lab." Carla did not want to mention the cylinder.

"Why do you think someone would try to run you over?"

"I think that we've stumbled upon some evidence that might explain why the **Golddigger** crew was murdered."

"Yes, I heard about that incident. Very unfortunate. Well, you have given us a few leads. We will investigate them and see what we can find out. Meanwhile, I am sure you are interested in getting some protection, while you are in Tegucigalpa."

"I'm mainly interested in getting to my hotel safely, tonight."

"Where are you going to stay?"

"The Hotel Honduras Maya, if they have a room."

"We will escort you there and to the airport, when you need it."

"I'm very grateful for your support." Carla did not make any mention of Brad Jacobs or the DEA, in her conversation, because she did not want to expose any U.S. operations.

An officer took her in a squad car to the hotel, which sat on a knoll on the eastern side of the city. It served as a landmark due to the fact that it was 12 stories high with Mayan art on the exterior.

The policeman left Carla, after she entered the spacious, air-conditioned lobby. He posted himself in his car, across the street from the hotel, to watch the entrance through the night. This was not missed by two dark-haired figures in another car a short distance away.

One muttered to the other in Spanish, "She told the police. Now, we won't get a chance at her until the airport." With that, they pulled away in their car, disappearing into the darkness.

Inside the lobby, Carla walked to the front desk where a neat-appearing female receptionist greeted her. Luckily, they had a room available. Just as she picked up her key, she heard a voice behind her say, "Hello, fellow diver."

A chill went down her spine, momentarily, then she remembered the password that she had been told, earlier, and turned to meet the individual greeting her. She faced a balding, middle-aged male in a tropical shirt and khakis, who was grinning widely. "Why, hello," she responded somewhat hesitantly.

"You remember me, Carla - Ted Litton. We met on the **Cayman Aggressor**," he affirmed, as he pumped her hand vigorously.

"Yes, of course," answered Carla, acting her part.

"Would you like to have a drink before retiring?"

"That sounds good."

Ted then led Carla, who was still slightly rumpled, to the bar. She had managed to comb her hair and brush off her clothing, while in the police car. Under his breath, he said, "My name is really Matt Douglas. Brad Jacobs told me where I could find you. I thought that you were going to arrive sooner."

"I stopped at the local police station to report the car that nearly ran over me. They were most kind and brought me here to the hotel. May I see some ID, please?"

"Of course," and Agent Douglas flipped open a wallet which held his passport and DEA badge. "That was probably a good idea to inform the police. Do you think that you were followed?"

"No, because the policeman, driving, said that he saw no suspicious-looking cars, tailing us to the hotel."

"I see," and Matt lowered his voice further, as he slid into a booth. In the background, a television, mounted on the wall of the bar, blurted out a weather report in Spanish. Carla could make out what appeared to be a satellite image of a large hurricane with its eye and spiral bands of clouds over what appeared to be the eastern Caribbean near Puerto Rico. She could interpret, roughly, from the Spanish broadcast that Tropical Storm Vicki was now Hurricane Vicki and a category 1 hurricane. Arrows on the televised map showed its projected path headed towards Honduras and Nicaragua. Before she could focus on the importance of all of this, her attention was diverted by Douglas reporting, "Well, since you left Guanaja, the DEA and FBI, have been piecing together some of the established evidence in the case. They are convinced a drug cartel is involved in the murders of the **Golddigger** crew, in view of the fingerprints found on one of the bodies and the execution style of the killings. Also, since the fingerprints found were those of Alfonso Caldas, the most likely perpetrators are the Cordillera Cartel run by Hector Ramirez. Do you know of Ramirez?"

"No." Carla was surprised that he was repeating much of what she had told Jacobs on the phone, but maybe Jacobs had not told him what she knew.

"He's a very ruthless man and he has a major grudge against the United States for the death of his former boss, Eduardo Rojas."

"I do recall reading about Rojas in the newspaper."

"Well, if this conclusion about evidence is correct, you two will need to be very careful during any further investigation. These people have neither remorse for their actions nor any capacity for human feeling. They kill dogs for sport. As Brad suggested, you would be wise to wait until FBI personnel arrive in a few days to resume the investigation."

Carla acknowledged, "I appreciate your warning," but at the same time, thought that she needed to get back to Guanaja, as soon as possible. There were so many unanswered questions. She was curious why Rod had so many contacts. He must have worked far afield.

Agent Douglas interrupted her thoughts with the offer, "I'll take you to your room and spend the night in a chair by your door, if you don't mind. In the morning, you can call the police to escort you to the airport, and I'll follow behind in a taxi, so I don't make them suspicious. I'll follow you to the gate and take the same flight as far as La Ceiba, where I'll disembark to make some further arrangements for our investigation. From there, you'll be on your own."

They started up to Carla's room on the fifth floor. She was grateful that the day was coming to an end because she realized, suddenly, that she was tired. Matt drew his gun out of a chest holster under his shirt, before opening the door and casing the room, thoroughly. He, then, let her enter. She took off her shoes and made an immediate beeline for the bathroom, where she locked the door and took a quick welcome shower. A hospitality robe was hanging on the door and she slipped into it before entering the bedroom, again. Agent Douglas was already stationed in a chair near the door to the hallway. Carla said "Good night" and asked him to wake her at six in the morning because her flight was to leave at 7:30 a.m. She crawled into bed, still wearing the robe, exhausted. Sleep came quickly.

21

While Carla was just drifting off to sleep, Maria Hernandez was finishing the first run of tests on the water samples. The results were interesting. She came up with an analysis showing a chloride-containing compound, which was also a hydrocarbon. She was aware of a similar constituent in some herbicides that had been used around the world. The idea occurred to her to call up a friend and colleague in Houston about the result, and she had just picked up the phone to do so, when a knock came on the front door of the lab. Ah, probably, the promised agents for protection. She walked to the door and leaned her head against it and asked, "How was the weather today?"

A male voice replied, "Snowing lightly."

Maria opened the door, but to her dismay, saw two longhaired Hispanic men, dressed in sweat-stained tropical shirts, standing before her. One, lifted his right hand which held a pistol with a silencer, and shot her swiftly in the head. Maria's surprised look was still on her face as she fell dead to the floor. The men moved her body aside and strode quickly into the lab, since they had a further objective. Of the two, one man, with particularly stringy hair and a scar on his face, walked to the hood and spied the cylinder with German inscription. He removed it from the shielded area and proceeded to carry it with him. He then set about breaking any beakers, containing fluid, in the lab sink. He did all of this while wearing gloves. His partner, meanwhile, had discovered the safe, but couldn't discern the combination after several attempts. The man with stringy hair finally signaled to him that they should waste no more time and leave, so they took the cylinder and

145

hurried out of the building, leaving Maria Hernandez on the floor where they had shoved her and the safe still locked.

Her body was not discovered until 9 a.m., when a fellow lab worker came in to relieve her. He called the police and then checked the safe, in view of the disrupted state of the lab. Therein, he found the labeled glass container with the water samples. Maria's precaution had paid off.

22

"We have a new problem," voiced Dr. Bruce Tapper, solemnly, to Paul Jonas in the small, hospital conference room, the morning of November 21st. "There is a Category 1 hurricane headed our way which should probably reach us in about 36 to 48 hours. It caused moderate damage in Puerto Rico and is gaining power. The Hurricane Center, in Miami, estimates that by the time it reaches us, it could be a Category 3 or 4 hurricane."

"Meaning, we could lose phone contact with the States and our sanitation capability, here, as well as our ability to get to outlying areas to vaccinate people," replied Jonas, continuing Trapper's line of thought.

"Precisely. To make matters worse, there have been a couple of new cases identified on Guanaja, in Savannah Bight, by one of our outreach teams. It seems that they are friends, who visited the boy, Felipe, while he was ill."

"Oh, great."

"The team has enough vaccine and immuglobin for a few dozen people, but it does not have enough to immunize the entire island. As it is now, the hurricane is scheduled to hit Guanaja, before it hits us. They will be cut off from us, entirely, at that point."

"OK, in view of that, let's have the Naval Force send a helicopter with additional supplies of vaccine and immunoglobulin, protective gowns, masks, gloves, and disinfectant to Guanaja, today. We'll alert our team, there, as to the impending weather development, if they haven't been so notified. They'll have to make arrangements to move any infirmary to higher ground, due to the risk of storm surge and flooding."

"We'll have to make the same arrangements here, most likely, because the hospital is too near the harbor."

"You're right, Bruce. Why don't you start initiating these measures, while I make a phone call back to the Center to request further provisions for our operation, before we possibly lose all communication with them, too."

"Will do. I'll meet with you at noon, to brief you in on what I've been able to accomplish."

"Sounds good. I'm going to check on the mother of that first index case, too. She came down with symptoms and we gave her VIG. I know that she has not developed lesions and I'm hoping that she won't get much sicker. See you at noon."

"OK." Tapper headed out the door.

Jonas immediately dialed for an operator to get an international line. He gave her the direct number to the director's office at the CDC. After approximately a minute and a half, a familiar voice erupted on the line. Dr. Tyner Chassen's southern drawl was unmistakable. "Ty, it's Paul Jonas."

"Well, hi, Paul. How goes the microbe war in the jungles of Honduras?"

"I think that we've made a fairly positive ID, microscopically, of a pox virus, probably smallpox, however, we're waiting for confirmation of the type from polymerase chain reaction tests that you guys will run, when you receive the skin lesion samples we sent, yesterday, by air express. I, also, sent some test tubes that a hyperbaric physician, who is investigating the **Golddigger** murders, found on a German U-boat wreck off the coast of Honduras."

"You're kidding."

"I'm not." Chassen whistled. "We are requesting that the contents of those tubes, which I believe may be scabs of old smallpox lesions, be submitted for the same tests, as well as back-up cultures on chorioallantoic membrane. The thing of concern, Ty, is that these tubes were found with other possible weapons of mass destruction on the wreck and someone is currently after them, as evidenced by the **Golddigger** murders."

"I'm reading you loud and clear. Do we have a location on the wreck?"

"That's only known by the physician and the photographer, who dove on the wreck and whoever else went after the stuff, aboard. However, we can get back to the physician to pin down the location."

"Good. How about, if I notify the Department of Defense and the National Security Council as to what has been found?"

"I was hoping you'd say that because we're obviously going to need more help here, and I don't know when I will be talking to you, again, in the next few days. I'm sure that the FBI has already made these groups somewhat aware of the situation, since they are participating in the investigation in Honduras. But, you still might want to touch base with them, too, about these developments."

"I'll contact everyone as soon as I hang up with you. What's your next move?"

"Well, we have a little complication to deal with. That's why I'm calling you. There's a potentially Category 3 or 4 hurricane headed our way in the next 36 to 48 hours."

"Jesus. As if you didn't have enough to deal with."

"I know. Anyway, we have to move the hospital patients to higher ground because there, undoubtedly, will be a threat from storm surge. Also, we need to make sure that we preserve relative sanitation ability, otherwise this epidemic will really get out of hand. Could be tricky."

"I'll say. Listen, Paul, before I call the DOD, I'll talk to the Honduran ambassador in D.C. and ask if we can get you extra military support from the country's government. If we can't, we'll try to get permission to send some of our troops to support any curfew and quarantine measures."

"I really appreciate it, Ty."

"Don't mention it. Is there anything else I can do for you?"

"As a matter of fact, there is. Could you call Kathy and tell her that I'm all right and that I'll call her as soon as things calm down here, a bit, today?"

"Sure, Paul."

"Thanks. I can't think of anything else, Ty, except wish us luck."

"It goes without saying, friend. Be seeing you soon."

"Bye, Ty."

"Bye."

Hanging up, Jonas wondered how long they would have the luxury of phone use, in the path of the advancing storm. One more problem to add to the list. His next concern was how the patient, Meribel, was faring. He made his way to the quarantine ward in the hospital. She was in a room, by herself, with a gowned, gloved, and masked nurse in attendance. The sight was not, all together, reassuring. She was ill, as evident from the sheen of sweat on her body and her frequent episodes of dry heaving.

'Meribel, how are you feeling," asked Jonas, gently, after donning protective clothing and a mask.

The nurse translated, "No good, doctor."

"I'm sorry to hear that. Do you have a headache?"

"Yes, small," translated.

"How about a fever?"

"Yes, I feel hot and then cold."

To the nurse, "Can I see her vital signs?" The chart was passed to Jonas. Meribel's heart rate was increased, but her blood pressure was within normal range. He listened to her chest with a stethoscope. Still clear. Heartbeat was fast and regular. No skin lesions, yet. "I will check on you, tomorrow. We may be moving you to a different place, because there is a big storm coming."

Meribel frowned and looked worried. "Will my husband and son be brought to the same place?"

"Yes, we will move all the patients to the new location."

After the translation, Meribel sighed, relieved. "OK, Doctor. Gracias."

"I will see you, tomorrow, Meribel. Get some rest."

Jonas strode out of the room, dumping his gown and gloves in the biohazardous material receptacle at the door. He did not remove his mask until he was off the ward. His next task was to find Dr. Lopez and learn if there were any new outbreaks on the ward or presenting to the emergency room.

As usual, Dr. Lopez was thoroughly occupied with patients in the emergency room, but looked less tired than when Jonas had last seen him. "Dr. Lopez," getting his attention. "Can I talk to you, for a minute?"

"Yes, of course, Dr. Jonas."

"Please call me, Paul. May I call you by your first name."

"Please. I am called Jorge."

"Good enough, Jorge. I just wondered if you had had any more outbreaks of the disease in the last 24 hours?"

"As a matter of fact, a new case has developed in one of the patients on the isolation ward. It is the policeman's wife. Your doctors vaccinated her, but she probably had already been exposed to active disease in her husband, before the vaccination took place. Her main symptoms are fever and a headache."

"No rash, yet?"

"None, but it is only the first day of her symptoms."

"Well, we may be late vaccinating some of these people. My only hope is that we can reduce the severity of disease with our measures, and prevent excessive mortality."

Jorge nodded. "I think only time will tell us, if we are are on the right track, Paul."

"I'm afraid that you're right. Unfortunately, we do not have the luxury of time, at the moment. You heard about the approaching hurricane?"

"Yes, an officer from the Naval Force called me this morning to alert me."

"My associate, Dr. Tapper is in the process of making preparations to move the patients to higher ground, as a precaution against storm surge."

"I am aware of these preparations and I, also, know that the Naval Force is sandbagging the harbor."

"Then, you, also, probably realize the danger we face trying to contain this smallpox outbreak, in view of the oncoming hurricane."

"Maintaining hygiene is going to be most difficult."

"Exactly. So, any suggestions you might have, in this regard, will be greatly appreciated."

"One precaution that we should probably take, immediately, is to start putting some stores of water aside, in the event that our water lines are disrupted by the storm surge. Water is precious in much of Honduras, anyway, and the tap water is not safe to drink, except, possibly in the Bay Islands. However, we need water to help disinfect things. We can stockpile bottled water for drinking." Jonas was nodding his head in agreement. "I will see if the Naval Force can help us in that regard. We might also get some assistance from the local churches."

"That is key advice. Thank you, Jorge."

"Not at all. You must forgive me, I must get back to patients."

"I understand. I'll check back with you later."

"OK, Paul. Until then." Dr. Lopez returned to his ER duties.

Jonas sought out Bruce Tapper, as it was almost noon. He found him in the same conference room, in which they had met, earlier. Tapper looked frazzled. "I'm afraid to ask if you had any success, Bruce?"

"Oh, yeah, Paul, I did. I'm just worn out from being endlessly on the phone and trying to make myself understood in pidgin Spanish. We secured a place to move the patients to higher ground. The Standard Fruit Company is going to let us take over a warehouse that they don't use anymore and which is about a half a mile out of town, on a hillside."

"You mean the processors of **Dole** pineapple?"

"The very same group. I have checked out the facility and it is fairly clean and even has a water source. The best part is that it's structure is comprised of concrete blocks, so there is a good chance it will withstand the storm. There is electricity, too, so we won't have to make major modifications. The warehouse sits off a road to the airport, and in the event, that the storm cuts us off from town with flooding, we can probably get to the airport, if needed. I already have Honduran military personnel cleaning the building and moving supplies to it from the hospital. If it meets with your approval, we will start moving patients over first thing in the morning."

"It sounds good. Why don't you proceed with your plan. Better sooner than later. How will the patients be transported there?"

"I took care of that, too. The Honduran military is providing canopied trucks for debilitated patients and buses for those who are ambulatory."

"Stellar, Bruce."

"The Naval Force has provisions and medical supplies en route to Guanaja, Roatan, and Utila. They are preparing to evacuate people from highly exposed areas in the islands."

"Now, I know why I've always been lucky to have you working for me. You anticipate all the problems and find solutions."

Tapper's tired face crinkled, and a chuckle escaped his mouth. "Paul, you're so thorough, if you didn't have me, you would have found another fix-it, kind of guy in short order."

"Ah, but I probably wouldn't have enjoyed his personality half as much." Big grin on Tapper's part. "Now, I'll tell you what little I've accomplished in the last couple of hours. I talked to Chassen, in Atlanta, and he will try to get us some additional military support from the country for curfews and quarantine, post-hurricane. He is, also, notifying all the appropriate authorities about the probable identity of our epidemic."

"That will, probably, raise a few hairs on the necks of some people."

"No doubt. By the way, I stopped to see the mother of that first patient from Guanaja. She is ill, but I don't think as ill as her son was. The VIG may be helping. I think her immune system will not allow the manifestation of the hemorrhagic version of the infection."

"That's reassuring news."

"I think so. The only problem is that she appears to be progressing toward the eruptive phase, which means she can still be contagious to others. That, also, raises a question about any unknown contacts of current smallpox cases, who are asymptomatic and who have not been vaccinated or isolated. Will they progress to illness? And if they do, during the storm and we lose the ability to maintain effective infectious precautions, who else will be exposed?"

"In light of that, what do you propose we do, Paul?"

"I think we are going to have to mass vaccinate the city of La Ceiba and the island of Guanaja, prior to the hurricane."

"You can't be serious?"

"I am. I've given it a lot of thought. Right now, we have no case reports out of this immediate region or in the other Bay Islands, other than Guanaja."

"That's true. Therefore, these areas are at the highest risk for transmission of the disease to the rest of the country, post-hurricane. And if it spreads to the rest of the country, we may not have enough vaccine or VIG to contain it, before it spreads even further afield."

"I'm following you, but didn't the World Health Organization find that mass immunization in Java did not prevent the outbreak of 1700 cases in 1969?"

"Yes, indeed, they did, but they did not face an impending hurricane and they had more awareness of smallpox, at that time, as it was more prevalent. As a result, there were greater stores of vaccine available because the organization was trying to eradicate the disease. They accomplished that objective in 1980. Smallpox has not been a threat for over a decade. We don't have that luxury, now."

"But, Paul, do we even have enough vaccine, here, to accomplish what you propose?"

"I don't know. All we can do is try." There was nothing more to say. Both men knew the task before them.

23

Carla awakened to gentle shaking by Agent Douglas, who said, "It's time to go, otherwise, we will miss our flights." It was 6 a.m., that same morning that Jonas was making preparations with Tapper. Further prompting was not necessary. She called the police station, first, and was promised a car in 15 minutes. She then dressed quickly in the bathroom, since she had showered the night before.

Agent Douglas checked the hallway, as they opened the hotel room door, then they both emerged and headed toward the elevator. Once, in the lobby, they separated, but not before there were some last minute instructions by Douglas.

"You go out and meet the police car, and I will follow a short bit behind you and flag a taxi. Have a good trip," he said more loudly for the benefit of any listening bystanders.

"I will," answered Carla, and she shook his hand and strode away toward the front doors. She saw a European-make police car parked at the curb and a policeman standing by the vehicle, scanning those emerging from the entrance.

She walked toward him and he queried of her, "You - Doctor Knight?"

"Si - yes," replied Carla.

"Buenos dias." He gestured toward the back seat of the car, indicating that she should get in. She climbed in the vehicle and they headed for the airport.

"My English poor," apologized the policeman. "Capitanear Ortiz tell me - give you information. Gray car, we find outside Tegucigalpa. Stolen. Many fingerprints. We will find who fingerprints. Also - grande huracan coming. You not go to Guanaja, maybe?"

157

Carla was all ears. "Excuse me, officer. You say, 'huracan'. Do you mean, hurricane? Grande wind?" She made a whooshing sound and moved her hands to signify trees blowing.

"Si. Grande."

"Oh." She was consumed by a wave of anxiety. Maybe the airlines had stopped flying to Guanaja, in view of the approaching storm. How would she get back to Rod? She would have to get help from Matt Douglas. By this time, she noted that they were winding away from the tree-lined cobblestone streets and out on the asphalt road to the airport. She turned, briefly, to look out the rear-view window and saw a taxi not too far behind them. Matt, she thought.

Her car pulled up to the low terminal building that serviced several airlines. There was a clutter of individuals and luggage on the sidewalk. Carla thanked the policeman for his escort and stepped out into the confusion in front of the airport. It seemed that the crowd was agitated. Probably, trying to get to their final destinations before the storm. She was so lost in thought that she did not see the greasy, longhaired man, standing off a distance, behind a pile of luggage. He watched her enter the terminal with a steady, predatory gaze. The policeman, who had waited until she had entered the terminal, and Matt Douglas, who pulled up in a taxi, did not miss him, however. The policeman got out of his car and approached the man.

"You appear to be loitering, senor," in Spanish.

"Not at all. I am getting some fresh air while waiting for a flight. Besides, there is nothing wrong with watching all the pretty women go by," replied the man, who Matt Douglas now remembered from mugshots, as Alfonso Caldas. The man moved off down the sidewalk and the policeman returned to his car. Matt hurried into the airport after Carla. He caught up with her at the airline ticket counter.

"Carla, we have trouble."

"I know. There is an approaching hurricane out in the Caribbean."

"No, that's not what I meant. I just saw Alberto Caldas, the cartel member who's prints were on some of the **Golddigger** bodies, standing outside the terminal and watching you enter the building."

Carla paled. "What did he look like?"

"Dark, long stringy hair, medium height, with a prominent scar on his right cheek."

"That was the same man who was watching me in La Ceiba, before I went to Guanaja to start the investigation."

"Well, then, there definitely appears to be drug cartel involvement in this case, as well as involvement, prominently, by Caldas. I will have to notify the DEA. Let's get to the gate and I will try to find a phone."

They made their way through the crowd toward the departure gates. Carla was not sure what was worse- a hurricane threat or the threat of a pursuing murderer. She wished that Rod were there with her.

Matt spotted a phone office with booths, on their way, and he hurried to the counter to give the operator the number to call in Washington, D.C., after instructing Carla to stay in an alcove out of sight. The operator pointed to a booth for him to enter when the call rang through.

Just then, Carla, who was waiting in the alcove across the hallway, noted two Hispanic men, one of whom she definitely recognized as the man in La Ceiba, walk into the phone office, to the booth where Matt was talking on the phone. She saw Matt look up, startled, and suddenly, she saw one man pull a knife from his pants and stab Matt repetitively. The phone office desk clerk screamed. She, meanwhile, gasped and clapped a hand over her mouth so she, herself, would not scream and draw attention. She then ran down the concourse to her departure gate, looking back, once, to see if the two men were in pursuit. They, instead, had run in the opposite direction from the office due to the commotion created and the arrival of security guards. Carla saw them as they just ducked into a side door off the hallway.

She was breathing hard by the time she reached her gate. The few passengers in the waiting area eyed her suspiciously due to her stressed state. Thankfully, some military officials were checking passports at the ticket counter and questioning passengers about whether their plans involved travel to La Ceiba or Guanaja. It was obvious that these areas were restricted in view of the quarantine being enforced for the smallpox epidemic. Many passengers were turned away.

With the commotion and screaming, farther down the concourse, the officials stopped their task. They regarded her warily because she was running. Forget telling them about the murder, they would just detain her for questioning. Better to flash the papers Jonas had given her, confirming her smallpox immunization and giving her clearance to return to Guanaja due to her role in the **Golddigger** investigation, than to risk missing her flight. The officials scanned her papers, quickly, and nodded for her to proceed. They, then hurried down the concourse to check out the tumult, as she was the only passenger allowed to check in for the flight to La Ceiba. The gate attendants were just announcing boarding and Carla was able to go out on the tarmac to the plane.

Aboard and in her seat, she was then sorry that she had not spoken to Rod by phone or radio, while she was in Tegucigalpa, or for that matter, Dr. Velasquez. With that thought, she let her head fall back against the headrest, realizing how the tension had emotionally exhausted her. She was afraid to fall asleep, as she was not certain who comprised the crew on the plane, so she stared straight ahead and thought about the many developments, concerning the case, that had been revealed in the past 24 hours. She, also, speculated about the hurricane. The plane was headed toward La Ceiba, first, then another flight would take her to

160

Guanaja. She hoped that her stop in La Ceiba would be mercifully short because she was fearful that someone, again, might be waiting for her.

24

Carla could feel the plane engines throttle down and the plane begin to descend toward La Ceiba, where once more she could see the Pico Bonito in green splendor through the window. She sucked in her breath, briefly, in anticipation of who might be lurking on the ground. However, upon disembarking, she was relieved to see no familiar, evil faces in the crowd. The stopover was short and she was back in the air, again, after more military clearance of her papers, to Guanaja. There had been greater military presence at the La Ceiba airport than in Tegucigalpa, and it was obvious that there was intense preparation for the hurricane, going on in the terminal. Due to the frenzy of activity, she did not have an opportunity to contact Dr. Velasquez. She felt isolated. Guanaja seemed like home to her, at this point. She was anxious to get there. It would be good to see Rod. She hoped that he would be waiting for her at the runway.

Her wish was answered, in the next hour, when the plane circled to land on the dirt runway and she saw a lone Caucasian male figure standing near the passenger shelter. Thank God. Somehow, he knew what flight to wait for. The door of the plane could not open fast enough. Carla bolted from her seat and rushed down the stepladder used for disembarkation. Rod saw the look on her face and hurried toward her.

"Are you OK?" He had been worried because he had had no word of her return from either herself or Dr. Velasquez and he knew of the approaching hurricane. Thus, he had simply come to meet the first flight that had landed that morning. "Yes, I'm OK, but a DEA agent that your friend, Brad Jacobs, arranged to protect me, is not." She was short of breath from speaking, rapidly. "He was stabbed, today, while making a phone call to the DEA. You were right - the drug cartel is involved. The man was just trying to help me," then, the tears came and Carla sobbed in Rod's arms, while he tried to console her.

"Carla," he said, softly, "we have to get back to the resort as soon as possible. Too much has happened and no one can be trusted. We, also, have a hurricane coming."

With that advice, Carla contained herself and looked up earnestly at Rod, and nodded her head in affirmation. He kissed her lightly on the cheek and said, "Let's go." It felt so right to her.

They strode off for the dock and the motor launch to the resort. The residents of Bonacca had already made some preparations for the hurricane. There was a high wall of sandbags stacked at the low end of the airstrip, near the bay. Several stilted huts in the town were boarded up. People were stockpiling water and other provisions, in the boats at the dock, to transport to their homes. Amid all of this, small Pepe ran up and exclaimed, "Doctor Knight, remember me - Pepe? I help you with your luggage. Remember me when you go. I help you, again - yes?"

Carla's tense face relaxed into a grin, "Why, yes, Pepe, I remember you. I will make sure to call you when I need your help."

"OK - deal," and Pepe stuck out a small brown hand, which Carla shook in agreement. He liked these two people. They were so interesting. Some day he would leave the island and be just like them.

Rod and Carla climbed into a small launch that he had brought from the resort. While they were motoring back, Carla commented, "These children, who meet the plane, really have an entrepreneurial spirit."

"Yes, they do. Their luggage carrying is quite competitive as you can see. Pepe is the nicest of the whole crowd, though, and he is a favorite of the resort personnel. His mother works in the kitchen at Posada."

"Where does he live?"

"He and his mother and brothers and sisters live in a stilted shack in Bonacca. His mother commutes each day by boat to the resort."

"Well, they all sound hard working." With that said, she went on to relate what had happened in Tegucigalpa and what she had learned from Dr. Jonas and Dr. Velasquez. Rod was silent through her entire account, his eyebrows showed his concern.

"After everything that you have told me, I am convinced that we have a spy in the resort, who is tipping individuals off, probably drug cartel members, about our activities. I am, also, convinced that Von Kreitler must be involved because there have been several planes taking off and landing on his island, of late, and one plane belongs to a known cartel member."

"How do you know that?"

Rod was slightly hesitant, answering, but he looked her straight in the eye, "I'm an undercover DEA agent."

Carla let out a small guffaw. "You can't be serious." Then, she saw he didn't smile. No wonder he had so many contacts.

"I was going to tell you, earlier, but I was afraid if you were detained and interrogated in a rough manner, my cover might get blown. I'm sorry. I don't want you to think that I'm not trustworthy."

"It's not that. I'm just surprised."

"Understandably. I have been down here, for a few years, watching to see if Von Kreitler had any drug involvement and this is the first break I've had in that direction. Are you game to help me scout out the activity on his island this evening, after dinner? I have a feeling that there is going to be some kind of meeting taking place."

She met his gaze, "Sure, particularly if it helps us get more answers about the **Golddigger**."

"I knew I could count on you." His grin was wide and reassuring.

Returning the smile, she settled back in her seat and watched the midday sun's rays shimmer on the water surface. All of a sudden, she realized that she was starving because she had not eaten breakfast that morning or dinner, the night before, due to the turn of events in Tegucigalpa. She had only been served orange juice on the flight to La Ceiba. Lunch would be welcome at the resort, even if the enemy was lurking on the premises.

25

While Carla was contemplating lunch, Alfonso Caldas arrived at a remote site on the Mosquito Coast of Honduras, via private plane. The plane taxied along a dirt strip, which skirted an uncharted backwater. A large, plantation-style house was visible at the far end of the runway, protruding through the palm trees. Its exterior was quite worn and, from the air, it was barely discernable amongst all the vegetation. This illusive appearance was intentional on the part of the residence's owner, Hector Ramirez, who used the retreat as a way station in drug operations. By day, the runway was covered with potted palm trees, unless it was in use, so Honduran drug officials could not spot it from the air during reconnaissance. A helicopter was parked in a clearing at the far end of the strip. Palm fronds, too, often covered it, during the day.

The prop plane came to a stop in front of a dirt path to the main house. Alfonso disembarked quickly and then, on second thought, sauntered to the structure's main entrance, knowing the reprimand he would be given by his superior, who would be displeased with the day's events. The earth smelled damp and steam rose from the sun-baked ground, as a result of a recent tropical shower. Exotic birds called from the surrounding trees. He opened the front door hesitantly and a Nicaraguan manservant ushered him toward an adjacent parlor. The interior of the building in no way matched the exterior. It was modern and luxurious beyond the wildest imagination. An elaborate rock wall with waterfalls met a large pool, surrounded by a slate floor in the cavernous entrance hall. Tall palm trees rose out of the floor around the pool. One almost thought that they hadn't left the jungle outside, as tropical birds flew back and forth among the trees climbing toward the huge skylight in the ceiling. The off-white upholstered furniture made everything bright in contrast to the shade created by the heavy jungle canopy beyond the house. Only the soft whir of ceiling fans could be heard in conjunction to the birdsong and water movement.

This serene scenario was broken by sharp footsteps on the slate. Alfonso looked up from his plush seat in the parlor to see the stern countenance of Hector Ramirez. His boss looked like he had just risen from bed, as his hair was slightly mussed and his shirt and pants were not completely buttoned.

"So, Alfonso, do you have good news for me, or bad?"

The hesitation on Caldas' part was enough of an answer for Ramirez.

Veins on Ramirez's temples bulged prominently during the silence. Caldas nervously picked at some dirt on his shoe. "What happened in Teguz?!"

"She got away, but we silenced a DEA agent who was with her," Caldas mumbled. "He was trying to make a phone call at the airport."

"I don't care what the bastard was doing!, screamed Ramirez, who picked up a colored glass vase and threw it against a white wall. It shattered into a myriad of pieces on the marble floor.

An exotic, young, Miskito native woman, who wore a filmy negligee, stuck her head in the door at that moment and whined, "Hector, what is all the noise about? Come back to bed. I'm lonely."

"Ina, leave us at once, you whore!, Ramirez screamed further and he threw another glass object at the door.

The woman quickly retreated with an offended pout. Alfonso had to repress a smirk. The manservant, who carried a broom and dustpan, replaced her, shortly. He, quietly, began to sweep up the glass shards while Ramirez and Caldas continued their conversation.

"The Knight woman is a nuisance. She has pieced together too much of the incident on the **Golddigger**. Both she and Dalton need to be eliminated before they discover our plan. I was counting on you, Alfonso. You have disappointed me."

Caldas became anxious that he was going to be punished on the spot. That could entail any form of quick death, or prolonged torture, for which Ramirez was legendary. He, therefore, quickly blurted out, "Dr. Knight did not get the cylinder from the wreck analyzed. We killed the lab technician and retrieved the cylinder, after the doctor left for her hotel. I have it in my possession, at this moment."

Ramirez's face broke into a relieved grin. "Bravo! I knew I could count on you."

"We also smashed every glass container in the lab, so there was no chance any water sample got tested," added Alfonso, perspiring visibly. "Remember, we retrieved the smallpox vials from the warehouse, too."

"Ah, yes. Excellent. All Dr. Knight can do, now, is keep guessing. Hopefully, we can get to Dalton and herself, before they find out anything else. We need to fly up to Bird Cay this evening to discuss further plans with Kapitan von Kreitler. I will have Ramon contact him by radio to let him know we are coming. I will also have the **El Mundo** moved north, just within Laguna Caratasca, so we can go directly from the Cay to the ship via helicopter, after the meeting. We need to resume our salvage operations as soon as possible." With that said, Ramirez let a colorful parrot that had landed on his opposite shoulder, climb onto his left hand and he began talking to it, softly.

Caldas was always amazed how fast Hector would switch moods. That's what made him dangerous. He reflected on Hector's past, briefly. Ramirez had been the youngest of four sons, born to a poor farmer in Columbia. He had been competitive with his brothers from the beginning and liked to be in control. There had been many bloody fisticuffs. Finally, his father, in frustration had sent him off to work for a wealthy landowner, who lived over a hundred miles from the farm, in order to keep peace at home. Ramirez was 14. He never returned home, again.

During his servitude, he developed expensive tastes by watching his master's lifestyle. He, also, evolved an obsession about being a member of the upper class. Therefore, his speech, diction, and mannerisms changed, over time, to mimic those for whom he worked. That left the issue of money, which he soon learned could only be obtained in great quantity, without formal education or family connections, through the drug trade.

A statement by Ramirez broke Alfonso away from his thoughts. "I have had the radio equipment, at the resort and aboard its vessels, disabled, so Senor Dalton can not communicate with the United States. That should slow down his intrusion into our operation."

"What if I slipped into the resort after our meeting, this evening, and slit the throats of Dalton and the Knight woman while they sleep? Then, we would be rid of them, for good."

"No, Alfonso. That would bring too much attention by the authorities into the area, again. We must be subtler. Kapitan von Kreitler will have an idea about their disposal, I'm sure."

"I will be glad when we return our full attention to our cocaine shipments. This operation is taking too much of our time and energy, and is exposing us to unnecessary risks," said Alfonso in an agitated manner, burning a fly that had alighted on a nearby ashtray, with a lighter he had produced from a pocket.

"Patience, Alfonso. We must avenge Rojas. This will all be over soon. The Kapitan's plan is perfect. Besides, you have had your fun along the way," encouraged Ramirez, as he thought of the woman aboard the **Golddigger**.

Alfonso slouched in his chair and looked bored.

"Come on. We have been through too much for you to give up now. You can help Ramon load some ammunition on the helicopter to take to the ship. Then, we can have some dinner and wine and leave for Bird Cay, thereafter. Our gringo friend from

Washington will join us for dinner and he will take the helicopter to the ship. We will take a plane to the Cay. So, go make yourself useful until dinner."

At the mention of the gringo, Alfonso had stiffened. He had not seen the informant in a long while. He did not trust him and hoped the gringo would not bungle things for the cartel. Ramirez was a fool to use him. He had another thought, which he voiced, "Are you not worried about the approaching hurricane?"

"I am aware of the recent weather reports." There was not a ripple in Ramirez's countenance. It was obvious that not even a storm was going to deter him from his mission. "We have taken precautions. That is why it is important to get the **El Mundo** to the wreck site, as soon as possible, retrieve the rest of the cargo, and get out of the area. We may not have a window of opportunity, again. Too much has been learned about the wreck by others. It won't be long before the authorities find the U-boat and salvage it, themselves. We don't want that to happen. Right, Alfonso?"

Caldas mumbled an affirmative response to Ramirez and rose lazily from his chair. "I will find Ramon and do what you ask." He sauntered out of the parlor, avoiding eye contact, his expression sullen.

As Ramirez watched him leave, he thought that one day he would have to put a bullet in Alfonso's head before his hitman did the same to him. It was only a matter of time. There would, eventually, be a disagreement between them that they could not resolve, peacefully. That was the way it was in the cartel.

Alfonso found Ramon outside, already loading the Bell Jet Ranger. The hot blast of moist air that surrounded them, surprised him after the cool interior of the house. Sweat poured down his forehead, immediately.

"Hey, Alfonz, did you see any action in Teguz?" Ramon gave him a knowing look and smirked.

"Not enough," answered Alfonso with a scowl and he returned to his task, without further conversation. They spent the next hour loading the helicopter in silence, except for an occasional, bawdy joke cracked by Ramon and some joint laughter. Alfonso noticed several Nicaraguan workers stacking sandbags around the airstrip and house, as well as nailing boards across many shuttered windows of the residence, obviously, preparing for the worst.

As dusk began to fall, a plane could be heard approaching in the distance. Alfonso looked up, when it circled overhead, and realized it was a STOL (short take-off and landing) craft. It idled in the air over the runway, briefly, and then landed like a helicopter. The cabin door opened, a portable stairway was wheeled up to the plane, and Brad Jacobs stepped out into the twilight.

26

Carla ate lunch in her room, upon the prompting of Rod, who could see the exhaustion in her face and wanted her to take a nap, afterwards. She was glad that he had convinced her to do this, because she was not anxious to talk to anyone.

Later, that afternoon, when she awoke, she walked down to the dive shop and found Rod sitting in a chair, frowning at the wall. He looked up and made an attempt to smile at her, but his look of concern prevailed.

"Hi. Has something else happened?"

"The resort communication system is down and I have not been able to reach Washington, D.C. to talk to Brad Jacobs or anyone else at the DEA. To make matters worse, the VHF radio on the dive boat has been tampered with and is not working, and my satellite phone has been destroyed. Someone definitely does not want us to communicate with the outside world. Our only hope is that Dr. Velasquez or Brad Jacobs have contacted the appropriate authorities and are sending aid to us. We, now, have the added danger that we can't monitor the progress and path of the approaching hurricane, unless we find someone with a portable weather radio."

"I see your point. Jacobs indicated to me on the phone, yesterday, in Tegucigalpa, that he was going to contact the FBI for help and that he also was going to come down to assist the investigation."

"Good because that's our only back-up at the moment. We need to get back to the wreck site, first thing, tomorrow, before that hurricane hits. You're still up for checking out Bird Cay?"

"Definitely. I don't feel comfortable, at the moment, staying in my room like a sitting duck."

"I couldn't agree with you more. We'll get our bathing suits and snorkeling gear, after dinner, and take a small skiff out to the Cay."

"OK." Carla helped Rod, during the remainder of the afternoon, make some preparations for the trip back to the wreck site the next day. Rod was anxious to get back to the site because he feared that whoever killed the **Golddigger** crew would try to return to the U-boat, soon, to retrieve whatever material they had left, and to destroy the wreck so it could never be found, again. He was hoping that they could get there, before these perpetrators arrived, and find out what was behind the sealed bulkhead door. The dinner gong sounded, suddenly, jarring him from his thoughts. He, subsequently, locked up the equipment for their trip in the dive shop and he and Carla walked to the dining room together.

Carla spoke little at dinner due to the thoughts racing through her head. The Campbell's watched her countenance, curiously, trying to read her mental state. They were full of questions. Rod fended them off politely and did not divulge what happened to Carla while she was in Tegucigalpa. She made an excuse, near the conclusion of the meal that she was quite tired and was going to retire early. Rod offered to walk her back to her room and he rose to pull back her chair. She accepted.

As the two of them strode out of the dining room, together, Bud Campbell murmured to his wife, "Chummy, aren't they?", and she sneered in agreement.

Back at Carla's room, Rod waited outside for Carla to put on her bathing suit, as he already had his suit on under his shorts. Soon, they were down the walk to the dive shop and dock, carrying nothing but towels and a flashlight with them. Both wore sneakers in anticipation of trekking around the Cay. Rod stopped at the photo shop to pick up an automatic pistol from a locked drawer and he put it in his towel. They loaded snorkeling gear into the same boat that had brought them from the runway dock, earlier, and climbed in. Rod kept the motor throttled down, so that their course across the lagoon would be as quiet as possible. What they did not see was the small figure, which watched them from some bushes on shore, as they pulled away from the dock. Pepe had come by small outboard boat to help his mother that evening, and he was eager to know what his two idols were doing.

Rod decided to go to Half-Moon Cay, first, as it would be a good vantage point from which to watch activity on Bird Cay. There was no breeze, which seemed eerie, in view of the forecasted, impending hurricane, and thus, no waves lapped against the beach, onto which they pulled their skiff from the water. Bird Cay was a quiet, dark outline in the distance. They gathered their towels and strode a short distance down the sandy expanse of Half-Moon Cay to a cluster of curved palms. Rod entered the water, first, after depositing his towel under a palm, and he rolled over into a backstroke. Carla followed eagerly as the water appeared so inviting. Once in, the liquid caress against her skin soothed her frayed nerves. She floated, for awhile, looking up at the inky sky punctuated by bright stars. She felt some movement in the water beside her and realized that Rod's head was not to be seen on the surface. Suddenly, she received a playful pinch on her flank and she let out a soft yelp. Rod surfaced near her and grinned. She could just make out his face in the starlight. The water was full of bioluminescence and any movement sent shimmers in all directions. He reached out an arm and pulled her toward him, his grin softening.

Carla smiled, in a light-hearted, reprimanding manner. "I thought we were on a reconnaissance mission."

"We are, but that doesn't mean we can't have a few light moments along the way." Rod gave her an innocent look, then his face sobered. "You know, you are quite an unusual woman. You meet everything head-on, in your life, never complaining, never backing down." Carla looked down at the water surface, uncomfortable with the praise. "And, I'm afraid that I'm becoming greatly attracted to you," and with that, he brought his face close to her own, as she looked up. He kissed her, at first, gently, then more passionately.

Carla was taken off guard by his comments. She wanted, badly, to let go of herself, but was wary. All she knew, was that she was happier than she had been in a long while. She wanted the moment to last forever.

Rod was fighting the desire to pull off her suit, after embracing her shapely body. He had done that with others. This situation was different. He really was interested in this woman and he didn't want to hurt her. She had been through so much in her life.

They kissed again and Carla then said in a throaty voice, "It's been awhile."

"Likewise," murmured Rod. She looked earnestly into his eyes after this statement, and he kissed her lips, and then her throat and the wet suit over one breast, and he ran a hand down her back. She was aware of feeling a mounting rush through her body, but this was interrupted by the sound of a turbo-prop engine approaching from the southeast and headed in the direction of Bird Cay. She pulled away from Rod with a jerk, reluctantly. She sensed his hesitance, too.

"Is that a plane, approaching?"

"I think so," Rod answered, suddenly alert. Both their pairs of eyes were riveted on the dark sky. Airplane lights were visible in association with the sound. Finally, the plane was discernable and they watched it descend on the island and land within a very short distance. Rod recognized it as a Pilatus PC-6 Turbo-Porter, a STOL(short take-off and landing) craft, usually used by many military operators. The time was almost 10:45 p.m. Rod noticed that a couple of bonfires were lit on Bird Cay, now.

"I've never had the chance to investigate those fires from any close vantage point. I think tonight's the night."

"Let's go. I am as impatient, as you are, for more answers."

"All right, but we'll have to be very careful. I am not sure if von Kreitler has guards on his island because I have never seen any when I have been near there, in the daytime. Keep your eyes open."

"Don't worry, I will. I don't want to end up like the **Golddigger** crew."

They motored quietly toward the Cay, then cut the motor 100 yards from shore. Rod grabbed an oar in the boat and paddled it like a canoe toward a secluded portion of beach, away from the main house and airstrip. He also picked the spot because some palms leaned low over the water to form a screen in front of the boat, thus effectively hiding it. They crept along the palm forest margin toward the house. As they came closer, they could hear some variably accented voices. The voices were speaking English. One sounded familiar to both of them.

At this juncture, they cut in amongst the palms behind the house, where a large veranda was evident, leading into a brightly-lit main room, whose shuttered doors were open to the night air. Several figures were visible inside. A number of these were dark-haired, Hispanic-appearing men, but one tall Caucasian man stood out among them. He was elderly, but fit and had silver hair. His back was toward Carla and Rod. He was doing most of the talking, with a clipped German accent. What he was saying astonished them. Rod whispered to Carla that the man, talking, was Von Kreitler. He was speaking directly to one of the Hispanic men, who appeared to be the leader. Rod recognized him from DEA photos as Hector Ramirez. He also saw Alfonso Caldas standing near him, who Carla remembered as the man at the airport and in the plaza, in La Ceiba.

Von Kreitler's voice could be heard saying, "I don't care if your men think that the salvage of the U-boat's cargo is too dangerous, with a hurricane approaching. You must get that uranium off the boat, tomorrow. The risks are far surpassed by what we are each trying to achieve. Think how surprised the United States will be and what chaos will ensue when we detonate our bomb. Just like the chaos they created for Germany in World War I and World War II."

For the benefit of others in the room, who, obviously, hadn't heard some of his reasons for salvage, he turned to the group and expounded, "During the First World War, the eventual, American involvement caused the war to last longer and, as a result, Germany incurred a huge amount of debt. This was complicated by a banking crisis in the Weimar Republic, after the war. The mark became worthless. When Hitler took over Germany, the Weimar Republic was failing. He began ethnic cleansing. Several scientists were driven out of the country in 1933, as a result. Even though nuclear fission had been discovered in Germany, the knowledge about the potential technology, utilizing this phenomenon, left with the exodus of these scientists. We had control of Europe's only uranium mines, but did not know how to use the material to make a bomb.

The Americans had the majority of our scientists and were able to make the atomic bomb and use it, eventually, against our allies in Hiroshima. We, meanwhile, had figured out how to make the unstable form of uranium for a bomb, by the end of the Second World War. We tried to send some by U-boat to Japan with plans for construction of a bomb, but U-234 was captured in 1945. A few months after this seizure, the Americans bombed Hiroshima. So, in a final attempt by the Third Reich to avenge itself, they sent me in a U-boat with 12 containers of uranium 235 to South America to hide our secret from the enemy forces and the world until the time was right for revenge. Along with that cargo, we carried a chemical herbicide, very much like Agent Orange, that we hoped to drop by rocket over the United States to destroy crops and vegetation and cause insidious disease in the general populace. We, also, carried one of the few deadly stores of smallpox virus that we had cultivated for unusual virulence in our laboratories and had, originally, planned to use during the war. It was necessary to scuttle the U-boat to hide the cargo until the time was right to use it.

The time for revenge is now, gentlemen. We, almost, have the technology and material for an atomic bomb in our grasp. We need to salvage the uranium and carry out our plan to build a bomb and plant it in Washington, D.C., near Georgetown, where it will be least suspected. What better way to throw the United States into chaos than to disrupt its seat of government. You have the opportunity of a lifetime to avenge your own situation. I don't think that you would disagree, Senor Ramirez," concluded Von Kreitler, turning back to the individual that he originally addressed.

"No, Kapitan von Kreitler," answered Ramirez, "you have made your point. However, our cause is simpler. We want revenge for the shameful death of our leader, who was killed like some animal slaughtered for market. We will get more protective equipment and try to remove the cargo in the next 24 hours, before investigation by the Americans continues. They have already found out too much."

"I wouldn't worry about the Americans. They will be taken care of," a very familiar voice said, and Carla gasped as she saw the red-haired figure of Bud Campbell step from behind another man. Rod, also, drew his breath in with this revelation.

A palm branch suddenly moved behind them and a Teutonic voice commanded, "Put your hands over your heads and don't move any further, or you will get a bullet through your head." Carla looked momentarily at Rod and he gave her a nod, indicating she should comply. "Now, turn around slowly with your hands on your heads," the voice directed further. They turned to find a fair, young male skinhead, of husky build, who was pointing a machine gun at them. Another skinhead male, who was of slighter build, accompanied him. He removed Rod's gun from the waist of his shorts. "You," he gestured his gun at Carla, "start walking toward the house, and you," pointing his gun at Rod, "you follow her.

Keep your hands on your heads." He marched them toward the house and up the steps of the veranda.

At the sound of their approach, the group, inside, became quiet and turned around. Carla saw the man, who Rod had indicated was Von Kreitler, set his icy, blue gaze upon her. It was much the same stare that she imagined some long-legged arachnid might lay upon its prey, before it ate it.

"Well, you must be Dr. Knight. How convenient for us that you should join our meeting. We have been chasing you all over Honduras. Good work, Hans."

"I found them behind the house, listening to the meeting," Hans, bragged.

"And Mr. Dalton, I'm sorry to disappoint you that I'm not a solid, law-abiding citizen of Honduras. We have had some nice conversations in the past, but this time, you have, unfortunately, stretched our friendship. Besides, Mr. Campbell tells me you are with the DEA. He has been onto you, for some time." Rod gave Campbell a scathing glance.

"Mr. Cambell is the least of your worries. Your biggest problem lies in what the two of you have discovered," Von Kreitler continued. We had hoped that when Mr. Campbell smashed your camera equipment your progress would have been hampered. However, Dr. Knight is too smart for her own good. Making the connection between the **Golddigger** crew's post-mortem findings and our chemical herbicide was quite brilliant. Yes, it's amazing what Dr. Velasquez will reveal under pressure."

Carla blurted out, "What have you done to him?"

"Oh, he will be out of work with some bumps and bruises," smirked Von Kreitler. And with that, he and Ramirez and his men and Bud Campbell erupted into laughter. Carla glared at the German.

"Regretfully, you have also learned of our plans for the radioactive cargo," Von Kreitler pointed out. "You are, now, both a major liability, a liability that must be removed. We must be subtle in this elimination, though. We do not want any new apparent murders, in the area, that people start investigating, while we are trying to finish our project.

Therefore, the demise I have planned for you, both, is natural. What more tragic mishap than two lovers out for a romantic night swim in calm water, when they suddenly run into a drift of sea wasps, those dreaded little cube jellies that have such a treacherous sting. They swim frantically toward shore in pain, only to get caught in more tentacles and stings. They have such terrible chest pain and abdominal aches that their breathing becomes difficult and they drown. The next morning, they are found washed up on shore with the pimply rash of numerous stings. The island residents are devastated. They mourn the loss of these lives and then forget them. Natural, don't you think?"

Carla shuddered, imperceptibly. She had heard of sea wasps, before. The most dreaded of these small, stinging jellyfish was *Chironex fleckeri,* whose venom was 350 times more lethal than the Portuguese Man-of-war. She hoped that Honduras did not have that variety. She could not remember. She looked desperately at Rod. His gaze was directed, unflinchingly, at Von Kreitler, who was enjoying the consternation that he was causing.

At this moment, Bud Campbell turned to Rod and with a snide grin said, "You're probably wondering how I became affiliated with Captain von Kreitler and Senor Ramirez? Basically, I'm for hire to the highest bidder. I, also, was a Viet Nam War vet, but I became a mercenary in South America, later, because I got a helluva lot more out of it than I did in Nam. Can't say that it has been a bad existence playing a tourist and performing guerilla tactics on the side for big bucks. It looks like you would have fared better doing what I do for a living."

"You couldn't pay me enough to turn against my country," retorted Rod.

"Obviously not. I pity your patriotic zeal," sneered Bud.

Von Kreitler turned to Hans and ordered, "Take the two of them to the dock on the leeward side of the island. Tie them to a dock piling with only their heads above the water and gag them. They will eventually slide down further. Then turn the light on the dock, so it illuminates the water around them. That will bring in the sea wasps. We will retrieve them later, while it's still dark and drop their bodies off the beach on Half-Moon Cay."

Hans and his fellow skinhead guard marshaled Rod and Carla from the room, but not before Hector Ramirez grabbed one of Carla's arms, briefly, and said, smiling sadistically, "It is a shame that such an attractive woman would get mixed up in our business. Otherwise, we could have met under different circumstances, and you could have been of some use to me."

Carla jerked her arm out of his grasp and Rod muttered, as he walked by Ramirez, "Obviously, you suffer from a delusional state. Give it a rest," at which point, Ramirez slapped him hard across the face. Rod recovered and grinned, "Hit a sore spot, I can see."

"Enough," Von Kreitler intervened. "Get them to the dock, quickly. The sooner this is over, the better.

They walked from the room. Hans followed them with a machine gun, as did his fellow guard and two of Ramirez's men. One of these was Alfonso Caldas. Carla's skin began to crawl. Dying by being stung repetitively by a bunch of jellyfish was bad enough, but not knowing what Caldas would do to her after her demise, was terrifying. He must have known the unsettling effect that he had upon her because he took amusement walking a short distance behind her, through the palms.

Rod was tempted to make a break, but he decided not to do so, for fear of what would happen to her if he were killed. So they plodded forward into the palm forest, an occasional lizard skittling out of their path. The night felt warm around them and there was still no breeze. Just the conditions Von Kreitler had been hoping for, to bring in a drift of sea wasps. The dock appeared a short distance ahead of them in the darkness. No light was on in the area. The water was glassy.

One of Ramirez's men had brought some rope and rags. Rod was bound and gagged, first, since he was their greater liability, and he was lowered into the water. Hans got into the water and quickly lashed Rod to a piling. Carla was bound and gagged by Caldas, who put a hand lecherously on her shoulder and bent his head near her ear to whisper, menacingly, "I will be waiting for you."

"Ah, you must mean in hell. I'm afraid I won't be there," answered Carla bravely.

Caldas lowered her roughly into the water, in response, and Hans tied her to an adjacent piling. Then, their captors filed away , making some obscene remarks in the process. A tin-shaded lamp, on the end of the dock, was suddenly turned on, electrifying their surroundings with stark light, and they were alone.

27

Carla eyed the glaring water surface, nervously. She began tugging at her bonds, but Rod indicated with head shaking, that she shouldn't do it, because with each tug, her body slipped slightly down the piling so that her head was barely above the water, risking that she might drown even before being stung.

Twenty minutes passed without incident, then suddenly Rod moaned and it was obvious that he had been stung. It was impossible to see the little cube jellies, long before their contact, as they were small and transparent. They were also extremely fast in their movement through the water. Carla had seen a picture of one in a textbook, a tiny, squarish transparent jellyfish with a ring of nematocysts (stinging cells) on its voluminous, string-like tentacles. Rod moaned, again, and Carla was now frantic to get loose because it was evident that a drift of sea wasps was closing in on him.

Just then, there was a motion on the opposite end of the dock, and a tiny figure ran down the dock toward them. Pepe appeared in the light to their amazement. Rod was now writhing in pain and slipping down the piling. Pepe untied a nearby dinghy and paddled it toward Rod. He pulled out a knife and cut the gag from around Rod's mouth.

"Pepe," gasped Rod, "cut Carla loose, first. The sea wasps haven't stung her, yet, so they probably aren't in the water around her, if you reach your arms in to cut her loose. Once she is free, she can cut me loose." His conversation was cut short by another moan.

Pepe hurried over to Carla and cut her loose. She took his knife and swam toward Rod, with Pepe cutting a path through the jellies, in front of her with the dinghy and paddle. She cut him loose and subsequently helped him into the dinghy, but not before, she, herself, was stung on the foot. She was grimacing, as both Pepe and Rod pulled her into the dinghy. Rod began paddling the dinghy with the one oar that was available, toward the beach. This would never do for crossing the channel to the resort. They would have to find a different boat, or get back to their own boat.

"Pepe, why were you here?", Carla asked incredulously.

"I saw you - from Posada, go to the Cay. Then, I watched you long time until you took boat to this Cay. I followed you in my boat. Saw the bad man take you here. I did not want for them to hurt you."

"Pepe, you saved our lives," said Rod, soberly. Pepe grinned. "Where did you hide your boat?"

"It is over in the bushes to the north."

"OK, let's get to it as fast as we can and get out of here, because they will be looking for us, shortly."

Despite the prickling pain racking his body and the developing headache, he pushed on beside Pepe, with Carla limping close behind. They reached the skiff which had been cleverly covered with palm fronds and pushed it out into the water. Pepe had used oars to row to the Cay. There was an outboard motor on the transom. Rod was thankful for this option, but oars would be quieter. Despite the slowness, rowing was their best alternative at the moment. They would have to make the most of a difficult situation. Carla sat in the stern and Pepe in the bow. Rod insisted on rowing. The going was silent except for the rhythmic sound of the oars in the their locks.

Carla knew Rod must have terrible pain from his exposure, as she was suffering from a moderate amount in her foot, despite only a glancing contact. While he was rowing, she began scooping up salt water and pouring it over his wound sites and then, over her own. Seawater was supposed to be better than fresh water for this kind of injury, since it did not stimulate nematocyst discharge. Wheals had formed on both herself and Rod at contact points, by this time. Rod also had some whip-like, purple lesions on his chest. She wadded up an old shirt that was in the skiff and attempted to pull visible tentacles off Rod's torso. When she got to shore, she would have to find a way to detoxify the envenomation for both of them. Pepe noted the consternation on her face, and she looked at him and asked, "Pepe, when we get to the resort, please go to the kitchen and look for some vinegar - that's V-I-N-E-G-A-R, vinagre en espanol. You know, your mother uses it on salads."

"Ah, si, Dr. Knight," acknowledged Pepe, eagerly.

After what seemed an eternity, they reached the cove in front of the resort. Pepe leaped out and tied the skiff to the dock. Rod had to be helped out of the boat by Carla, as he now had chest pains and a raging headache. Carla ran into the dive gear room and rummaged for her gear bag, which contained a first aid kit. Pepe had already gone to find some vinegar. By the time she returned to where she had left Rod, Pepe had arrived with what she sought. She poured vinegar on Rod's wounds and her own, for five minutes, in order to prevent nematocyst discharge. She asked him if he had some shaving cream and a razor, and he nodded affirmatively, pointing to the photo shop and telling her the items were in an athletic bag, there. Pepe ran to retrieve it. Once in hand, Carla sprayed the cream on all the affected areas and shaved them to remove any residual nematocysts. She, then, applied hydrocortisone cream. Rod watched the ministrations with a puzzled look. He had seen the vinegar used before, but had never seen the shaving cream treatment.

"Where did you learn to do that?"

"A dive medicine course."

"Well, I'm glad because it is already helping." Some of his pain was lessening.

She handed him an aspirin and a Benadryl tablet from her first aid kit. "This will relieve your headache a bit and the itchiness."

Suddenly, in the distance, a motor could be heard starting and several voices were audible over the water. Rod looked at Carla.

"They know we've escaped. We have to get out of here and we have to try to get back to the wreck site." He turned toward Pepe. "Pepe, you must get back to Bonacca any way that you can, right away. In the morning, try to get your family to take you to La Ceiba, because there is a hurricane coming and you would all be safer there. Find the police in La Ceiba and have them notify the FBI in Washington, D.C., in the United States. Remember F-B-I. Tell them that we have found the drug men and German captain, who killed the people on the **Golddigger**, and that we need their help. Tell them we are going back to the shipwreck site, south of Guanaja. They need to bring many men and guns. Can you remember that?"

"Si, Senor Rod."

Rod turned to Carla. "We won't be able to take a boat from the resort because they will see us and overtake us. We must go across the island and see if we can find a boat to get us back to the wreck. You'll need some shoes. Do you have some in your gear bag?"

"Yes, there are a pair of sneakers in the bag."

"Good, go get them. I'll grab a pair of mine in the photo shop." The boat motor now sounded closer. "Go, Pepe. Get us help. You saved our lives, already. Thank you." With that said, Pepe scurried off into the darkness.

Rod grabbed Carla's hand and led her behind the main buildings to the jungle at the perimeter of the resort. It covered a high hill, towering immediately in front of them.

"We're going up there?"

"Yes, I'm afraid that we have no other choice. Bonacca and Savana Bight are too far along the shoreline in either direction, and they will be searching this side of the island for us. Our only hope is to make for the Bayman Bay Club on the other side and find a boat. We must hurry and get a bit of a lead, as they are not far behind us."

Rod ran briefly into a nearby maintenance shed. He returned with a machete and an old pack, in which he put a bottle of water and Carla's first aid kit. They started to make their way through the thick, tropical vegetation, scrambling up a rocky slope with vine holds, not knowing what lay ahead of them, but, certainly, knowing what was behind them.

28

The climb uphill was initially hard and didn't get easier. A number of insects were plying the night air looking for sustenance. The exotic caw or hoot of a tropical bird sounded above them, frequently. Carla would, occasionally, feel something land on her bare arms, but didn't dare look to see what it was, and would rid herself of the creature by shaking her extremities. Once, a snake slithered across her foot and she let out a small yelp and leaped away. They were moving at such a rapid pace, clinging to vines and whatever other handholds they could find, that there was no time to focus on the unpleasantness. Both of them sustained a number of bites from various insects in the process.

Carla was relieved to see that they had nearly made the summit of the first mountain behind the resort, but to her chagrin, a number of smaller hills lay in front of them, as Guanaja, unlike Roatan, was wider and more steeply mountainous. One summit that they would not have to scale was Michael Rock Peak, the highest on Guanaja. It was more centrally located on the island and northeast of the Bayman Bay Club, Rod indicated.

Voices could now be heard in closer proximity behind them and it was obvious that the party, pursuing them, had reached the resort by boat. Rod decided to navigate toward Bayman Bay Club with Michael Rock Peak as a reference point and as a result, he and Carla stayed due west of the mountain, which he could see on occasion through the breaks in the dense foliage. The air was exceedingly warm and humid and both of them were drenched in perspiration. They stopped, briefly, to drink from their water bottle.

During this interlude, Rod smelled smoke in the air and he stood up, abruptly, appearing alarmed. Small animals started to scurry out of cover past them. These included numerous lizards and rabbits, from the direction they had just come. Rod spoke urgently, "They must have started a fire with gasoline to flush us out and ambush us."

"Oh, my God. You don't think they set the resort on fire, too, do you?"

"Hard to say. It would act as a distraction for the locals if they had to put out a fire at the resort and were, therefore, too occupied to follow Von Kreitler's men into the jungle, or back to the Cay. We just have to try to get to Bayman, ahead of the fire. I don't think that we have much more than two and a half kilometers to go."

"We don't have much choice, do we?"

"No, I'm afraid we don't."

"Well, let's plug onward because I never want to meet up with that Caldas fellow, again."

"They were both tiring at this point, but focus on their objective and fear of capture drove them forward. Their legs and arms bore numerous scratches and sand fleabites. The roar of the fire pursued them, as well as the occasional crash of a burning tree. It was finally necessary to tear up a shirt in the pack and wet the pieces to hold over their noses and mouths against smoke. There were pine trees in the forest that they ran through. These had been there for centuries, even at the time that Columbus had landed (he had named Guanaja, "Island of Pines"), and these trees provided better fuel for the fire than the rain forest vegetation, and helped it spread.

Rod and Carla came upon a sudden obstruction in their path, while the fire was close at hand. It took the form of a vertical rock wall with a smooth, even surface that spanned a long distance on either side of them, and that was approximately 45 feet high . A tiny stream of water trickled over its upper edge, making the surface slippery. There were no obvious footholds. Vegetation hung down the wall, due to the moisture it provided. They would have to try to find a way around it. However, when they turned to do so, a burning tree fell in their way, forcing them to return to the wall and to attempt to scale it, or face burning to death.

Carla was trying hard to stay calm, but she felt trapped. She also was afraid of heights, and looked helplessly at Rod. "I'm not sure that I can do this."

"Sure, you can. You go ahead of me, so I can catch you if you slip. Now, grab onto this vine with both hands." Carla reached for the long plant stem and yanked on it. "See, it will support your weight. I want you to pull yourself up the vine with both hands while climbing up the wall on your feet. If you slip, hold on tightly to the vine, or grab an additional one, and gather yourself up again, so you can place your shoes flat on the wall for grip, or try to wedge your toes into any crack that you find. I will be right behind you. We don't have much time. Let's go."

With that, Carla began creeping up the wall as instructed. Her hands were shaking badly. About halfway up the face, her sneaker slipped and she screamed. However, she didn't lose her handhold, but dangled from the vine like a loose leaf. Rod got abreast of her, and put an arm around her for support. She was, thus, able to reestablish her traction on the surface and proceed. Eventually, they made it over the top. Mud streaked their faces and hair. They lay on the ledge, coughing for a short period, due to all the smoke inhalation and exertion. Rod helped Carla to her feet and they forged onward, anxious to get across the island. She could see the exhaustion on his face, from trying to cope with the pain from his sea wasp stings.

An hour passed, and just as they thought that they could not go much further, they heard waves striking against a beach. Morning light was infiltrating the darkness. The sound of the fire was more distant behind them and they no longer heard any pursuing voices. Pushing the foliage away, Rod saw the promontory of Michael Rock and the bay in front of Bayman Bay Club stretching before him. The resort was several yards south of them, along the beach. It consisted of individual hardwood bungalows with louvered doors and windows, set into the foliage of a hill. A main building was situated amongst them. All were connected by a wood plank walkway and steps. From the hillside, a dock extended some 300 feet out into the water. Some boats were moored along it and a dive shop was perched midway along the structure.

"I've got to find Rudy Lentz," Rod stated emphatically. "He's an American dive master at the resort and he can get us a boat and some equipment. I hope he's here and not in Bonacca, this morning. He normally stays in the most remote bungalow on the beach."

They made their way across the soft sand beach to a solitary, lighted bungalow tucked just behind the perimeter of palm trees. Some rock music could be heard wafting from the open doors. A muscular dark-haired male in his late 20's was sitting under a ceiling fan, on the edge of a bed, cleaning some dive equipment.

"Rudy," Rod called softly.

The young man looked up startled, but then grinned when he saw Rod. However, slowly, his grin receded into a frown of concern, when he noted Rod's purple welts and Carla's scratched and insect-bitten limbs. "What happened to you guys?"

"We have just run through the jungle from Posada del Sol, trying to get away from Kurt von Kreitler and a very nasty group of drug dealers, who were involved in the **Golddigger** mishap," Rod answered.

"You've got to be kidding."

"No, I've never been more serious in my life. There is, also, a fire burning across the island, that was set to flush us out."

"Holy shit! Do you need me to hide you two?"

"No, Rudy, we need a boat and some dive equipment. By the way, this is Dr. Carla Knight. She has been working to solve the **Golddigger** murders with me."

"Nice to meet you," greeted Rudy, sizing up the rumpled, yet attractive woman before him. "Hopefully, we can meet again under calmer circumstances."

"Yes, it's nice to meet you and the sentiment is likewise."

Rod interjected, "Does the resort have any torches used for underwater work, Rudy? I also need a wrench, some dive lights, and a pair of wire cutters."

"Well, you're in luck. I can, actually, supply you with everything. There is a magnesium torch with an oxygen source in the dive shop and I can get the tools from maintenance. May I ask what you are going to do with all of this?"

"It would take too long to explain, friend. Simply, we are going back to a wreck that was near the location, where the **Golddigger** was found."

"You know that there is a hurricane, forecasted? Most of the guests, here, have tried to head for the mainland, but ended up trapped in Bonacca because of the smallpox quarantine."

Rod had forgotten about the epidemic, in the course of all their other trials. How was Pepe going to get to La Ceiba? He could see from the look on Carla's face that the same thought was occurring to her. "I know there's a hurricane coming, Rudy. This is the only window of opportunity we have to hamper the **Golddigger** murderers' operation."

"OK, man, you seem to know what you're doing."

Rod turned to Carla. You don't have to come with me. You could stay with Rudy and he could hide you."

"I wouldn't consider staying here. You need my help. Let's get there as fast as we can. How are your stings faring?"

"The pain has lessened and my headache is gone. However, I look like I had a plate of red-brown spaghetti splattered over my chest and legs. How is the pain in your foot?"

"Minimal. After that mad dash through the jungle, I almost forgot it was there. I'm afraid you're going to have some discolored marks for a long time, as sea wasp stings are notorious for scarring."

"Better scarred than dead." Rod turned to Rudy and asked, "Do you remember Pepe, the entrepreneurial little porter at the airstrip?"

"Everyone knows Pepe," answered Rudy, while they made their way down the dock to the dive shop."

"Well, we asked him to go to La Ceiba to contact the authorities, so that they would in turn notify the FBI in the United States for help. However, I'm afraid, with the quarantine in effect, he will never get there. As a back-up, could you try to radio the police in La Ceiba with our whereabouts, so that the Honduran navy can locate us?"

"Sure, I'll try as soon as you leave. Rudy was gathering some wet suits for them and masks, fins, tanks, weight belts, and BC vests, as he said this. "You can take **Sea Dancer** over there. She has a generator aboard, to which you can hook the electric cable for the torch. Also, it is our fastest boat. You, probably, could use some food to eat on the trip." They nodded, vigorously. He ran back to his bungalow and brought back a sack of fruit, bread, and cheese, as well as some soft drinks.

"I can't thank you enough, Rudy."

"Don't mention it. One of my friends was aboard the **Golddigger**. I want you to get those guys."

"We're going to try. Be wary of anyone around you and stay safe. Tell the police, we are going to a location 16 degrees 1 minute North latitude and 85 degrees 1 minute West longitude, off Cabo Cameron."

"I'll tell them." Rudy helped finish loading the boat. "Good luck out there. Batten down the hatches." With that, he shoved the vessel off the dock, as Rod started the engine aboard the **Sea Dancer**.

The 32-foot boat was equipped with twin 210 horsepower diesel engines and it literally raced out through the waves, heading south. They left Rudy, waving, on the end of the dock. The fire had died out a distance behind the resort, as it had started to rain, and all that remained of it were some curls of black smoke in the air. Fortunately, it did not appear that their pursuers were still after them. No one had arrived on the beach from the depths of the tropical forest, while they had been there or since they had departed on the **Sea Dancer**. Rudy was the solitary figure visible in front of the resort. They only hoped it stayed that way, so he could radio for help.

Clouds were bunching up high on the early morning horizon, in front of them, organizing into a thick band. Showery rain started coming down and the wind picked up, in gusts. It was obvious that the outer-hurricane squall line was not far away. The two of them had spent the entire night trying to escape and, now, it was morning. That could work to their disadvantage, Rod told Carla, if Ramirez's ship was already anchored on the site, because they could not approach without being seen, and they would have to wait until they had the cover of night, again.   However, Rod thought, with the hurricane approaching, the rough seas and sheets of rain would provide cover, and they might be able to get close without drawing alot of attention. He and Carla both hoped the weather would remain in their favor, but not cost them their lives.

29

Pepe had sought cover after he left Carla and Rod. He realized that he could not take off in a boat right away, or he might be pursued. Therefore, he concealed the motored skiff that he had brought from Bonacca, on the other side of the resort, under some palms and then, hid in a cabinet in the resort's kitchen, until he heard the ominous voices, which eventually arrived, recede away into the night. From the direction of the landing party voices, it was obvious that they had headed for the jungle, so he ran in the opposite direction, from tree to tree, watching for any danger. After a few minutes, he arrived at the beach, south of the resort, where he had stashed his boat. Quietly, he rowed along the shoreline, until he was far enough away to start the small motor. He reached Bonacca after 45 minutes. In the interim, flames were evident from the edge of the tropical forest and the outer buildings of the resort. He hoped that Carla and Rod had gotten to safety, and that the resort personnel were aware of the fire.

In Bonacca, he ran to his parents' dwelling which was on the second level of a stilted structure by a canal, and which was more like a large one room apartment with curtained divisions. It was, now, boarded up, in preparation for the storm. He, his parents, and four brothers and sisters lived here. They were poor, but between his mother's earnings from the resort and his father's unpredictable earnings from fishing, they were able to get by. He and all of his respective siblings, ages 6, 7, 9, and 11, worked odd jobs to help his parents.

His mother was sitting under one of the two electric light bulbs in the hut, sewing, despite the late hour. The rest of the family was asleep. She made additional money for them, by being a seamstress for the resort, as well. Upon his arrival, she looked up smiling, but concerned, because she had heard shouting in the direction of Posada del Sol. "Where have you been?"(in Spanish).

"Out fishing for lobsters," replied Pepe in Spanish.

"I was worried. The hurricane is coming soon and I heard loud voices in the night."

"That's because a fire started behind Posada del Sol."

Pepe's mother paled. Her job was at risk. "Did you see if the fire was put out?"

"No, mother, because I hurried home to tell you and father."

"I must wake your father and have him go to the resort to see if his help is needed."

"Mother, we must go to La Ceiba, tomorrow, to escape the hurricane."

"No, my son, this is our home and we will stay here. Besides, we could not leave, if we wanted because of the quarantine."

"But we have gotten needles in our arms, you remember?"

"No matter. That was done to protect us, here, but we still cannot leave the island."

"Pepe had forgotten. He was sure Rod and Carla had forgotten, too. He would just have to get to La Ceiba, anyway he could, by himself.

After his father was awakened, he described, once again, the fire he had seen while "lobster fishing", and then he went to bed, planning to be up early to go to the airstrip to meet the first flight. His mother watched, curiously, as he retired. He seemed calm, despite the night's event. Little did she know that her son was, possibly, the only hope for two individuals, who were facing a lot of danger, alone, and who were trying to avert an international disaster.

30

November 22, 1993

As the sun barely crawled above the horizon, Pepe left his home and made his way to the airstrip by boat. His mother heard him leave and thought he was going to his job as a porter at the airstrip. She called out that he should return in a couple of hours, so that the whole family could go, together, to the shelter inland on the island, where the town would wait out the storm. She was no longer worried because Pepe's father had returned that morning, reporting that only the maintenance shed and one bungalow had burned at the resort.

At the airstrip, Pepe waited, anxiously, for the plane to arrive. It was one thing to help unload luggage from the planes, but quite another to try to stow away on board. He saw the black swath in the jungle to the northeast and wondered if the evil men had caught Carla and Rod. Several people had responded to the fire during the early morning hours and contained it, but they could find no evidence for cause other than an empty gas can.

Finally, he heard the drone of the plane engine approaching from the southwest. His plan was already formulated. He would pick an individual, who needed luggage carried from the rear compartment, and when they and the flight crew weren't looking, he would set the luggage out where they could find it and then, disappear into the rear compartment, hiding behind some cargo that wasn't being unloaded. With any luck, no one would check the compartment again before take-off. Next stop was La Ceiba, anyway, and if they found him there, he would be turned into the local authorities. Perfecto!

He watched the plane land without incident. To his dismay, it was an empty flight except for cargo. He spotted the pilot and one crewmember, unloading boxes from the rear compartment. He waited until they had completely unloaded the plane. When they turned to talk to quarantine check officials and sign papers, Pepe made his move. He stood on some boxes and climbed into the rear luggage compartment, unnoticed. He overheard the crew telling the officials that this would be the last flight before the hurricane. They had brought food and medical supplies, issued by the government, because they were not sure when the next flight would be. Pepe heard the pilot walk toward the plane and close the luggage compartment doors. He found a large maintenance tool box, behind which he hid. The prop engines started and the plane taxied down the runway, then it turned, accelerated, and took off. He had made it!

After approximately 40 to 45 minutes, the plane began to descend and he heard the pilot request the control tower, by radio, to land in La Ceiba. He had grown cold during the flight and had huddled under some cargo blankets. The plane landed with a jolt and braked quickly to a stop. Pepe crawled from under the blankets and prepared to leap out of the compartment, once the plane stopped in front of the terminal and the cargo door was opened.

Suddenly, the cabin door was opened, but not the luggage compartment door. He could not stay here. The crew disembarked. Pepe waited almost a minute and then, climbed over the seat into the main cabin. The door was still open and he made his exit. He jumped off the wing and raced across the tarmac, out of reach of a baggage handler, who yelled at him. However, shortly thereafter, he was detained by an airport security guard near the terminal. "Where do you think that you are going?", he asked Pepe in Spanish, grabbing his arm.

"I am going to the police station. I need to report a crime on Guanaja. It is important!"

"Calm down." The guard smiled patiently. "Just what crime do you want to report?"

"I know where the murderers of the **Golddigger** crew are."

The guard straightened to attention. He had read of the incident in the La Ceiba newspaper. Maybe he should listen to this little waif. "Very well, I will drive you to the city police station and you can tell your story to the captain, there."

"Gracias, senor."

The rotund man had a kind face and smiled. He had learned not to discount people's stories because often they were telling the truth. This child might actually know something about the murders. He led him to his patrol vehicle and helped him into the front seat.

Pepe had never been to La Ceiba. He marveled at the paved streets and the long pier with a lighthouse out in the harbor. When they drove up in front of the official-looking building, which was the police station, he became intimidated. The guard, whose name was Geraldo Torres, led him to the captain's office. Therein, sat a thin, severe-looking man in his early 40's. His name was Captain Ramon Gonzalez and he had been a career policeman, as had his father. He looked at the diminutive figure in front of him. "Well, what brings you here?", he asked sternly.

"Senor-Capitanear, I have come to get help for my friends."

"Who are your friends?"

"Senor Rod and Doctor Knight on Guanaja. Bad men - drug men, are following them. The bad men and the German capitan, they kill the people on the **Golddigger**, too."

Pepe had Captain Gonzalez's undivided attention. "Where are these drug men, now?"

"They go back to shipwreck, south of Guanaja. Senor Rod says to call F-B-I in Washington. He says to bring many men and guns."

Captain Gonzalez looked at Pepe, incredulously. This was possibly the biggest tip on a crime that he had had in his entire time on the force. If the story was true and he acted, correctly, he could be up for a commendation, perhaps a promotion in rank. "You say, Senor Rod said to call the FBI in Washington, in the United States?"

"Si, Capitan.

"Do you know Senor Rod's surname?"

"I think it sounds like Dolton, or Dalton, something like that."

"Very well, we will call Washington to see if they know of this Rod Dalton."

It took several minutes for Hondutel, the telephone company to locate the number in Washington, D.C. and connect Captain Gonzalez with it. The phone rang two times and then was answered by a female, who said, "Federal Bureau of Investigation."

Captain Gonzalez responded, "May I speak to your Office of International Investigations?"

"Certainly, sir. One moment, please."

In a few seconds, a firm male voice answered, "International Affairs - Agent Grant."

Captain Gonzalez then introduced himself and his position and location. He related that he might have a lead on the murders that occurred aboard the American ship, **Golddigger**, from a child who lived on Guanaja. He described Pepe's urgent attempt to get to La Ceiba and mentioned the names of the individuals Pepe was trying to help. He alluded that drug cartel members appeared to be involved in the crime. Specifically, he asked Grant if he knew if Rod Dalton was a FBI field agent in Honduras.

"No," was the reply by Agent Ben Grant, who was all ears receiving this information. He asked Captain Gonzalez for his phone number in Honduras and said that he would confer with his superiors and then get back to him within the next few hours about the matter. Captain Gonzalez thanked him and hung up. Ben Grant stared at the file on the **Golddigger** incident, resting on his desk. He was concerned - very concerned - as the evidence in this case was very disturbing. The FBI knew about the German U-boat and its bulkhead's nuclear symbol from Dave Krueger's film, retrieved from the flashlight, aboard the ship. They knew about the Agent Orange-like compound found in Carla's water sample, saved from the vandalized lab in Tegucigalpa. Also, the concurrence of the smallpox epidemic on the Honduran east coast had been worrisome. And, they knew that Dr. Velasquez had been beaten badly and left for dead in La Ceiba, but he had survived. However, they did not know absolutely, until now, who might be behind all of these developments. The possibility that a drug cartel might be involved with a German expatriate was disconcerting, indeed. It was clear that those individuals were after the cargo on the U-boat and they would be there again, shortly. They had tried over the past twenty-four hours to reach Rod Dalton, to no avail. Brad Jacobs with the DEA had already left, reportedly, to meet with Dalton. Agent Grant decided he had better not only contact the DEA and CIA, but also the White House. It was going to be a long day.

31

November 22, 1993
12:01 p.m. EST

The men gathered in the Oval Office, that afternoon, sat soberly while information on the **Goldigger** case was presented to them by the young man named Ben Grant. Their mood matched the leafless appearance of the trees, outside. They consisted of : Arthur Jenkins, head of the CIA; Richard Moore, director of the FBI; Harold Morgan, the DEA chief; Charles Tompkins, National Security Advisor; Carl Edwards, Secretary of State; William Taber, Secretary of Defense; General Walter Thomas of the U.S. Air Force; Admiral Sid Weatherby, head of the U.S. Coast Guard and a member of the Joint Interagency Drug Enforcement Command; Carlos Hurtado, the Honduran Ambassador; and President of the United States, John Claymore. Representatives of the Department of Energy, the Environmental Protection Agency, FEMA, and the CDC's Tyner Chassen were, also, there. No one interrupted Ben Grant until he revealed all of the known facts on the case.

Finally, FBI Director Richard Moore interjected, "It would appear that there is a plot underfoot to cause some destruction to some part of the world by these people. Director Morgan has given me special intelligence on the probable drug cartel involved. It is most likely the Cordillera Cartel headed by Hector Ramirez, who is a notoriously ruthless drug lord. He took over the cartel after we arrested Eduardo Rojas and sent the man to the gas chamber for his perpetrated murders in the United States. I am sure that Ramirez is consumed by hatred for the U.S., as a result. The puzzling aspect is the German U-boat. We are still trying to figure out how they discovered it or knew about it. We suspect from intelligence reports on Honduras, provided to me by Director Jenkins, that one Kurt von Kreitler is involved, since Mr. Dalton alluded to the participation of a 'German captain'. He has been a resident of Honduras since the 1950's. We knew that he was a U-boat commander during World War II and that his sub disappeared at the end of the war. No one ever looked for it because German records indicated that aerial bombs had sunk it, even though our war data did not confirm this information. We know Germany had finally developed technology for the atomic bomb by the conclusion of the war, but we assumed it was not disseminated anywhere after the fall of the Third Reich. We were obviously wrong. I will let Directors Jenkins and Morgan fill you in on Von Kreitler's background and recent activities."

Arthur Jenkins stood up and turned on the slide projector. An image of a young, uniformed Teutonic man with steely, cold blue eyes appeared on the screen. His eyes, even in a projected image, pierced the audience in the room. "Meet Captain Kurt von Kreitler, "der Eismann" - "the Ice Man", as he was affectionately known by his peers. He grew up in Hamburg and was notorious for turning in his Jewish neighbors to the SS. He received his naval training from the academy at Kiel. Very early on, he became one of Hitler's favored officers and was privy to many secrets within the Reichstag. His nickname came from the heartless way that he treated his subordinates, who differed in opinion with him. He was, once witnessed, putting a gun to the head of a first lieutenant and shooting him because the officer questioned a maneuver, while they were pursuing an enemy sub. His superiors took no action against him, as he claimed that his officer had tried to incite mutiny during engagement in warfare. The remainder of the crew was too afraid to speak out against him. Hence, his nickname evolved. He disappeared after the war for five years and then surfaced as a resident on a cay off the island of Guanaja, in Honduras. No unusual activity, on his part, has been apparent until approximately ten years ago. The DEA has had him under surveillance since that point in time, because there was suspicion that he might be involved with drug smugglers.

DEA Chief Morgan took over the slide projector at this point. "Rod Dalton (a smiling, rugged male face flashed on the screen), one of our field operatives, and several others have been ·in Honduras the past few years, watching drug activity. The nearby Mosquito Coast has provided an excellent stage for smuggling operations due to its remoteness. We knew that cocaine was being flown out of Honduras, but we were not sure from what location. Finally, we noticed some patterns arise in the Bay Islands. At least once a week, a fire would appear on the beach of Bird Cay near Guanaja and a plane would land on the small airstrip, there. One of our operatives checked out this activity, on one occasion, and found Von Kreitler and several other Caucasian and Hispanic men and women having, what appeared to be, a beach barbecue. They could not be caught actually transferring cocaine, but it was suspected. Now, we finally have proof that there has been a connection between Von Kreitler and the Cordillera Cartel by the events that have occurred and the confession of a small boy to the La Ceiba police. We know that the drug cartel and, probably, Von Kreitler were involved in the **Golddigger** murders. We do not clearly understand why Von Kreitler would court the drug cartel's alliance, but we suspect he bears some wartime grudges. Two Americans, Mr. Dalton and a Dr. Carla Knight (a slide flashed of an attractive brunette in a doctor's lab coat), were captured on Bird Cay, tortured, and then escaped thanks to the help of the little boy that I just mentioned. We know that Von Kreitler and the drug cartel are after them, most likely, for what they have learned about the **Golddigger** and the U-boat's cargo. From the efforts of Dr. Knight and Mr. Dalton, we have found out that this cargo consists of weapons of mass destruction, namely chemical, biologic, and probably nuclear. Local labs have confirmed an Agent Orange-like compound aboard and Dr. Chassen's CDC lab has shown that the currently identified smallpox outbreak in Honduras is related to an initial exposure to vials, containing the virus, that were aboard the U-boat. We don't know Von Kreitler's and the cartel's exact whereabouts, but we surmise that they are converging on the U-boat wreck, because they need to unload the remainder of the cargo before any other individuals discover the wreck site. A satellite has confirmed that a large vessel is now in an area of the Caribbean south of Guanaja, off the Mosquito Coast. Mr. Dalton and Dr. Knight are on their way back to the wreck to stop the unloading of cargo, according to the boy." Director Morgan then paused.

President Claymore, a distinguished man in his mid-50's, who had spoken little during the meeting, thus far, looked at the Security Advisor Tompkins and said, "Well, what do you propose we do to capture these criminals and avert a future disaster? Also, how do you propose to rescue the two Americans who are pursuing them?"

"I propose that we enlist the help of the Honduran Naval Force and have them join our Coast Guard, which can be sent to the area to surround the wreck site. Additional strategic support can be supplied by our Air Force. FBI and DEA personnel can arrive via boat and helicopter. Can you foresee any diplomatic problems, Ambassador Hurtado or Secretary Edwards?"

"No," replied Ambassador Hurtado, a polite man with well-oiled hair. "We want to help in anyway possible and rid our country of this menace."

Secretary of State Edwards basically concurred, but added, in a calm manner, "The Colombian Ambassador to the United States needs to be contacted about the impending arrest of some of his country's citizens. I'm sure he will be happy to hear that there is finally some hard evidence against the drug cartel." Everyone in the room nodded in agreement.

Director Moore looked at Secretary Taber, Admiral Weatherby and General Thomas. "Does the plan sound reasonable to both of you?"

"Yes, I can have a cutter, which is currently off Key West, there, in the next six hours," avowed Admiral Weatherby, a tall man in his late 50's. However, I am concerned that we have an approaching Category 3 hurricane in that vicinity. Last weather report, an hour ago, had upgraded it and revealed that it was approximately 100 miles off the east coast of Honduras and moving at 15 miles per hour."

Ambassador Hurtado interrupted, "I will talk to our Naval Force commanders about getting a ship to the area from Trujillo. That would save some time and, hopefully, beat the hurricane to the wreck site."

Secretary Taber, a tight-lipped, balding gentleman, offered to Ambassador Hurtado, "We can be ready to deploy ground troops to Honduras, if extra military support is needed to contain the cartel and assist in hurricane preparation."

"Any support would be greatly appreciated in this emergency," Hurtado replied.

"I hate to be negative, but does anyone actually know where this wreck site is?" asked General Thomas. "I can send A-10 Thunderbolts from Texas, but it sounds like some reconnaissance may need to be done first."

"You're right. We never got that information from Dalton," related Director Morgan. He called Brad Jacobs at the DEA, but never told him the GPS location. What about the fellow who sponsored the **Golddigger** operation - Peter Beck? Maybe he has that information."

"It would be worth a phone call to find out," concurred Director Moore.

"I agree," affirmed CIA Director Jenkins.

"If you are unable to learn the location, a plane or helicopter can be dispatched from Trujillo to scout the area," offered Ambassador Hurtado.

"Let's not waste any more time, gentleman," urged President Claymore. "Director Moore, why don't you put that call through, now, to Mr. Beck?"

Moore nodded and rose to use a protected phone line on a nearby table. However, the same phone rang at that very instant and he strode over and picked up the receiver. He heard the voice of one of his FBI agents on the other end. Rudy Lentz had, finally, made radio contact with La Ceiba and managed to contact the FBI office in Washington. What he was now being apprised of, were the latitude and longitude coordinates of the wreck.

He turned to face the men who had been listening intently to his phone conversation, in disbelief. "Gentlemen, our problem has been solved. A friend of Dalton's just called in the location of the wreck - 16 degrees 1 minute North latitude and 85 degrees 1 minute West longitude. He also asked us to send help for Dalton and Dr. Knight."

"Our mission now seems clear," stated President Claymore. "I suggest we get started. I imagine, Director Moore, that you and Director Morgan will send several armed agents to Honduras."

"Yes, we will probably send them by Air Force transport to Trujillo, where they can board a helicopter bound for the wreck site. I am estimating five or six hours for this transport, if they leave within the next hour. That may put us right up against the time that the hurricane passes the site, in which case, we will have to have a back-up plan. Does that sound accurate, General Thomas?"

"I think so, but may we look at a map?"

"Certainly," answered President Claymore, and an aid produced a large GPS map of the Gulf of Mexico and the Caribbean region.

General Thomas then plotted out the coordinates given for the wreck. He conferred briefly with Admiral Weatherby and then spoke to the group. "Let's all synchronize our watches. It is now 13:04. Our A-10 Thunderbolts will depart Pasadena, Texas at

14:15 Eastern Standard Time and converge on the wreck site at approximately 17:15 Eastern Standard Time, or 16:15 Central Standard Time, or Bay Island Time."

Admiral Weatherby, then, requested, "Ambassador Hurtado, please contact your Naval Force commander and have them dispatch a ship, if possible, from Trujillo at 15:30 Honduras, or Central Standard Time. That will enable the ship to converge on the wreck site at approximately the same time as our Thunderbolts. Our cutter from Key West will be dispatched, immediately, and should arrive not long after your Naval Force ship. That will concentrate heavy fire power in the area, nearly simultaneously."

"The FBI and DEA agents flying in from D.C.," General Thomas added, "can be transported by helicopter from Trujillo, 30 minutes after the Naval Force ship departs, thus, coordinating their arrival with the other forces. With any luck, only the outer hurricane squall line will hit the site, since the location is somewhat south of the predicted hurricane path. If the prediction is wrong, we may have to move the converging ships and helicopters south of the site, and have the jets fly reconnaissance around the storm, or above the eye, until the hurricane passes. I doubt Von Kreitler and his group will salvage anything, successfully, or live through the event, if the hurricane hits them directly. The same risk, I fear, holds true for Mr. Dalton and Dr. Knight."

"I believe General Thomas is right and I think his back-up plan is reasonable. Does anyone disagree?" Silence. Claymore could tell that the group was anxious to put the wheels in motion, due to the time constraints. "Any further questions, gentlemen?", President Claymore queried.

"I don't have a question, but I do have a request," posed Dr. Tyner Chassen.

"Go ahead, Dr. Chassen."

"I ask that everyone dispatched to Honduras, in this effort, be vaccinated for smallpox. We still have an epidemic going on, down there, with the impending complication of decreased hygiene secondary to hurricane damage. Everyone needs to take maximum precautions. The CDC will send supplies of vaccine, immediately, along with staff to administer it, to all staging areas."

"Good point, Dr. Chassen. We have to protect everyone in this process. Any other suggestions?" Claymore looked about the room. The group shook their heads. "Very well, then, good luck on all your efforts. The security of our countries and the lives of two Americans are at stake."

Everyone stood as the President left the room. Admiral Weatherby was already on the phone, dispatching the cutter from Key West. General Thomas was on another phone contacting Ellington Air Base in Pasadena, Texas to alert the A-10 Thunderbolt squadron. Director Morgan was huddled in conversation with Director Moore. Everyone else had left the room. Morgan's face looked concerned. The FBI Director was telling him that it had been reported, in the earlier phone call to him, that there had been no word from Brad Jacobs since he had left the country. He had missed his contact in Tegucigalpa. Where was he? Had Ramirez's men taken him out? He was afraid of the possibilities.

32

While Pepe attempted to get to La Ceiba, Rod and Carla were making their way back to the U-boat site aboard the **Sea Dancer**. Even though danger lurked ahead, it was good to get out on the open water, again. Rod had formulated two plans: if Ramirez and Von Kreitler had already reached the site then he would seek to board their boat and sabotage it, to buy time for the authorities to arrive; if they had not arrived, he and Carla would dive on the wreck and try to find a way to make the remaining cargo difficult to retrieve. He realized that they did not have protective suits this time. It would be a risk. His only hope was that, by the time they surfaced, the authorities would have arrived. Otherwise, they, most certainly, would be killed.

The wind was picking up around them and the sea became choppy, as a result. Overhead, the sky was angrier-looking than it had been, earlier. It was going to be a slower crossing than planned. Hopefully, it would be slower for Von Kreitler and Ramirez, as well. A storm might actually be to their advantage because it would distract Ramirez's crew and they might be able to get within a short distance without being seen. Also, they could scuba dive in rough seas, without their bubbles being seen, as easily, on the surface.

After another two hours of careening through the waves, they could see the faint outline of land, in the distance, which they assumed was Cabo Cameron as they were nearing the GPS coordinates of 16 degrees 1 minute North latitude and 85 degrees 1 minute West longitude. To their chagrin, a large ship was barely visible in the blinding sheets of rain, anchored near the location.

Rod turned to Carla, "Get on your gear, now," and he idled the engine of the boat which, now, rocked wildly in the waves. He, also, hurried to don his gear, but it was a struggle on the lurching

215

deck surface. Some tanks had come loose from their bungee tethers and they were rolling around, clanging against the bulwarks. The tanks that they did strap on had 3000 psi of air, apiece, and were full. Rod's demeanor was serious. "We have a long shallow dive ahead of us to get to their ship, unnoticed. We are just under two-thirds of a nautical mile from their vessel, which should take us approximately 60 to 65 minutes to scuba dive there, if we move at 60 feet per minute. Most of our air will probably be gone. It will be imperative to get to a depth where we are out of the surface turbulence, yet shallow enough that we can dive for 60 minutes. I will take a compass heading on their ship, once we get in the water."

"What will we do with the boat? It's too deep to anchor here," Carla pointed out.

"Good question. We will have to set it adrift. The waves are moving in a direction away from their ship, so they will move the boat in that direction. That may act as a decoy for us. Unfortunately, we will not get a chance to use the torch on the wreck. I am going to take the wrench and wire cutters in my BC, in the event that they can be of use to me aboard the ship. Are you up for this?"

"Absolutely. We are in this pursuit, together." Carla managed a sincere smile. "Besides, I want to get off this rocking boat, soon."

He reached over and touched her cheek, affectionately. "Let's go, then." They proceeded to roll off the port gunwale into the churning seas. The boat drifted away from them, rapidly, leaving them to their own resources. They descended, immediately, letting the air out of their buoyancy vests. At approximately 40 feet, they were clear enough of the wave motion on the surface to proceed forward. Rod had taken a heading, quickly, before they descended, from the compass on his gauge console. He was, now, holding it straight-armed, in front of him, following the heading. Carla was directly behind him, paddling her fins and keeping pace, well.

Swimming had always been her forte. They were traveling approximately 65 feet a minute.

After 24 minutes dive time, more turbulence could be sensed above them, slowing their progress. Rod turned and signaled to descend a short distance. There must be stronger winds causing even greater wave activity, thought Carla. They descended to 47 feet, all the while continuing forward. Carla was just starting to feel some fatigue. Her pressure gauge read 1900 psi of air. She glanced at Rod's console and saw he had 2100 psi. It was obvious that he had been diving more regularly and could conserve his air consumption. They were not likely to get bent, as they could be at 60 feet for 60 minutes by Navy Tables without requiring decompression. There was more to fear from the lingering menace on the surface.

Bottom could not be visualized from the depth at which they were diving, as they were in nearly a thousand feet of water. They, also, were a couple of thousand feet, out to sea, from the ledge that the wreck was sitting on. A thick bull shark that appeared out in the deep blue perimeter, curious about the storm on the surface, broke the monotony of the dive. It swam off into the depths after what seemed an interminable period, as it became bored with sensing their activity, which was not erratic, but purposeful. Carla never lost sight of it while it was in visual range. Rod, however, stayed focused on the compass heading.

Another 31 minutes passed, before a noticeable change in the water occurred. The illumination had lessened and Rod, looking overhead, realized that they were almost under a large hull, 21 feet above them. He could not make out the ledge holding the wreck due to the turbidity of the water caused by the storm. However, he knew it would be below them. No other divers were in their vicinity, but bubbles were visible, emanating from the depths.

There must be a crew working within the wreck, thought Rod. They needed to act fast, before they were seen. He checked his air pressure gauge - 650 psi left. He motioned to Carla - she had less than 500 psi. They had to try to surface away from the pitching hull, although, not too far, otherwise, they would never get to the ship in these rough seas. They, also, had to try to stay together, while surfacing. He indicated to Carla, by hand signals that she should hold onto the high-pressure valve on his tank. She could tell from the animation of his signals "to hold on" meant "for dear life and looking above her at the turbulence, she understood. She, therefore, clenched the valve with a vise-like grip.

They started to ascend at the rate indicated on Rod's dive computer. Carla was still hanging on, but was nauseated by the jostling motion. Her regulator was beginning to tug hard when she inhaled, and she looked at her pressure gauge, which registered less than 300 psi of air. She hoped they would reach the surface, soon.

They broke the surface not knowing if gunfire or angry voices would rain down upon them. Neither occurred, but the seas were furious around them. Large waves threatened to separate them and smash them against the ship. The wind gusts of the outer convective bands of the hurricane had struck, but were not as great as those in the rain shield, around the eye, which was eighty miles north of them. Lightning slashed the sky, frequently, while rain showers punctuated the sea's surface. Carla still clung to Rod's tank valve. He motioned to the starboard side of the ship, where a steel boarding ladder was banging against the hull. A safety line was clamped to the lower rung of the ladder and extended about 30 feet out on the water's surface. They were not far from it. Rod indicated, again by signals, that they should try to swim for the line, separately, in order to make a successful approach. Carla let go of Rod's tank valve and tried to maintain her position by paddling furiously with her arms and legs. She was rolled in the troughs of large waves, her regulator getting knocked from her mouth. She put the mouthpiece of the snorkel in her mouth, but the apparatus filled with water, so she groped wildly for her regulator and put it back in her mouth.

Rod darted for the line on the crest of one wave. He was able to grab it and hang onto it, perilously, waiting for Carla to approach. She also attempted to ride the crest of one wave toward the line, but missed Rod's outstretched hand by a finger length. She fought to swim back, again, as the waves tried to pull her away. This time, Rod caught the nozzle on her tank and pulled her to the line, where she hung on desperately. They pulled their way toward the ladder with difficulty, taking their fins off, before reaching the ship, with one hand and threading their arms through the straps, so they would have two hands and two feet free to climb the ladder.

No heads peered over the side above them. This told them how much the individuals on the ship cared about their own diving crew. They crept up the steel ladder, precariously, as they were buffeted around by the motion of the boat and force of the wind. Carla slipped twice in the process, hanging only by her arms. Rod, alerted by her small cries of alarm, was able to help her regain her footing, each time, either by coaxing her or holding on to one of her arms for stability. He got to the starboard gunwale of the ship and pulled himself over the edge. No one was visible on the lurching, upper deck. Rod threw himself forward on its surface and Carla crawled over behind him, exhausted. They noted scuba tanks strapped to the bulwarks of the ship. Two individuals were visible in the wheelhouse, bracing against the rocking of the ship. They were not looking in their direction.

Carla nudged Rod and said in a low urgent voice, "Maybe we should change tanks, now, while we are still undiscovered?"

"Good idea, but we need to be fairly mobile to find the engine room, so let's ditch our used tanks here, and when we come back, we'll grab some full ones." Carla nodded.

After considerable pitching on deck, they managed to slip off their vests and unfasten their spent tanks, tethering them so the tanks would not roll and bang against the bulwark. Their masks, fins, and regulators were stashed in large coils of rope, nearby. They put on their vests, again.

Rod drew near Carla and whispered, "We need to find the engine room. I'm guessing that the main group must be gathered somewhere, talking - a main salon or galley." He started toward the aft door of the house of the ship, using handholds the whole way in the gale force wind. Carla tried to follow behind him, having more trouble because of her lighter weight. He made it to the door and pulled on the handle, gently, bracing himself against the door, so it would not fly open. A soft light flooded the hallway in front of him. Another closed hatch door was visible a long distance along the corridor. Beyond, some voices could be heard, faintly, above the howling wind outside. He stepped quickly inside, followed by Carla. They had to brace themselves with their arms on the walls of the corridor due to the severe pitching of the ship.

The voices, down the corridor, continued in conversation. It sounded like seven or eight people were present. Their voices could also be heard more distinctly with the outer bulkhead door closed. Bits of conversation became clear.

"The divers are finishing setting the charges," Ramirez's voice could be heard saying to someone. Rod looked at Carla, alarmed. It was obvious that they were going to try to blow up any traces of the sub!

A Teutonic voice that could be discerned as Von Kreitler's, replied, "How much longer do you think they will be down there? We have retrieved and loaded the cargo. We need to depart soon. This storm is not getting any better and we don't know what authorities they may have notified, if they made it across the island. It is also imperative that we move off this location before the charges detonate in the wreck!"

"They are doing the best they can, under the circumstances," responded Ramirez. "We should be under way, shortly, and the charges are only set to go off in the next hour and a half."

220

Rod whispered to Carla, "We don't have much time. Let's get to the engine room." She nodded quickly.

Through another bulkhead door, they found a companionway to a lower deck and, subsequently, two more companionways to even lower decks. The air was heavy and hot, here, and it smelled of oil. There was the rhythmic whine of engines close by. They knew they were in the right place.

With a little more reconnoitering, Rod found the cooling water pipes to the four large diesel engines. He climbed to a platform near two of the pipes on the aft engines. Valve knobs were visible above the main cylinder leading to the pipes. Rod attempted to turn these knobs, but they would not budge. He pulled the wrench out of his vest and adjusted it to the width of the one knob, and leaned his weight against it. The knob creaked loose and he was able to turn it in the opposite direction from its opened intake valve position, until it stopped in its closed position. He did the same thing to the next valve knob. Now, both these engines would have no circulating cool ocean water around them, and they would eventually overheat and shut down. He did not touch the remaining two valve knobs. No use losing all four engines in this storm. Rod's only objective was to slow Ramirez's group's escape from the area. To Carla, he urged, "Let's get out of here. They'll be all over this place in a short bit."

"Maybe we should hide out somewhere on the ship, rather than try to get new tanks and get back to the wreck?"

"We can't let them detonate that wreck and destroy evidence of their intended covert operation. We're going to have to try to find the explosive's charge and defuse it. Again, you don't have to come with me."

"I'm coming."

"OK, then." Rod took hold of her arm and pulled her toward the engine room's bulkhead door. "We're going."

During their interlude in the corridor and below, Alfonso Caldas had heard the whoosh of air beyond the salon door and knew the outer bulkhead door had been opened. When no one appeared through the inner door, he became uneasy. He, also, did not hear the outer door close, but he noticed the sound of the wind had become more distant, again. He motioned to a couple of his cartel members to come with him and they exited the salon.

Caldas and his men searched the corridor, looking in every space. All of a sudden, he noticed some puddles of water near the aft door and followed a path of wet booty prints toward a bulkhead doorway. Someone had recently headed to the lower decks. It might be crew, but it might not. Better to check.

Rod and Carla were coming up the second companionway from the engine room, when Caldas' party reached the first lower deck. They were spotted and they tried to return to the second lower deck to hide. However, once again, their wetsuits revealed them by the wet marks on the deck. Their cover was quickly exposed. Caldas pointed a knife at Carla's throat, while another cartel member jammed a machine gun butt in Rod's back.

"Don't think I wouldn't cut you like a pig, right here, if you try anything! Move!," hissed Caldas, and he prodded her along with Rod back up the companionways to the salon.

The group in the salon eyed them, suspiciously, as they entered the harshly lit room in their dive gear. Rod's mouth dropped open when he recognized one individual, who turned to face him. It was Brad Jacobs!

"No hard feelings, Rod," Jacobs offered, smugly. I know we've known each other since Nam, but sometimes loyalty to a cause is not enough. The DEA could never pay me what my work deserved. Mr. Ramirez has been very generous to me over the last few years and I have been able to live a totally different lifestyle than I would have, otherwise. Besides, what does a little information traded either way, matter in the long run? We weren't given straight information by the CIA in Viet Nam, and look where it got us. So, I figured selling the information, I collected for the

DEA, to the highest bidder was the best form of security for myself."

"Yes, and your 'security' has probably cost a number of lives in recent investigations, which have been botched due to your 'innocent passage of information'." Not to mention the agent you had bumped off, who was trying to protect Dr. Knight in Tegucigalpa." Jacobs glared back, indignantly, as a human life meant little to him.

"Senor Dalton," Ramirez interrupted, I am really very touched by your dialogue with Agent Jacobs, but we have some explosive charges about to go off beneath us in the next hour and we need to move off this spot. Therefore, Senor Caldas will escort you and Dr. Knight to a remote portion of the ship and dispose of you both, for you have become a nuisance."

Rod looked at Carla, knowingly, as each of them realized the ship would not leave its location easily. There was some satisfaction in this, even though their own lives were at stake.

Von Kreitler addressed them, as he stood in the center of the gathering before them. "Yes, Caldas, take them away and dispose of them in any manner that you wish. Let them be a lesson to the United States that no one interferes with the plans of the Cordillera Cartel and the new Third Reich." His two, marble-like blue eyes blazed at them beneath his head of stark white hair.

Caldas shoved them through the salon door and passageway toward the outer bulkhead door. The group in the salon turned their backs to them and returned to their deliberations. Two other men accompanied Caldas, one was Hans from the encounter on Bird Cay. Both had machine guns.

Once on the open deck, which was careening in the storm, the three men grabbed Carla and Rod and pushed them toward a stern hatch. They were shoved through it, after it was opened, down a dimly lit companionway. Caldas dragged Carla into a storage room and the door was closed behind them, leaving her trapped with the vile man. Rod, meanwhile, was led further down a passageway to another storage area.

Caldas sneered at Carla with his back against the closed door and pointed his long stiletto knife at her. "Take off your dive suit," he barked. "Hurry!"

Shaken, but not ready to give up to such an animal, she began to unzip her dive suit. She did not remove her buoyancy vest, as she needed to keep it on her at all costs. She would remove her weight belt next because it could be used as a weapon, if the opportunity presented itself.

"You are going to take everything off! Do you know what it is like to have your throat slit? You can't talk or scream, and you are gasping for air. That's just how I want you, when I take you," he tormented her.

Trembling badly, she unclipped her weight belt. Just then, there was a violent lurch of the ship. Caldas stumbled and fell against a bulkhead, dropping his knife. Carla saw her chance and lunged forward, hitting him on the head, as hard as she could, with a full swing of the eight-pound weight belt. This stunned him and he slouched to the floor. She heard a burst of machine-gun fire at close range and feared for Rod's well being. Caldas had fallen in front of the door and she was trying to move him out of the way to open the door, when he stirred suddenly and grabbed one of her legs. She screamed.

Her cry was answered by the door bursting partway open and Rod appeared. He had a machine gun and he riddled Caldas with bullets. The hit man let go of her leg and became motionless on the deck, in a pool of blood. Carla broke into tears, relieved that she was not going to be one of Caldas' victims.

Rod shoved Caldas's body aside with the butt of the machine gun and opened the door further. He grabbed Carla by an arm, gently, and pulled her into his arms, and said, "We have to get out of here and get back into the water. It's the only place where we have a chance until help arrives.

Carla nodded. She was still shaking. "How did you get free?"

"Probably with the same lurch that caused Caldas to lose his balance. I was able to knock one fellow against a bulkhead and get his gun, and then I shot them both." Rod could see that Carla was still suffering from the shock of Caldas almost getting her. He shook her and said, "It's OK, Carla. Caldas is dead. Come on, let's get out of here."

She nodded, hesitantly, and pulled on her weight belt, following him out into the passageway, while avoiding walking near Caldas' body. On the blustery deck, they found their masks, fins, and regulators, where they had left them, and put on new tanks. An occasional wave spilled over the deck, making walking treacherous. It was obvious that the ship was not holding its position well, because it was taking the full brunt of the waves. The ship had probably lost the use of two of its engines. Their sabotage plan was working. Rod still carried the machine gun for protection. Clinging to the rungs of the boarding ladder, they inched down toward the water surface, and Rod threw the machine gun into the sea. They finally stepped off with their regulators in their mouths. Their fins were still strapped over their arms, due to the inability to wear them, while climbing down the ladder. They put on their fins and, immediately, dumped air out of their vests with the push of a button on a hose valve. The two descended, not knowing if help would arrive in time.

33

Back on Guanaja, the eye of the hurricane had passed over the island, in a southwesterly direction, heading along the coastline toward La Ceiba at 14 miles per hour, a few hours before Carla and Rod descended on the wreck, again. Most of the island residents had found shelter. Those, who had not, lost their lives or suffered serious injury. The storm had already raged for almost half a day. As the eye passed, blue sky appeared and the winds calmed. The birds started to sing again. People crept out of their shelters to survey the damage.

The island was unrecognizable from its former state. Palm trees were stripped of their leaves and hills were blown clean of their vegetation. It looked like a gigantic shaver had run over Guanaja. Docks were ripped apart or collapsed. Dwellings were blown off their pilings and deposited on land like discarded toys, along with several boats. The sand beaches were worn away. Power was out on the entire island because generators had been flooded. Everywhere there was debris. Bonacca had been engulfed by 9-foot storm surge, despite the protection of the fringing reef and cays, and was heavily damaged. Most of the residents had taken refuge in a church, a mile inland on the island, built against a hillside. Amazingly, it had remained intact despite high winds and horizontal rain that had battered it for hours. Water lapped at the church's doorsteps, however, because flooding extended across low parts of the island for a distance of two miles. The airstrip had been spared as it had been constructed on a slight rise in the terrain from the water's edge. It was littered with fallen trees and debris, though, making the runway invisible. The Posada del Sol resort still stood proudly by the shoreline, due to its resilient adobe structure. Its roof had been denuded of its tiles. Bayman Bay Club had not fared as well. Its pier had been demolished by wind and storm surge. Several of its cabins were missing. Rudy Lentz had stayed in Bonacca, after making contact with Washington, D.C., and had sought shelter along with several of the residents of the village. Only six roofless dwellings in Savannah Bight stood upright amongst the stripped palm trees. As for Von Kreitler's residence on Bird Cay, it was completely destroyed by storm surge, when the low pressure of the hurricane drew the normal tide up into a 14-foot dome of water. The entire Cay was submerged except for an occasional skeleton of a palm tree rising up above the water surface. No one had been there during the storm, however. The site had been deserted. Most of Von Kreitler's men were now on the **El Mundo** and his servants had taken refuge in Bonacca.

The respite from the hurricane was temporary. The winds built up momentum, again, and blew from the opposite direction, as the outer hurricane bands, beyond the eye, approached. Rain pelted surfaces, horizontally, once more. The familiar howling of the wind resumed. Darkness engulfed the island, since evening was approaching and the electrical power was still out. Here and there, occasional candlelight could be seen flickering or light from a Coleman lantern could be seen through the cracks of a boarded up window. Further damage ensued.

Pepe's family comprised some of the people, who had taken shelter in the church. His mother had come under some duress, as she had been frantic not being able to find her son before the storm hit. She refused to leave their home, initially, but then she realized that she was jeopardizing all the children in doing so. Reluctantly, she now huddled with others in the church waiting out the storm. She hoped that Pepe had done what he had suggested, that they go to La Ceiba. If he had gone, she couldn't figure out how he had gotten past the quarantine checkpoints. He had been vaccinated before the storm, like the rest of the residents of Guanaja. But how could he have had enough money for the trip? She feared that he, was somewhere out in the hurricane, instead.

Her face was so etched with worry that it drew the attention of one of the CDC team physicians. The short, blond-haired doctor was making her rounds of the building, in lantern light, checking on the disease status of the individuals taking shelter. This was because there were now two threats - further spread of the smallpox epidemic and the risk of cholera and dysentery due to the dwindling sanitation. A small wing of the church had been converted into an infirmary and any high-risk smallpox contacts were kept there, along with anyone who was manifesting symptoms or signs of smallpox. At the moment, there were two patients in the infirmary, who had been moved from Savannah Bight before the hurricane hit. They were friends of Felipe's family, who had visited the fisherman's son while he was ill. It was decided to move them to Bonacca, as there was no adequate shelter in Savannah Bight, from which to administer their medical care during the storm. They had both received VIG, as soon as it was learned that they were contacts of the first case. The hemorrhagic form of the illness had not manifested. They were not as sick as Felipe had been. The patients did develop diffuse, large pustules, though. Their lesions were not extremely confluent, like unvaccinated ordinary-type smallpox. The patients' appearances had alarmed others in the church, but these affected individuals were kept strictly isolated in a curtained corner of the makeshift infirmary and wore masks, making the villagers less uneasy. There had been no other new cases identified on the island.

The CDC physician bent over Pepe's mother and, gently, asked her some questions, looked in her mouth, listened to her heart and lungs, and examined her extremities. Pepe's mother had been so distraught that she hadn't noted a rash on her right ankle. There was a pustule, surrounded by redness. "How long have you had this, senora?" the physician asked in Spanish.

She looked at the area, puzzled. A couple of days ago, she had scratched the area on the splintered edge of a door. Today, she had waded knee-deep in standing water, outside of the church, when the hurricane abated, briefly. In Spanish, the woman answered, "I cut the leg, only a little, two days ago. I have not covered it."

"I see," responded the physician, glad to hear that there was a more benign, probable source of this infection. The wound had abscessed. Undoubtedly, the woman had not washed the area, after wading in the floodwaters, as clean water was in short supply. Who knows what was in that water? Septic tanks had overflowed as a result of the flooding from storm surge. Not to mention, other contaminants that may have seeped into the water, as it engulfed the land. "Listen, I will take you to the infirmary and we will open that infection, clean it, and put you on antibiotic medicine? OK?"

"I can not leave my children and husband, now, and I must find my son, Pepe." The woman's voice was urgent, almost wailing. Her other children, who were standing nearby, looked frightened.

"Where did you last see your son?"

"Before the hurricane, at our house. He wanted us to go to La Ceiba, but I told him, 'no,' we had to stay here. I thought he had gone to the place where the planes come down, to help carry people's baggage this morning, but he never came home. Oh, I know that I have lost him!" Pepe's mother started to cry.

"Come now, we will help you find your son. Possibly, he did manage to get to La Ceiba. If so, he is safe because he is away from this hurricane. Once the storm passes, we will try to get on our satellite phone and call the La Ceiba police. They can help us find him."

At that, Pepe's mother brightened and nodded slowly. She followed the doctor to the infirmary. The physician incised and drained her abscess, dressed the wound and gave her some antibiotics. She was just about to return to the nave of the church, when a large rumble was heard outside of the building in the midst of the howling wind. The building shuddered suddenly and the wooden beams groaned. People started screaming and clinging to one another. Mud oozed through the cracks in the rear door of church, which accessed the infirmary area. Members of the CDC team and Honduran military that were in the building rushed to push a heavy armoire with religious garments against the door. Everyone prayed. The rumbling stopped and there was only the howling wind and pelting rain, again. A few villagers rushed to the front entrance of the church to open the door and see what happened. The door would not budge. There was something heavy against it. Cries of fear issued from the occupants. Pepe's mother returned to her family's place in the room. Her husband tried to comfort her and their children, but all were agitated. The military officials discussed the matter. Obviously, there had been a mudslide from the hill behind the church. It had surrounded the building and blocked the doors. The windows had been spared, but were too high and narrow to climb out of and had been boarded up, as well. They were trapped inside for the duration of the hurricane with a limited supply of food and water, not to mention, rapidly dwindling sanitation due to a backed up toilet and two sick smallpox patients. Time was against them. Only an abrupt change in weather would make a difference.

34

The rain shield of the hurricane was pummeling La Ceiba, seventy or so miles, southwest of Guanaja. Wind gusts had reached 175 miles per hour. Five inches of rain had fallen in a couple of hours, augmenting the flooding by 15-foot storm surge. The great pier, along the waterfront, had collapsed. Rising water in the streets had engulfed cars and flooded main floors of buildings. The main canal in the city had overflowed, as well. Carcasses of dogs, cats, and chickens floated by, as well as the occasional, bloated body of a drowned human being. The death toll would number in the hundreds. Trees were ripped out of the ground, roots and all. Any windows that hadn't been boarded up were imploded. The hurricane had reached full Category 4 status.

Many hours before the first high winds battered La Ceiba, Pepe had been rushed from the police station to the hospital to be examined for any signs of smallpox, in view of the quarantine on Guanaja. He had been determined to be disease free. Also, Dr. Lopez had noted his vaccination mark. Despite his cleared status, it was felt that he should be observed in the hospital, and, as a result, he was moved, along with the other patients, to the Standard Fruit Company warehouse on higher ground. That was where he was located when the hurricane struck La Ceiba. Dr. Velasquez was there, too, because an assistant had found him, a couple of day's prior, at the morgue office, after he had been badly beaten by Ramirez's men. He was being treated for multiple broken ribs, a collapsed lung, a broken forearm, broken nose, and a concussion. Not only had he survived the beating, but also he would probably survive the hurricane as a result of being moved to his current location. Flooding had extended inland over flat terrain for a distance of four miles. Most single-story dwellings were immersed. The warehouse still stood safely on its hill above the rising water.

Drs. Lopez and Jonas were making rounds in the makeshift isolation area that had been curtained off for smallpox cases, while the wind screamed outside. The sailors afflicted with the illness had not survived, as they had all succumbed to complications of hemorrhagic smallpox. A few cases of nonhemorrhagic disease had surfaced in some of their family members. Meribel was still alive. She had not manifested hemorrhagic-type symptoms. No pneumonia had surfaced. She did not develop any pulmonary edema. However, her skin had erupted diffusely with pustular, confluent lesions. Most were on her face, followed by her extremities, and trunk. The lesions had evolved quickly and appeared to be fewer in number than in an unvaccinated case. Meribel had had no fever during the eruption. She had been quite ill prior to the rash, though. Jonas was convinced that she had a case of modified smallpox. He was ecstatic because it meant that the combination of vaccination and VIG was effective against this more virulent strain of smallpox. He voiced this to Dr. Lopez, "You know, Jorge, the key was immunizing her during the incubation period of the virus."

"I think that you are right, Paul. I am just glad that we had enough vaccine and immunoglobulin to immunize the number of people that we did. We have not had any new cases present in the last few days, which is promising."

"I agree."

Dr. Tapper approached the two physicians. "Hey, is anyone hungry? The military has made a temporary canteen for us in the warehouse, and the food smells pretty good. I think that we're going to have to eat every chance we get, because the number of casualities from the hurricane, piling into the intake area, is increasing and we're probably going to end up working non-stop."

"Excellent suggestion, Bruce. You lead. I'll be right behind you, beating a path to the food," Jonas replied, grinning.

"Me, also," Jorge rejoined.

The three men headed toward a corner of the concrete warehouse, where the smell of meat and rice filled the air. Some benches and tables had been set up near a counter and a propane cookstove. At one of the tables sat Pepe, along with one of the policemen from the local station. He gave the men a curious look. Despite his fear, he was having the adventure of a lifetime. He was anxious about his family, though, and his friends Senor Rod and Dr. Knight. He could see his mother worrying about where he was, wringing her hands under the sole light bulb in their small home.

Dr. Lopez recognized the little boy, after picking up his tray of food, and he went over and sat down beside him. Jonas and Tapper joined them. "Hello, Pepe. How are you?"

"Hello, Dr. Lopez," the boy mumbled, shyly.

The Honduran physician introduced the boy to the two men. "Pepe, I'd like you to meet two American physicians, who have helped us with the sickness here and on your island. This is Dr. Jonas and Dr. Tapper."

The answer, even more reluctantly, "Hello." Pepe's eyes remained downcast.

To Jonas and Tapper, Jorge elaborated, "Pepe is a very brave boy. He hid away in a plane on Guanaja, before the hurricane, to get to La Ceiba to tell the police about the murderers of the **Golddigger** crew and to tell them the whereabouts of the Americans, who are seeking them." Pepe brightened.

"You know, Pepe, I have a son about your age and I hope he grows up to be as brave as you are," Paul Jonas praised.

Pepe looked at this adult before him, with new interest and smiled. Perhaps, he would be able to help him find out what happened to Senor Rod and Dr. Knight. "Can you help me find my friends?"

Jonas looked amused. "I can see why you made it here by plane. You don't waste any time and get right to the point. "Who are your friends?"

"Senor Rod and Dr. Knight."

"Oh, I met Dr. Knight before. She seemed like a very nice lady and brave like you are."

"Yes, she is. I am very afraid because I left her on a beach with Senor Rod and bad men were coming for them."

Dr. Lopez interjected, "Pepe, the police you saw here in La Ceiba are having the Naval Force go help them. Do not worry. They will do everything that they can."

"Oh, that is good. I will have to go home soon, or my mother will be angry."

"We will get you home once this hurricane has passed, son," Dr. Jonas reassured. Pepe seemed satisfied and nodded.

The men finished eating, bid Pepe a good night's sleep, and bussed their trays to the dishwashing area. Outside, the wind kept howling. Dr. Lopez returned to the intake area to see new emergency patients. Paul Jonas decided to visit Dr. Velasquez, while Bruce Tapper checked on current sanitation arrangements. He had not seen the older gentleman, since he was brought to the hospital for his beating injuries. He was surprised to find the coroner, sitting up on a cot, reading some notes. The man's right arm was in a sling and he held papers in his left hand. His face was black and blue beneath both his eyes, but his spirit seemed intact. He appeared relieved to see Jonas.

"How are you doing, Dr. Velasquez?"

"I am glad to be alive. How goes your war against smallpox?"

"I think that we have made progress containing the severity of the cases. Also, we have not had any new cases present in the last few days."

"That is wonderful news. Any word on the whereabouts of Dr. Carla Knight and Senor Rod Dalton?"

"All we know is that they are pursuing the murderers of the **Golddigger** crew, somewhere out in this hurricane. They had been held, briefly, by the perpetrators, but then escaped, and are reportedly headed back to the site of the U-boat wreck. We are pretty convinced, from police reports that the perpetrators are returning for the wreck's cargo. Thus, the reason for Dalton's and Knight's journey, back to the site."

"May God protect them, both, through this hurricane and from those animals, who did this to me."

"I couldn't agree with you more. Can I get you anything?"

"No, Dr. Jonas, but thank you for asking. Hopefully, you can get some rest soon."

"Oh, I will. You get some, too. Good night."

"Good night." Dr. Jonas left the curtained cubicle and was headed to a briefing area to find Dr. Tapper and be updated on the sanitation system, when he heard shouts outside, in front of the building. He noticed several individuals, including Dr. Lopez, run toward a small side door in the warehouse and opens it with some difficulty. The blast of wind blew papers, cups and dishes on tables, and linens on the floor. Dr. Lopez stepped outside into the chaos to face two frightened soldiers, who were pointing down the hill, toward the road. A small figure could be seen in the increasing darkness, huddled in a blanket against the horizontal rain and immersed in about three feet of floodwater. The soldiers spoke in frantic Spanish to Lopez. They kept shaking their heads and pointing, and then rushed past Lopez into the building, despite his shouts to them to stop. Jonas cautiously pushed out into the furious wind, to get to Lopez, who was holding onto the stump of a tree, so he wouldn't be blown over.

"What's the matter?" shouted Jonas.

"There is a pregnant woman down on the road, who is covered with sores and who is bleeding from her mouth and nose. She was trying to climb up the hill to the warehouse, but was too weak. The soldiers are afraid that she has smallpox and won't go near her."

"Ridiculous. They have all been vaccinated and can wear masks, gloves, and gowns," yelled back Jonas.

"I know, but their fear overcomes their reason."

"The poor woman, she still may be able to be saved. We have to get to her."

"I agree. I will get us some masks and gloves and some rain ponchos."

"Don't bother. I already grabbed the gear for us," Tapper's voice could be heard shouting behind them.

"Bruce! You're a champ."

"I'm coming with you."

"No, I need you, here, to oversee the operation. I appreciate the offer. Jorge and I can manage, together. Besides, he can translate for me."

"Let me at least keep a rope on you both, while you make your way down the hill. You can't stand in the open in this wind force."

"Very well, but get some soldiers to help you."

"OK."

Gear donned and ropes secured around them, they made their way down the hillside precariously. They were knocked off their feet several times by the wind. The tension on the ropes helped them get to their feet, but they eventually stayed hunched over, low above the ground, grabbing handholds where they could.

The woman was not far from them, now. She appeared forlorn under her soaked blanket with a protuberant abdomen, hanging onto the door of a stalled car to maintain her position in the rising water. Jorge called to her. She did not move. It was obvious that she was very ill, maybe dead for all they knew. Jorge eased himself into the muddy water on one side of her and Paul eased in on the other side of her. When they pulled the blanket away from her face, they could see blackened pustules covering her cheeks, forehead, and nose. She was maybe eighteen or twenty years old. Her eyes had subconjunctival hemorrhages and there was blood oozing from her nose and on her lips. She was breathing shallowly.

Her stare was glassy. Occasionally, she moaned. It was a severe case of early hemorrhagic smallpox.

Damn, thought Paul, it always hit pregnant women harder. Their group might have even vaccinated her, but the pregnancy would thwart her successful immunity. Or maybe, she was a friend of one of the sailors' families that they hadn't discovered and vaccinated. No matter, now. She had the disease. To Jorge, he yelled, "We need to get her out of here fast. I don't think that she has much longer to live. We might be able to save the baby."

Jorge nodded grimly. "I think she is in her last trimester, by the size of her abdomen, so you are right, the baby may be salvageable." He pried her right hand from the car door and put her arm over his left shoulder and around his neck. Paul did likewise with her left arm, putting it over his right shoulder.

They were about to haul her out of the water, when a large rumble sounded above them on the hillside to the west of the warehouse. The two men froze at the sound. A huge wall of mud and debris broke loose and roared toward them, so fast that they had no time to react. Bruce Tapper looked on in horror, after he had screamed himself hoarse trying to warn them. The mud hit the three figures like a freight train. They were immediately buried and swept away. The ropes were ripped out of the soldiers' hands and snaked away rapidly out of sight.

Bruce collapsed in a heap on the other side of the warehouse door, sobbing and croaking "no" over and over again, after someone had yanked him inside to take cover from the slide. He had lost his mentor, not to mention a good friend, and the La Ceiba hospital had lost one of their most dedicated physicians. What was even more tragic was that the two men had tried to contain a potential new index case of smallpox in vain and at the cost of their lives.

35

Over a hundred miles east of La Ceiba, two A-10 Thunderbolts screamed over the **El Mundo**, information, at low altitude through the abating storm. They made a large circle and passed overhead, again. Von Kreitler and Ramirez raced to the wheelhouse to talk to the captain. Their divers had returned while Rod and Carla were aboard, so there was no reason to stay longer. Now, with jets passing overhead, it was imperative that they leave immediately. However, the captain gave them bad news. He had shut down two engines, already, because they had overheated, mysteriously, and the two, yet functioning, did not provide enough power to help the vessel motor away at a fast speed.

"Find Dalton!", screamed Von Kreitler. He was hoping Caldas had not killed him yet (even though he had heard machine gun fire), because he suspected Dalton had sabotaged the ship.

Two crew members returned, shortly, to report that Dalton and Knight were gone and Caldas was found dead along with a few other cartel members, all riddled with bullets. Von Kreitler's eyes bulged and his veins showed prominently on his forehead and neck. His wrath could not be contained. "Get more men to the engine room and check every inch of it. See if there are any signs of sabotage. Also, have some divers return to the wreck and see if Dalton and Knight have been foolish enough to go back there."

Ramirez looked semi-defeated. He was losing hope in their operation, which so far had been costly, and now whose outcome seemed questionable. He didn't want to end up like Rojas, in some stinking American prison, waiting for a death sentence. He had just lost his best lieutenant. He would fight to the end. "I will find Dalton, myself," and he stormed from the wheelhouse, leaving Von Kreitler to ponder their fate.

On the way to the gear room, Ramirez encountered Brad Jacobs, who was alarmed by the current circumstances and wanted to know what they were going to do. "It would appear, Senor Jacobs, that with Senor Dalton's escape, your cover is gone and you are no longer useful to us. Jacobs paled at this comment, but had no chance to reply before Ramirez pulled out an automatic pistol and shot him in the head. Ramirez left him where he dropped, as he had more urgent matters to attend to.

Less than an hour remained for the charges on the wreck to blow. The captain suddenly reported seeing a large ship, which appeared to be a naval vessel, on the horizon. Von Kreitler felt a pain in his stomach. It was obvious that Dalton and Knight had gotten to the authorities in their flight across the island. Why had he worried if their death would look natural, when he had them tied to the dock to be stung by sea wasps? He should have had them shot on the spot.

His thoughts were interrupted by a marine radio transmission on frequency 2182. "This is the Honduran Naval Force vessel, **Torbellino**, calling the ship **El Mundo** off Cabo Cameroon. Please respond."

Silence.

"This is the Honduran Naval Force vessel, **Torbellino**, calling the **El Mundo**. You are surrounded by United States Air Force jet fighters. They will fire upon you if you attempt to move off your anchorage: on attempt any act of aggression. Do you acknowledge?"

Silence.

Von Kreitler considered his alternatives. He could be captured and face humiliation and imprisonment for the remaining years of his life. Or, he could join his U-boat in its ultimate fate, and at least resist surrender. Hitler had chosen his own death, and so could he. He instructed the captain to hold steady and not attempt to move the ship. Then, he left the wheelhouse in search of dive gear.

Ramirez was already suiting up, when he entered the gear room. He was told that the entire ship had been searched by the crew and Dalton and Knight were no where to be found, so they must have returned to the wreck. Ramirez was arming himself with a spear gun and a large knife. He noted Von Kreitler starting to assemble gear and asked him, "Where are you going?"

"I am going down to help you find Dalton and make certain he doesn't dismantle the charges. We are surrounded. There is no point remaining on board. The only thing we can hope for is that some of the Honduran Naval Force boards the ship, before the wreck explodes. It might set off a fire or explosion on the ship and, at least, eliminate some Honduran and U.S. naval personnel. The U-boat will be destroyed, so they will only be able to retrieve the unloaded cargo, if they are lucky."

"I will lose many men," Ramirez stated soberly.

"There will always be new men and another drug cartel.," avowed Von Kreitler.

"That is not much consolation."

"It will have to be enough, for now."

Once they were completely suited up, the two men made their way to the boarding ladder. The seas seemed to be calming, somewhat. Bad news, in view of the approaching vessel. They took leaping strides off the lowest rung of the ladder into the water and descended. The U-boat wreck was barely visible in the late afternoon light and bubbles issued from the conning tower hatch. Someone was obviously within the wreck.

36

Carla and Rod had made all due haste toward the wreck, once they were in the water, as they wanted to find the explosives' detonator. Their biggest problem was that they had no good light source. However, Rod had noticed that they had unused cyalumes (for night diving) tied to the valve knobs of their tanks, so he pulled them off and bent the sticks to activate the chemical light. He gave one to Carla. Enough of a green glow was provided that they could see within the dark confines of the wreck. Carla stayed close behind Rod to prevent getting lost.

Suddenly, Rod noticed some waterproof firing circuit wires along the floor of one corridor, leading down a ladder into the cargo area that they had discovered before. They led to several shaped plastic explosive charges that were sealed in sections of metal pipe with waterproof covers. The charges were lashed to a metal stud on the side of the hull with wire. No detonator device could be seen. Rod turned and followed the wires back up the ladder and down the corridor into the control room. The wires forked, at this point, and he motioned to Carla to follow one and he would follow the other.

Several minutes into this task, she heard the clang of metal hitting metal, a distinctive sound underwater. She thought that Rod was signaling her to come back with the cyalume. Upon retracing her path, she found the corridor lighted by dive lights discarded on the deck and Rod trying to fight off Ramirez and Von Kreitler, who were grabbing him around his neck and arms. She still had a dive knife with her and she pulled it out of its scabbard and launched herself toward Von Kreitler. He did not see her quickly enough in the surrounding darkness and she was able to grab the low-pressure hose to his regulator mouthpiece, and cut through it. He, immediately, let go of Rod and clutched at his own throat. He, then, grabbed for her mouthpiece and she slashed at his hand with her knife. A plume of blood issued from a gash in his glove. His actions became feebler as he swallowed more water, gasping for air. Carla kept slashing at him to prevent him from grabbing her. Her last memory of him would be of his cold blue eyes boring into her. He finally became unconscious and sank to the floor.

Meanwhile, Rod had managed to wrest a knife out of Ramirez's hands, but Ramirez was attempting to strangle him. He had pulled off Rod's mask during the struggle. Carla came up behind Ramirez and cut the hose on his regulator. She watched him let go of Rod and flail, trying to find his spare regulator, known as an octopus. Rod moved out of Ramirez's reach, picking the knife up off the deck of the boat, and then, swiftly grabbed the octopus hose and cut it. Ramirez seemed to convulse and, gradually became flaccid, eyes staring blankly into the darkness.

Rod picked up his mask and put it on, clearing it by blowing air out of his nose, while tilting the mask away from his face and looking upward. He pointed to the light coming through the open hatch in the conning tower, indicating that they should go toward it. He signaled that they did not have time to dismantle the detonators and he pointed to their instrument panels. It was obvious that they were well beyond no decompression limits and they, barely, had enough air to make it to the surface. Therefore, they quickly headed through the hatchway and out into the surrounding water, trying to make a steady controlled ascent even though they were out of time. The warning tone on their computers kept beeping that they were ascending above their ceiling limit, but they had no choice. Finally, they could see the rippled motion of the surface above them. Their regulators tugged hard, suddenly, and gave no air. They still had another 20 feet to ascend, so they unclipped their weight belts and shot to the surface, exhaling in the process.

Above the sea, much was going on. A Naval Force helicopter was circling overhead, fanning out the water around them. They began waving a distress signal because they knew the wreck would explode soon and they needed a hyperbaric chamber for decompression treatment. A voice called from a bullhorn that a hoist would be lowered and would pick them up. The hurricane had abated, considerably, by this point, as much of its center was north of them. The waves were smaller. They noticed that the **El Mundo** had been moved a distance away, off its anchorage, and must have been boarded, because there was a grey, Honduran Naval Force vessel tied to it. Several sailors in white uniforms could be seen aboard the **El Mundo**. The authorities had been notified and had arrived in time.

A metal basket was lowered on a hoist and Rod helped Carla crawl in first, after she dumped her fins, BC vest, and tank. She was lifted up without incident. The basket was lowered, again, and Rod crawled in after dumping his gear. He was immediately hoisted away and the helicopter moved off. Not a moment too soon, however, as an immense underwater explosion occurred, shooting water and debris a hundred feet into the air.

Beneath the surface, **U-2359** broke into a myriad of pieces, which plummeted off the ledge into the depths below. It's skipper, Captain Kurt von Kreitler, followed it into the murky darkness along with his accomplice. The wreckage of the **Isabella**, also, had laid beneath the sand near the U-boat site for hundreds of years, unbeknownst to the **Golddigger** crew and others. Its frame was widely scattered, as well as its treasure, during the U-boat explosion, thus, eliminating the chance for full recovery by a future salvage operation. It had, however, provided a greater bounty because it had helped to expose a diabolical scheme, which could have claimed a multitude of innocent lives in the years to come.

37

17:11 CST

The helicopter, which picked up Rod and Carla, headed immediately toward Roatan to get Carla and Rod to the island's hyperbaric chamber for recompression treatment. Dusk was beginning to fall. They were laid on their backs in the aircraft with 100% oxygen by mask. This was done to minimize the effects, on the brain, of any bubble formation in the blood, caused by excessive dive time and rapid ascent. A medic also administered IV fluids to both of them to reduce the sludging of the blood vessels by gas bubbles. Neither of them had difficulty breathing or any loss of consciousness, but they did begin to have aches in their joints.

Director's Richard Moore and Harold Morgan, were aboard the helicopter. They briefed them about the events surrounding the capture of the **El Mundo**. The Naval Force vessel overtook the **El Mundo**, as divers were trying to return to the wreck to assist Von Kreitler and Ramirez. Under some duress, the captain of the **El Mundo** finally confessed that explosives had been set to go off underwater in a brief period of time. The **El Mundo** was, thus, moved as fast as possible, off its anchorage under the guard of the Honduran Naval Force, which also moved its vessel off the site. A search ensued aboard the cartel's ship and the **U-2359** cargo was discovered in the stern compartment of the cartel's ship. The cargo had not been inventoried, thoroughly, but there appear to be biologic and chemical agents of mass destruction, as well as components and plans for a nuclear agent.

Rod related to Director Morgan that they had killed Hector Ramirez, while they were in the process of trying to avert the explosion in the wreck. Alfonso Caldas' fate was, also, discussed.

249

He divulged Kurt von Kreitler's involvement and plans with the cartel and explained how Carla had done away with the U-boat captain, and how she had saved his own life. She looked uncomfortable during this description, but Rod and the other men regarded her with admiration

Morgan looked at both of them and said, "In the space of one day, two people, who have evaded our agency's attempts to arrest them for years, have been removed as problems. Amazing! You are both to be congratulated. On the other hand, sadly, we learned of the duplicity of Brad Jacobs and we found him with a bullet through his head on the **El Mundo**. Evidently, he had exhausted his usefulness to Ramirez. I understand he was a friend of yours, Rod."

"Yes, he was," Rod nodded his head wearily. "However, he wasn't the only person who had changed since Nam and couldn't be trusted." Carla caught the implication, but said nothing.

"Well, I hope we don't have any similar disappointments in the future," replied Morgan. "The agency wants to thank you both for all of your efforts in this investigation and for protecting the United States from the planned acts of terrorism, originally intended by this group."

"I also wish to add my sincere thanks," concurred Director Moore.

Carla asked at this point, "Does anyone know if the chemical analysis of the water samples from the wreck was completed in Tegucigalpa? And also, do you know what happened to Dr. Velasquez, the coroner of La Ceiba. We heard that he was beaten by cartel members?"

"The sample was safely analyzed," reported Director Moore, "and did show a break-down product of a compound like Agent Orange, but the analysis was not done in the lab in Tegucigalpa, because Ramirez's men broke into the lab, killed the technician, and stole the material being tested (Carla gasped at this information). Fortunately, the lab technician had put a remaining sample in a safe before they arrived, and thus, it was delivered intact to the authorities and run through further analysis in the States. You will be happy to know that Dr. Velasquez is alive and recovering in a hospital in La Ceiba with a broken bone in one limb, a concussion, and some broken ribs. He was worried about you, after his experience, and wanted to make certain that no harm had befallen you."

"Tell him, I will contact him as soon as possible and I am glad he is alive." Carla smiled, but was upset that Maria Hernandez had died, trying to help her. "What about the possible biologic agent test tubes that I left with Drs. Jonas and Velasquez at the La Ceiba airport? Was there a positive ID made on the organism?"

"Yes. The CDC revealed, this morning, to the members of the National Security Council and Department of Defense that they had made a preliminary microscopic ID of the test tube material, that you submitted to Dr. Jonas, of smallpox Variola virus, to be confirmed further by culture," Moore answered. Carla shook her head. "We still do not know the status of the presumed smallpox epidemic on Guanaja and in La Ceiba, due to the telephone communication interruption caused by the hurricane. We are confident, however, that the epidemic will be contained because there was mass immunization conducted in the two areas before the storm."

"What of the little boy, Pepe, who we asked to try to get to La Ceiba?" inquired Rod.

"He has become something of a national hero. He successfully stowed away in an airplane to La Ceiba and got the authorities to contact us in Washington, D.C. The police captain in La Ceiba did not believe him, initially, but upon contacting us and learning of the situation in Guanaja, he personally escorted Pepe to the hospital in La Ceiba to be examined, because he was concerned that the boy broke quarantine on the island. At last report, he was ok and was being observed in the hospital, but there is a Category 4 hurricane raging there, now, and we have had no other reports.

The President of Honduras, as well as the President of the United States, have indicated that they want Pepe and his family to be well taken care of in the future," informed Director Moore.

"He saved our lives," stated Rod simply.

"I think he may have saved a number of lives," affirmed Moore. "Your friend, Rudy, was instrumental in getting help to you, as he successfully reported your location coordinates in time."

"I am lucky to have such good friends," Rod conceded. It was a relief to know that some of his friends could be trusted. "Director Moore, there are two individuals who tried to sabotage our investigation and who were in league with Von Kreitler, that you should have your men look for at Posada del Sol. They are Bud and Gloria Campbell, or so they are named."

"We will follow up, immediately, on that," replied Moore.

The helicopter touched down on Roatan, at this point, and they were shuttled to the recompression chamber at Sandy Bay by an open bed truck. They were kept supine. Director's Moore and Morgan had taken their leave of them at the helicopter, stating that they would return later to debrief them further.

The chamber attendants took their medical histories while they positioned them in the chamber, Carla on one berth and Rod on another. One attendant placed masks, delivering 100% oxygen, over their noses and mouths and they were then pressurized to a depth of 60 feet, or 2.8 atmospheres of pressure. This treatment was pursued because they had no neurologic symptoms, only pain as the predominant symptom. The theory behind recompression was to simulate going to depth again and increase pressure, in order to shrink the size of problem-causing bubbles in their tissues and bloodstream. This, also, gave time for oxygen to wash out inert gas and fluids, before they were decompressed back to one atmosphere of pressure at sea level. The entire process would take two hours and fifteen minutes for their level of symptomatology. During this time they would breathe 100% oxygen for 20-minute periods, then air for five-minute periods to prevent toxicity.

Carla knew the whole procedure. After all, it was her job to utilize these chambers day in and day out. Rod must have read her thoughts, for he looked over at her and asked, "This must seem like work to you."

She laughed and answered, "Well, I must admit that I have spent more hours than I care to, in these things."

He smiled back, sincerely, and said, "This was not exactly my idea of spending a night with you."

They both burst out laughing. He continued, "I propose that we get something to eat and then, sleep after we are freed from this contraption, considering we haven't slept in over 36 hours and haven't eaten much in over 16 hours. After that, we can resume where we left off on Half-Moon Cay last evening."

The boldness of this invitation took her off guard, slightly, but she looked back and gave an earnest nod. He reached out and squeezed her arm, affectionately. The chamber attendant, inside, smirked briefly when he heard these comments and returned to his duties recording vital signs and instrument readings.

Two hours seemed like five due to their hunger, but they were finally released in the late evening, pain-free, and taken to the Anthony Key's Resort for dinner and a night's lodging, compliments of the manager who had heard about their ordeal. The resort had not sustained much damage, despite high winds, because it had missed the brunt of the hurricane. After a substantial meal in the lodge dining room, during which they were alone, spoke little and ate voraciously, they retired to the bungalows that they had been given. Before parting, they gazed longingly at one another, but knew they were too fatigued to attempt a night together.

Rod took Carla into his arms and looked deep into her blue eyes. "You are amazing. Not only are you pretty and smart, but you are the best damn partner I ever had in an operation. You never complained. Not once." The smile widened shyly on her face, then confidently. He drew her face to his and kissed her. A mixture of passion, fatigue, and the desperate desire to relax kept them locked together for another few minutes.

Carla put her forehead against his, looking down toward her feet, and said, "I never thought I'd find someone, again, who was so brave about facing life. You never question what you have to do, you just do it."

"The same could be said about you," whispered Rod, and he kissed her once more. They separated, knowing fatigue had won them over. A hot shower was a weak, but welcome, substitute for their company and made sleep inevitable.

38

November 23, 1993

The next morning started a sad day for the city of La Ceiba. Heavy rain continued in the area. Surviving residents saw, for the first time, the full extent of the destruction caused by the hurricane. The main pier was no more. Most one-story structures were underwater. Several buildings were blown apart like matchsticks. Amazingly, as if by an act of God, the original hospital was still standing, but was surrounded by water. It would take several weeks to clean up the muddy mess inside. There was the stench of death and decay in the air, coming from what was floating in the flooded streets or what was buried under mud or buildings. Those walking about had to wear masks, distributed by the military because the smell was so overwhelming. The search and rescue process had started, but this was often reduced to search and body recovery. Such was the case, near the Standard Fruit Company's warehouse on the hill. Bruce Tapper was there with several others, attempting to dig through the mudslide to find the bodies of Dr. Jonas and Dr. Lopez. What guided them was the appearance of some portions of rope protruding from the sea of mud, and the increasing stench. After several hours, they found the mangled bodies of the two physicians. They were not far apart, buried under about twelve feet of mud. Tapper could not bring himself to look at the bodies. He just turned away and wept. He collected himself, abruptly, when he heard that they could not find the smallpox-infected body of the pregnant woman. This presented an extremely dangerous situation for the city and, maybe, the outlying regions because of the lack of sanitation and the diseases being spread in the mud and water. Who knows how many individuals, would eventually come across her corpse and if they would be wearing adequate protection, or if they had been vaccinated. A whole new epidemic could occur with another index case. Paul must have realized this possibility. No wonder he had risked his life. Tapper realized that he must reach the CDC director, Dr. Chassen, as soon as possible.

He returned to the warehouse to find a military official, who could get him to a working phone line. While Tapper was making a search of the facility, Pepe was having arrangements made by the authorities to reunite him with his family on Guanaja. The boy was to be taken there by helicopter in a few hours. Meribel and her family would remain at the facility until her sores began to scar and she gained more strength. As for Dr. Velasquez, he had no office to return to, at the moment, and he was still recovering.

Bruce Tapper found an official, outside the warehouse, who was coordinating emergency medical supply transportation to outlying communities. The non-commissioned officer informed him that a satellite phone was available at an army installation on the outskirts of town. Tapper left word with the hospital staff and other CDC team members where he was going and why. All were mourning the deaths of Drs. Lopez and Jonas. They understood his need to reach the CDC. The epidemic had seemed to be under control. Now, the possibility of further future outbreaks loomed.

Tapper endured a hair-raising ride by jeep over debris and through flooded roads to the phone location. He reached an operator in Tegucigalpa and had her dial the CDC director's number on an international line. A familiar Southern voice answered at the other end of the connection.

"Dr. Chassen, this is Bruce Tapper calling. I wanted to reach you right away to let you know that Dr. Paul Jonas is dead." He heard the gasp at the other end.

"Oh, my God, what happened?"

"He was trying to rescue a new smallpox victim with another physician and was hit by a mudslide, during the hurricane here."

"I'll need to reach his wife, as soon as possible. What a tragedy." There was a brief silence. Chassen's voice broke, "He was a good friend. Did they recover the diseased woman's body?"

"No, not yet." Another pause in the conversation.

"Have you had any other new cases?"

"No, and our current cases seem to be improving with VIG and vaccination."

"Well, that's good news amongst the sad. How are you holding up, Dr. Tapper? I know Paul was a good friend of yours, too."

"I'm doing ok, sir, better than a little while ago. The Honduran government is arranging for Dr. Jonas's body to be sent home to the States as soon as possible."

"I'm relieved to hear that. I know his family will be grateful. Bruce, you take care of yourself and get the rest of the team back here, safely, when you're done with your work.. You know that you can always come back sooner and we can send down a replacement team."

"I know, sir, but I want to finish what Paul and I set out to do here. Dr. Chassen, I need to ask you a question."

"Go ahead, son."

"If we face a more widespread epidemic, here, or new outbreaks, elsewhere, do we have adequate reserves of vaccine and VIG available?"

"No son, we do not. It would take some time to manufacture new supplies."

"You've answered my question."

39

Rod and Carla ate breakfast, eagerly, that morning, unaware of the tragedy in La Ceiba. They were taken to the airport outside Coxen's Hole for a helicopter flight to Guanaja and a day of revelations. Plane flights to the smaller island were not in operation, yet, because fallen trees, there, obliterated the airstrip. The two of them were not prepared for the sight that met their eyes, as they approached the isle. Guanaja was devoid of upright trees. Water extended inland for almost three miles. There was evidence of several mudslides, one of which appeared, from the air, to have surrounded a church. People could be seen, outside of the building, digging and removing mud from in front of the main entrance. There were no identifiable intact structures in Bonacca. All had sustained moderate or major damage. No boats were seen moored, nearby. Only a jumbled mass of vessels was evident, beached on the shoreline. There was, however, a large Naval Force ship anchored at a distance southwest of Bonacca. This was where their helicopter landed.

A motor launch from the ship took them to Posada del Sol. Along the way, the scene of devastation appalled them. The once lush island was bare except for broken structures and vegetation, and its perpetual hilly landscape. The canal traversing the island was unrecognizable from its prior state, as it had overflowed its banks and merged with other floodwaters. Bird Cay did not exist anymore. Villagers could be seen removing debris from their collapsed dwellings in Bonacca. It was, at least, reassuring to see human life. Posada del Sol looked somewhat stark sitting on its point, without the surrounding palm trees. It no longer had a tile roof.

They received news, at the resort, that Pepe's family was among those trapped in the church by the mudslide. Many surrounding area, surviving residents had started working, that morning, once the rain stopped, to free the doorway of the mud piled against it, so that the occupants could get out. Bryan Reynolds, the manager of the resort, was with them. He had gone to participate in the rescue, to let Pepe's parents know that he had received word that their son was safe in La Ceiba and would be brought back to the island, that afternoon. No deaths had been reported within the church, by a CDC physician yelling through the wall to a villager, outside. There were a few cases of dysentery. The number of smallpox cases still remained only two, and they were improving. Most, in the church, considered themselves lucky. All told, there were nine confirmed deaths on the island, so far, from Hurricane Vicki.

There was a somber air in the resort. However, it was relieved by the arrival of Peter Beck, who had flown down from Miami on a private jet to Roatan and had taken a helicopter to Guanaja. The intense, dark-haired man with graying sideburns and an athletic frame appeared serious, at first, viewing the devastation on the island, but, quickly, became animated lauding Rod's and Carla's success in solving the **Golddigger** murders. He, also, was impressed by little Pepe's efforts to bring the murderers to justice and promised to provide the boy with a fully paid college education in the United States, someday, as thanks.

To Rod, he offered a position in his company, as he believed that Rod had several talents, which could be useful in future, ventures. However, Rod declined, saying that he had "never been cut out to be a businessman," but he thanked Beck warmly for the offer. Beck was appreciative, as well, to Carla for her insights during the investigation. He indicated that she would be the first person he would call about any diving accidents related to his operations, in the future.

Finally, grinning, he divulged some interesting news to both of them, "Yesterday, after the explosion on the sub, U.S. divers on the Coast Guard cutter that arrived from Cuba, went down to survey the area and found very widely scattered debris consisting of some unusual things. These items included some Spanish pieces of eight and gold doubloons, as well as a few gold crosses encrusted with gemstones and other jewelry, not to mention chard's of pottery and fragments of old coral-encrusted wood. The **Golddigger** crew would appear to have successfully found the wreck of the **Isabella**, even though they didn't know it and didn't bargain for the discoveries of the U-boat and its treacherous cargo, which ultimately cost them their lives."

This last statement conjured up the vision in Carla's mind of the Bermuda Triangle, which inexplicably claimed ships and planes within its perimeter. In like manner, it was curious that two vessels could sink in the same location, hundreds of years apart, and then invoke more trouble in the same area, later.

Her disturbing thought was interrupted by Beck, who continued, "Of course, the Honduran government will lay claim to the treasure discovered, as no salvage rights are registered by other parties and the treasure was found within their waters. That's the story of my life, about money - easy come, easy go. Oh well, on to the next treasure quest. I do plan to make a large donation to the people of Guanaja for disaster relief and rebuilding the island. Can I offer my plane to either of you to reach your final destinations? It's the least that I can do, considering all that you both have done for me."

Carla spoke first. "That is very kind of you, but I was hoping to stay another few days to help the islanders here, as well as to see Dr. Velasquez and file a report."

"Understandable. How about you, Rod?"

"Peter, thanks for the offer, but I, like Carla, am going to stay put and help out here." Rod was not sure what his next DEA assignment would be, since the purpose of his current post had been accomplished. He was, actually, a little dumbfounded because he had been at Posada for three years and had started to accept it as a permanent residence. Rod's local employer, Bryan Reynolds, still did not know that his employee was a DEA agent. Neither, did Peter Beck. Their ignorance had been maintained to keep Rod's cover and, also, to protect his identity for future assignments. Thus, Rod had no immediate travel plans.

"As you both wish. However, I don't feel that I have rewarded you for your efforts. Please stay in touch, in the future. If you need anything, call."

"We promise," Rod answered. Hence, Beck, with further pressing matters in Miami and the media to answer to, took his leave of them.

Shortly after his departure, a launch arrived carrying Admiral Weatherby, FBI Director Moore, and DEA Director Morgan. They had come to debrief Carla and Rod, further, as to the previous day's events and to offer President Claymore's personal thanks for their heroic deed. Bud and Gloria Cambell had been found and detained at the Tegucigalpa Airport by Honduran customs officials, the previous evening, while trying to leave the country. The FBI had learned that they had long records of selling secrets about the U.S. military to foreign sources. They were slated for extradition to the United States, to be prosecuted as accomplices of a multiple homicide and for acts of high treason.

Additionally, further investigation into Brad Jacob's financial affairs revealed that he had been acquiring large sums of money in a Swiss account, deposited by a Colombian bank, the past five years. He had led a modest lifestyle while in D.C. as a DEA agent, but was known to take exotic vacations and, undoubtedly, was planning to retire early.

A number of the Cordillera Cartel henchmen had been rounded up on the **El Mundo**, thus reducing their ranks considerably in Bogota. Director Morgan reported this fact with some satisfaction. The cartel was left without any immediate leaders and Colombian police were seeking remaining cartel members for their participation in the terrorist plot. They were vulnerable without the ruthlessness of Ramirez and Caldas. However, there would always be others to take their place and continue the cocaine production.

The FBI also detained a few remaining members of Von Kreitler's Teutonic army, on the **El Mundo** and at Ramirez's compound on the Mosquito Coast. Most were young German skinheads and, therefore, not candidates for any past war crimes, but they were to be extradited to the United States for acts of planned terrorism and homicide, involving American citizens. Documents, dating back to 1945, were found on the **El Mundo**, which indicated that, as the Third Reich fell in World War II, various members of Hitler's party, were designated to escape with advanced war technology to use at a later date for acts of terrorism and destruction in Allied countries. Such was the case of the German submarine, U-234's crew, which had surrendered to U.S. forces in May 1945, en route to Tokyo, with a cargo of uranium oxide that was a raw material for atomic bombs and plans for chemical rockets, aboard. However, U-2359 was never found until a week ago and the cargo it contained was far more sophisticated than that of U-234, Director Moore pointed out. It carried uranium 235, which was far more fissile than uranium oxide, as well as agents of biologic, and chemical warfare. This had been discovered, yesterday, when the cargo was retrieved from the **El Mundo**. The fact that uranium was in 235 U form would have saved one expensive and tedious step for Ramirez and his cohorts, however, it made the material more precarious to handle and store. As a result, it had been placed in heavy lead containers behind a steel bulkhead with a lead liner all these years. Rod realized, upon learning this information that it was fortuitous that the material had been taken off the wreck before it exploded.

The small cylinders found in the U-boat's corridor were another story. A lab in the United States had been sent the remaining water sample, retrieved from the safe in Tegucigalpa. They made positive ID on the substance, it contained, as 2,3,7,8-tetrachlorodibenzo-p-dioxin, otherwise known as TCDD, the most toxic member of a group of chemicals called dioxins, contaminating some types of herbicides. Thus, it appeared that the cylinders contained such a substance. The largest prior contamination, by this compound, was achieved per the Agent Orange used in Viet Nam, as a defoliant. Subsequently, it had been found to cause chloracne, cancer, and other ill effects in humans.

Rod whistled. "Carla, you were right about those post-mortem findings and your hunch."

"Yes, a good bit of detective work, I'd say," Director Moore lauded.

"I just remember seeing pictures, in a dermatological text, of South Vietnamese, who had been exposed, and the similarity was remarkable," responded Carla. "It's obvious Von Kreitler and his crowd did not plan any conventional herbicide use of this substance."

"No, indeed not," said Moore. "In fact, we found additional documents on the **El Mundo** giving elaborate instructions for other chemical agents of mass destruction. And, we believe there are more different types of biologic agents in the cargo, besides smallpox. There is testing being done to confirm this, as we speak."

"You know, they planned to set off a nuclear bomb in Washington, D.C. We overheard a discussion at Bird Cay, a couple of nights ago, about this scheme," Rod said.

"A number of cities were specified in the documents as targets. D.C. was one of those," Moore added. He continued. "I do have something sad to report. We learned from our contacts in La Ceiba, now, that some communication is being reestablished after the hurricane, that the city incurred great damage and loss of life during the storm. One of those that was lost was Dr. Jonas, whom you met briefly, Dr. Knight."

"Oh, no! He seemed like such a good man. How did he die?"

"He and a local emergency physician tried to rescue a pregnant woman, who had an obvious, active smallpox infection and was caught in floodwater near a makeshift hospital. All three perished, when a mudslide let loose from the hillside above them and engulfed them. The two physicians risked trying to save her because the smallpox epidemic had been, believed, contained, prior to the hurricane. This woman represented a new, unreported case."

"Those poor people. Did they find their bodies?"

"They found the two physicians. They have not found the woman's body, yet."

Carla was silent, a moment. She realized that the specter of a possible, uncontrolled epidemic remained, after all of the CDC's efforts. "I feel badly that those physicians died, in vain."

"Over a thousand others died, as well," Moore added, to put things in perspective.

Carla nodded, appreciating his point, but became worried. "What about Dr. Velasquez? Is he still alive and safe?"

"Yes, he is alive and well, within the makeshift hospital in La Ceiba."

"Oh, thank God. I must go see him, soon."

"You might want to wait until some of the initial disaster recovery is over and the city is made more secure."

"You're probably right. Thank you for letting me know about Dr. Jonas."

"You're welcome. Once again, you two, the country is grateful for what you prevented. The nation of Honduras is thankful that you solved an international homicide for them and drove out an infiltrating drug group," Director Morgan extolled. Admiral Weatherby and Director Moore nodded. "What do you each plan to do, now?" Morgan inquired. "I imagine you need some down time, after your ordeal."

"I plan to stay for a few days and then, return to work," Carla indicated, while looking covertly at Rod. The three men talking to them did not miss this.

Rod didn't answer immediately.

Morgan spoke for him. "Rod, why don't you take a couple of weeks off? After that, you can report to D.C. and we can figure out your next assignment." He was looking at the cube jelly scars on Rod's legs and said, "By the looks of the beating your body has taken, I'd say you need a doctor, my boy." He looked at Carla, smiling, while saying this.

Carla blushed slightly. Rod nodded back at Morgan and answered, "I'll consider taking some time off. The break would be welcome."

Director Moore took Carla's hands in his and said, "It has been a pleasure and honor meeting you. If you ever get tired of running your chamber in Seattle, please call us. We can always use individuals with your medical knowledge and a good sleuthing mind. The same goes for you, Rod. If you get tired of the DEA, there is always the FBI."

They all shook hands, then, and made their farewells. The launch transported the three men away from the resort and toward the Naval Force ship that was anchored off Bonacca. A helicopter was awaiting them, there, which would take them to the mainland for a plane connection to the United States.

Carla and Rod watched them leave. Rod turned to Carla and suggested, "I thought that I would go join Bryan Reynolds, digging the church free of mud. I'd like to find Pepe's mother and father and let them know what Pepe did for us. Do you want to come?"

"Sure, I was actually going to suggest something similar, myself. The townspeople probably need a great deal of assistance clearing debris from their dwellings, too, not to mention medical assistance."

"My thought, exactly. Let's go, then." They set off for Bonacca in one of the resort's small boats, carrying food and medical supplies, and planned to return in time for dinner.

At the church, they met Reynolds, who was just helping to dig away the last bit of mud, obstructing the door. He was delighted to see them and grateful that they had solved the **Golddigger** murders. Two villagers pulled on the church door and it opened, abruptly. A steady stream of exhausted people rushed out of the entrance. Behind them, remained a few, masked CDC team physicians, tending to the resolving smallpox cases. They decided to keep the patients in the building, after it had been evacuated, as the sanitation would soon be improved and it served as an effective isolation area. Besides, it was one of a small number of intact structures, remaining post-Hurricane Vicki.

Rod identified Pepe's mother and father in the retreating crowd. He and Reynolds rushed toward them. Pepe's mother let out an exclamation. "Have you seen my son?!"

"We just got word that he is safe in La Ceiba and will come home, today," Reynolds related in Spanish.

"Oh, thank the Blessed Virgin!" Pepe's mother, Ana, folded her hands and pointed them toward the sky. "I prayed to her."

"His father, Ramon, sighed in relief. He looked puzzled, though. "What was Pepe doing in La Ceiba?"

Rod answered. "He went there to tell the police who had killed the **Golddigger** crew and where to find Dr. Knight and myself, since we were tracking the criminals. We owe him many thanks, Ana and Ramon, because he saved our lives. You can be very proud of him." Both parents were joyous and hugged each other, and then, they hugged Rod, Bryan Reynolds, and Carla.

The three Americans accompanied Pepe's family to Bonacca, by boat, and helped them, during the remainder of the afternoon to clear debris from their collapsed house, as well as from the homes of several of their neighbors. All worked hard, constructing some temporary shelters on the residential sites. These consisted of cotton sheets or canvas thrown over quickly erected wood frames to protect occupants from the elements and provide some privacy. Hammers were heard pounding nails until dusk.

Many individuals talked during the clean-up process, others were silent and grief-stricken about what they had lost. When the counting was done, Hurricane Vicki had claimed 11 lives on the island. That was far less than the number of deaths in La Ceiba, which was confirmed at 1,924 by this point in the recovery process.

It was felt that this number would increase, as more reports came in of discovered bodies. Most had died in mudslides or drowned during flooding. A few had died from being struck or impaled by flying objects. The people of Guanaja considered themselves fortunate to have not lost more residents than they did, as news filtered in from La Ceiba.

It was getting late in the day. Rod and Carla were becoming tired after all of their work. Bryan Reynolds had already returned to the resort to help make preparations for Pepe's 'welcome home' dinner. Rod brought up the subject of his son, while they finished their labors. He mentioned how he had planned to introduce the boy to baseball, when he was old enough. His own dad had done that for him and he was grateful for the experience. Rod became silent after this confession.

Carla sensed his pain and touched his arm, gently. "Rod, why don't you visit your son, in the near future? How old would he be now? Sixteen or seventeen?"

"Seventeen."

"I'm sure that his mother has explained circumstances to him. He is not a little boy any longer. He would not be confused about his parental situation. He would probably welcome the acknowledgement and affection from his true father."

Rod was silent, frowning into the sand. Then he stopped and drew Carla against him, hugging her tightly. "I'm afraid," he whispered into her hair. "I'm afraid he won't want me as his father, after all these years."

"You won't know unless you try. There is no shame in that."

"Maybe you're right. I'd really like to see him." He squeezed her again. "You're a good woman, Carla. I'm lucky to have met you." He stroked her face and kissed her, earnestly, releasing her as he did so, because it was getting hard to hold back more advances. "Let's go back to the resort. It's almost dinnertime and we will want to clean up, beforehand. I'm afraid that it's going to take awhile because there is no running water, yet."

"Good idea." Carla was relieved at his suggestion. She was feeling emotions that were getting difficult to control. They walked back to the boat, hand in hand.

"Tonight, I'd like you to stay with me," Rod declared, as they climbed in, his eyes echoing the statement. "I hope that you won't say no."

"I can think of no place that I'd rather be," Carla answered, her eyes meeting his evenly. "Besides, there's no power and it will be dark, and it will be nice to have the company," she added, mischievously. Rod grinned at her levity, in the face of this proposal. That was one of the things that he liked about her. They talked little, motoring back to the resort. They didn't have to, their eyes spoke volumes.

Each returned to their lodgings and prepared for dinner. They could have forgone the meal, but knew they were expected. Besides, Pepe had finally arrived from La Ceiba and they wanted to see the little boy, to whom thy owed so much.

When they walked into the dining room, which had been swept clear of clutter by the staff, the little boy ran over to them and hugged both adults, while they showered him with compliments and gratitude. Reynolds had a table set for them, away from the remainder of the resort's guests, in the kerosene lamp-lit dining room. Even though two days from now, it would be Thanksgiving, he felt it was appropriate to have a special dinner that evening. After all, they had just lived through a hurricane. He and his wife sat with Rod and Carla, along with Pepe and his mother and father, Rachel Vega, and even Rudy Lentz, who, still, had been stranded on that side of the island after the hurricane. Rudy was delighted to see Rod and Carla, as they were to see him. Rod emphasized, to those at the table, how important Rudy's achievement had been, reaching the U.S. authorities with the GPS coordinates of the wreck site. Everyone was impressed and Rudy, grinned, shyly, in the face of the praise. Pepe's brave venture, was discussed, again. He was enjoying his newfound celebrity and the adulation of his two idols. All of the adults at the table looked a bit haggard from dealing with the aftermath of Hurricane Vicki. The meal, prepared on a gas barbecue, was delicious, or it might have been that their hunger was excessive after the last few days' ordeal. Talk was kept light and minimal about the recent rescue. Reynolds, politely, did not ask too many prying questions. He was vocal, though, regarding his amazement about the Campbell's' true identity and their arrest. All he and the media would ever know, was that a hyperbaric medicine physician and an underwater photographer solved the Golddigger murders. No mention was made of the U-boat's cargo. It was, simply, reported that the **Golddigger** crew had been murdered after discovering a drug trade going on at sea between the Cordillera Cartel and Von Kreitler. No one ever questioned the validity of this. The CIA and FBI made sure that they had no reason to. The cargo had been confiscated by the U.S. government and was on its way to the States, to a military weapons repository.

Talk, subsequently, at the table, was dominated by Pepe, who discussed his plans for the future. He was such an entrepreneur. Already, he was speculating where he might go to school in the United States. He wanted to return to Honduras after his education and start a computer game business.

Soon enough, dinner was over and biddings for 'good night' said. Rod took Carla's hand as they walked over the cobblestones toward his bungalow. They were both silent, hearts beating hard. Rod fumbled with the doorknob and they were suddenly inside. The air was still and humid because the ceiling fan was not working. His arm wrapped around her and her arms wrapped around his neck. The kisses came quickly and endlessly. He arched back her neck, gently, and his mouth trailed down her neck and found her firm breasts. She moaned softly. They pulled each other's clothes off and dropped them on the floor, where they stood. Their skin, touching, excited them and was a balm for all those old scars in their lives. Eventually, they ended up in bed.

Carla felt that she could let go and trust this man. She had not been intimate with anyone in a long time. Rod, similarly, had not been with anyone since an interlude with a girl in La Ceiba, during Carnival, the previous spring. The longing had been suppressed. Now, it was raging for both of them. He was, soon, inside her and they climaxed in close succession, after a deliciously, prolonged interval. After their cries died away, they laid back spent. Neither spoke for several minutes, but they touched hands.

Rod spoke first. "Will you return to work in Seattle, after another week?"

"Probably. I only arranged coverage for a specified period. Do you know where you'll be going next?"

"Not yet. It's always up in the air at the end of an assignment."

"Well, maybe you'll get posted back in the United States," she said, hopefully.

Rod could hear the hope in her voice and became defensive. This woman enthralled him, but he was afraid of changing his lifestyle. There was security in the way he lived. He could control it. There had been no security with his wife, Laura. Besides, he had lived this way for years. "Carla, I have to be honest with you. I have never felt so good being with someone, as I have with you the last two weeks, but my job has never been easy on relationships and I have not been with anyone for a long time, since Laura. I have become somewhat of a loner. You deserve someone who's able to be with you, most of the time."

The words cut her like a knife. This man had seemed so sincere. They had been through so much, in such a short time. She wanted a sense of belonging and to trust again, not a weeklong tryst in the sun. She had been a loner, too, going on trips, by herself, often, to remote locations. However, she valued her friends and respected the brevity of life. On the one hand, the solitude of single life was an opportunity to have clarity of one's own thoughts, but in the long run it was a vacuum.

Rod could feel her grip lighten. He rolled over and hugged her. "Carla, you make me feel wonderful," he whispered. "I hope you believe that. I just can't promise anything, right now. We have the whole week before us to do things and talk. Right now, I want to fall asleep in your arms." He smiled and she smiled back, emptily.

She knew what she must do. Good-byes had gotten harder since Philip's passing. Each one was like a small death. She tried to savor what pleasure they had had, while Rod held her in his arms. They finally said 'good night', and he fell asleep. She waited until his sleep seemed deeper and he rolled over, then, she eased herself off the bed and dressed. On a table, she found some paper and a pen. She wrote him a short note and put his name on the folded overleaf and left it on the nightstand. Softly, she let herself out of the bungalow and returned to her room to pack.

40

November 24, 1993

Her only chance to get off the island, quickly, was to have the resort provide a motor launch for her to be taken to the Naval Force vessel, offshore. There, she could get a helicopter to the mainland. It was 4 a.m. If she had the night desk attendant make arrangements, now, she could probably be off the ship by daylight. Forget her dive equipment. She could have it sent to her, later. Besides, her new plan was to go to La Ceiba for the remainder of her time-off, check on the recovery of Dr. Velasquez, and see if she could provide medical support in the city's disaster relief operation.

Rachel Vega was on duty at the night desk, where a lantern provided the only light. She looked bewildered to see Carla at this particular hour of the morning, with her bags beside her. "Is something wrong?" she asked.

"Something has come up at work, home, in the States, and I am needed, urgently. The message was relayed by a messenger from the Naval Force ship, after dinner, last evening. I will need a launch out to the ship, so I can take a helicopter to the mainland. Could you see if you could radio the ship and let the crew know that I am coming?"

"Why, yes, of course, Dr. Knight. I am so sorry to see you go."

"Me, too, Rachel, but work calls." The young woman could see the sadness in Carla's face. She wrote Bryan Reynolds and his wife a note explaining why she had to leave, unexpectedly. She thanked them for their hospitality. The next note that she left, was for Pepe, with her address in the States, indicating that she would like to stay in touch with him. She left him her dive watch in an envelope, as a gift. These, she deposited with Rachel Vega, who still could not understand her sudden departure. She thanked the young woman for her help and kindness. A driver for the launch was summoned from the sleeping resort staff. The man looked puzzled to be transporting a guest in the black hours of the morning.

As the launch motored away from the previously idyllic place and the darkness enveloped her, Carla thought about what she had been through the past two weeks. She supposed one could say that she had tested life to the hilt on this trip. However, there was more to life than just chasing criminals. She would not wait for someone to figure this out.

The sailors aboard the Naval Force vessel were surprised to see Carla disembark from the small craft, with her luggage, in the first rays of daylight. However, they were courteous and led her to their commanding officer, which was glad to accommodate her request. After all, this young woman had done their country a great service.

Rod was broken out of his reverie of sleep, at approximately 6:30 a.m., by the sound of activity in the resort. He had relaxed so completely and slept so deeply, that he had not heard Carla leave, nor had he stirred until now. His eyes snapped open and he looked over at the pillow next to him that was empty. He saw the note on the nightstand and opened it.

It simply said, "I'm not very good at 'good-byes', anymore. - Carla."

Damn, he was an idiot. He pulled on a pair of trousers and ran to Carla's room, knocking on the door. No answer. Next, he ran to the main office of the resort, where Rachel Vega was just ending her shift. "Where has Dr. Knight gone?"

"She said that she was needed urgently at work, home. She didn't say much more than that. We made arrangements for a boat to transport her to the Naval Force vessel. She should probably be leaving soon on a helicopter for the mainland." Rachel Vega looked puzzled at his sudden concern.

Rod wasted no more time. He thanked Rachel and raced to the dock, just in time to see a Naval Force helicopter lift off over the island in the blood-red dawn and head southwest. He had been deluding himself about women during the past several years. No more. This was the nicest, most courageous woman he had ever met. He knew that he loved her. He had taken her for granted. She had helped him subdue a terrible adversary and saved his life. That was more than anyone had done for him since Viet Nam, or for that matter, since he had been a DEA agent. Others had betrayed him. There was more to life than the agency. He would go to the States and get her back.